CHASED BY FAME

MELISSA BRANDT

Brandt.Melissa.M@gmail.com

Cover Design by G. S. Prendergast
CoverYourDreams.net

Book Design by Lia Rees
FreeYourWords.com

Printed in the United States of America

First Printing 2015

ISBN: 0692561277

Blue Veranda Publishing

For my preemies,
delighted in and treasured.

CHAPTER 1

Thirty-six men grinned at Colette Halbrook, each looking his best. Several new faces enticed her and the choice was hers. After twenty minutes of deliberation, she plucked two from the lineup.

"Michael from Medford, let's start with you." She skimmed his online profile and highlighted the only three hobbies he advertised: movies, camping at the coast, and hiking. It would require an organized manhunt to locate an Oregonian who didn't share those interests. She read on. It was the last paragraph that earned him the date.

I captured alligators in the bayou for almost a decade, but I'm still on the hunt for an athletic, devoted wife.

She grinned. "Do you carry a diamond in your wallet just in case?" The seventeen-year age gap was out of the question, but that didn't exempt her from enjoying tales of swampland danger over dinner. His flashing name indicated he was online, so she sent him a generic greeting. Even with dial-up, it wouldn't take him five seconds to check her bio which stated her age, twenty-nine, and a false location, Portland, Oregon.

Two years into the addiction, and not one guy had turned her down. Her headshot was cute enough, but it was her curls that kept her calendar full. A stranger once described them as hickory-colored. Curiosity sent her to Home Depot's cabinet section and, sure enough, the wood was a combination of lights and darks.

Michael agreed to Saturday, so she clicked back to bachelor number two. Wallace was an actuary who felt no shame in flaunting his six-figure salary. It was repugnant the way women would boost a guy's ego simply because of the numbers scribbled in his checkbook, but she wasn't about to miss out over a technicality. His bio stated he likes to bring a guest on the first date. Most likely it was his son or daughter, but there was only one way to find out and she was game.

*

The hallway leading to the Neonatal Intensive Care Unit had been painted pastel blue three weeks ago, and Colette was still in awe. A co-worker caught up with her, confiding that if her shift didn't get switched from swing to days, she was going to look elsewhere for employment. Colette encouraged her to be patient, but at the same time, wondered who would take her place. Rumor had it, they were looking to hire more men.

When they got to the nurse's station, Colette learned it was going home day for her baby, Chad, who had a relatively smooth ten-day stay in the NICU. She was told mom and dad had been ready for discharge an hour ago, but wanted to say goodbye before they headed out.

Colette hurried to the last room on the left, Pod Four, and noted that all eight incubators and cribs were occupied. After getting an update on three of the babies, Colette smiled at Chad's parents. "You guys get to go home today."

"It's about time," said the mother, snorting as she laughed. "You'd think Junior here stole a car. The law was keeping him here, you know. A nurse told me I had no say. She claimed some nonsense about CPS getting involved if I took him before them doctors gave the go ahead. CPS? Give me a break."

"He must have gained weight again." Colette ran her index finger across the chart. "Twenty-three grams. Good boy."

"Gain weight or else, right? Eat good or you get pricked with another needle." She fluffed her thick bangs and blinked away tears. "Compared to some of these others, Chad's situation was a cakewalk. But you try spending your newborn's first week-and-a-half in here." She covered her chest as if she were pledging allegiance. "What I'm trying to say is... I don't know what I would have done without you."

"It was my pleasure, seeing those big brown eyes every afternoon."

The father wiggled his right arm loose from under his sleeping son. "Thank you," he said as their hands met. "My wife goes on and on about you."

"I hope not," Colette grinned. She twisted Chad's sock in place. With those chipmunk cheeks, he looked full term. "You got your wish. You guys get to spend Valentine's Day as a family."

"I was sure them doctors would keep us penned up in here for another week. I didn't know until this morning." Licking her lips, she peeled a frilly valentine off the end of the crib. "I don't want to forget this. Did you see these?"

"Aren't they cute? Second graders made them. Their teachers brought them by last night." Colette watched as the mother dabbed at the gold glitter sprinkled liberally across the fire engine cutout. The NICU had given her a new perspective on Valentine's Day. It wasn't about romance and roses, or feeling unloved and lonely; it was about mothers finding joy in the toughest of times, celebrating a holiday, often for the first time, with their newborn. It was love in its purest form.

The mother put her hand on her husband's shoulder. "Honey, let Colette say goodbye. I'm ready to get out of here."

Unsure of himself, he carefully leaned toward Colette, offering her the baby. She scooped up Chad and studied his face wondering when her day would come. Twenty-nine years and childless was hardly a reason to rush to the nearest sperm bank. Sooner or later she would meet Mr. Right-For-Her, elope to Fiji, and nine months later—POP. The haunting *what ifs* would be silenced. That's what she told herself for comfort anyway. It rarely worked.

Chad yawned. On his shirt was a picture of a basketball drooling with the caption "dribble, dribble, shoot." The top of his jeans was rolled down like a cinnamon roll, exposing a plump belly begging to be tickled. Moments later she found herself giving up yet another baby she wanted to keep forever. Chad was carried out of her life in a dinosaur car seat. The longing that plagued her was difficult to conceal. Her biological clock wasn't just ticking—it was demanding new batteries.

Avoiding the empty crib, she began charting vitals on another patient. As she worked, she imagined taking a baby away from the pricks of the hospital's needles and into a beautiful nursery, affectionately decorated for that special son or daughter. Discreetly, she dabbed the moisture building on the inside corners of her eyes.

"Ha! You owe me twenty bucks," said twenty-three-year-old Jazmine Anderson.

Colette spun around and framed her face with her hands. "Does this look like crying to you?"

"Pay up." Tucking a layer of dyed-black hair behind her ear, Jazmine gestured to the third nurse in the room. "Nick saw it. Tell her, Nick."

He laughed nervously. "I think I'll stay out of this one."

Jazmine pointed at him. "You have a moral obligation to be truthful. Don't make me come over there." She walked toward him before detouring to the sink.

Nick grinned, shaking his head. Colette admired his easygoing nature and supposed him to be the only respectable man she knew, if there was such a thing. He was shy, polite, and according to his wife, a good husband. "Thank you, Nick."

"Never mind, Colette. You're off the hook. Now Nick owes me twenty dollars for obstruction of justice."

A monitor began sounding steady dings indicating Colette's four-pound baby, Joshua, wasn't getting enough oxygen. Other than a quick glance, she ignored it. "No you don't, Nick. I never agreed to her obnoxious bet."

"You had that baby for what... a week?"

"Two weeks." She silenced the alarm and noticed that his skin color was decent. Most likely he would catch his breath.

"Colette, I bet you were one of those kids who boohooed on the last day of school."

After making sure no parents were standing in the doorway, Colette said quietly, "You, on the other hand, gave personalized goodbyes to half the football team."

Jazmine laughed hard. Lowering her voice, she grinned at Nick. "She thinks I'm such an s-l-u-t."

The alarm sounded again, but this time the dings were twice as fast. After sanitizing her hands, Colette unlatched the incubator and let the side down. Vigorously she rubbed his back.

5

"Take a breath, Joshua." His heart-rate was dropping quickly. She spun a dial allowing more oxygen into the cannula positioned just inside his nostrils.

"I need to meet Summer," said Jazmine. "I bet she has all kinds of dirt on you from your high school days."

"Take a breath, buddy." She flipped him onto his back like an overcooked pancake, mindful not to tug the wires stuck to his skin. It wasn't just his hands and feet that were pale; his face was also dusky. She rubbed his stomach hard enough to cause discomfort. His chest started to rise and fall as if he were panicking. "There you go, Joshua. Good boy." Within seconds, his color returned from a dark purple to a nice shade of pink. She lifted his head, turned it to the left, and gently set it back down. Then she bent his arm and tucked his fingers against his chin. "There we go. Nice and cozy now." She unplugged two of the wires leading to his chest and began untangling them.

"She does, doesn't she?" Jazmine continued. "High school girls spill everything to their bestie. I bet she got some middle of the night phone calls from your college days too. Am I right? It might be in my best interest to contact Summer to find out who you really are."

Colette laughed. "Summer knows some stuff, but it's nothing that would shock you."

"Like what? C'mon. You privatize everything as if nothing interesting ever happens to you. I know you've got issues just like the rest of us." She turned to Nick. "Close your ears. Girl talk."

Nick turned his back. "Say no more."

Colette closed the door of the incubator and headed to the warmer for a fresh blanket. She looked over her shoulder, narrowing her eyes. "Jaz, you get the full scoop on my dating life and you know it."

"I would hardly classify those as dates. They're more like verbal encounters with strangers you'll never see again. I don't get how you have the nerve to tell man after man that you had a great time, but you're not feeling a connection. Doesn't it bother you that you're hurting them?"

"After one date? No. Maybe if we were three dates into it. The guys I go out with are in their thirties or older. If they were serious about finding a wife, they'd already have one."

"Then why even date?"

"It's fun. I get to dress up and try out new restaurants. You should hear the stories some of these men tell. It's free entertainment."

"Not for them."

"I laugh at their jokes. I'm engaging. They have a good time. They get their money's worth."

"Not if they thought they were buying more than dinner."

"A guy buys me a salad and I'm supposed to put out?"

Jazmine narrowed her eyes. "You don't ever want to fall in love?"

"If the right guy happens to come along—"

"Say he does. How's he going to get past your 'one date only' rule?"

Colette could feel the heat rising to her face. "You're never going to drop that, are you? I wasn't serious."

"Ha! Someday Summer and I are going to have a chat, and I'm going to get the full, uncensored scoop on Colette Halbrook."

"Sounds boring," Colette grinned.

"Nick, you don't believe Colette's life is perfect, do you?"

"I thought I was banned from this conversation."

"You see? Even Nick can see right through you."

"I never said my life is perfect."

Jazmine raised an eyebrow. "But you've never said it's not."

There was truth behind her accusation, but Colette's darkest moments were nobody's business. "There's nothing pretentious about a positive attitude."

"Perfect people get under my skin. I'm your friend, Colette. You're supposed to share your grievances so I can feel better about my own life. Don't I do that for you?"

She had a point.

Shrugging her shoulders, Jazmine slid the tip of a bottle into her baby's mouth and stared at his face adoringly. She lowered her voice, keeping her gaze focused on her work. "You know who else I hate? Flawlessly beautiful women. That's two strikes against you." She dabbed the corner of his mouth with a towel and looked up. "Please give me a reason to stop envying your existence." Jazmine's smirk suggested she was only kidding, but she eyed Colette as if she were waiting for an answer.

Jazmine's little charade was now bordering hurtful. A fat stomach, varicose veins, and a plain face were some of Colette's more obvious flaws. And as far as her personal life, nobody had the ignorance to suggest life could be perfect for anyone, especially a woman. Not with those crazy female hormones that like to show up every four weeks to shake things up.

The next twenty minutes were spent in silence. Nick quietly excused himself for a break, and his replacement seemed to be in her own world. That, or she picked up on the tension in the room.

8

Jazmine finally broke the silence. "You know what you need?"

Here we go, thought Colette. The woman doesn't know when to stop. "A vacation. I need a vacation and so do you. Let's go to Hawaii. Or Aruba. I need to know the sun still exists. I haven't seen it in months."

"I'll tell you what you need."

When Colette glanced at the other nurse, she quickly looked away as if she wasn't eavesdropping. "Seriously, Jaz. You can stop right there. I've heard it all and I've taken notes." It was one thing to be ridiculed in a fun-loving way, but Colette had a strong hunch that whatever Jazmine was about to say next would become the latest gossip-in-the-workplace.

"Hold on, Colette. Hear me out. This is good stuff." She pulled out a preemie-sized Huggies diaper while Colette looked on, completely helpless. "Sweetie, what you need is a baby of your own. You really do."

Her words struck hard. A baby was exactly what she needed, what she longed for every single day. Colette watched as her dear friend went about her business, oblivious to the potency of her remark. Colette was touched to the core by her sincerity. It was as if intuition had given her a glimpse into the deepest part of Colette's soul.

Jazmine winked playfully. "But it takes two to tango, young lady, and I know plenty of guys who would be happy to—"

"No, thank you very much," Colette cut in sharply, eyes widened with embarrassment. "No. I'll be fine."

CHAPTER 2

The moon was full, the hour nearly midnight. Colette made her way up the stairs to her third-floor apartment drooling over her date—a large Oreo blizzard with extra Oreo. When she reached the landing, she paused momentarily to relish the cloudless view Eugene winters seldom allow. The sky was shimmering, electricity lit up the valley. It was a recipe for enchantment on the most popular date-night of the year.

Had Valentine's Day not fallen on a weeknight, she too would be dining at an expensive restaurant, getting high on dark chocolate, and perhaps making out with a stranger she didn't care to see the next day. Her lips parted as she guided a spoon along the inside edge of the DQ cup. "It's just another night," she whispered. "Not a big deal."

When she leaned against the banister her optimism slipped, tumbling down a mile of forested hill. Each year she vowed to remain unaffected by the holiday, but that didn't keep her from recognizing the obvious; Valentine's Day was needlessly cruel. Sure, there were some who enjoyed its superficial traditions, but it plagued millions of others with misery, as if there was something wrong with being single.

Personally, she enjoyed her drama-free life. She didn't have to fret over the whereabouts of her boyfriend, she carried within her a confidence that her toilet seat was down, and she had the freedom to cry to her heart's content to classics like *While You Were Sleeping*.

Before turning around, Colette dug into the pit of her bag for keys. She would bet her two front teeth that Stuart, her neighbor, was waiting up for her.

"Happy V-Day, Colette."

Smiling politely, she walked under the covered breezeway and stepped onto her doormat. "You too." She had never met anyone quite like Stuart. He was quirky and tried too hard, and after a year of knowing him, she was sure he preplanned their daily conversations. "It's chilly tonight. My hand is frozen to this cup."

Stuart rocked slowly in his weathered chair. "Did you know Valentine's Day originated from the festival Lupercalia?"

"Really?" She longed for the warmth of her apartment. "Shoot. My ice-cream is melting."

"Oh yes. Men in goatskin thongs used to run around Rome beating women to make them fertile."

"Stuart!" Colette reprimanded with a grin. "What are you saying?"

"It's true. Did you make any plans for this evening?"

"I did. Ten hours of sleep. What about you?"

"Just shooting the breeze."

She slipped inside the door directly across from his. "Have a good night."

"Watch out for Cupid's arrow."

She locked the deadbolt. The mystery she saw in Stuart was comparable to that of her former middle school teachers. Did they really exist outside the classroom?—or in Stuart's case, the front porch?

The first order of business was getting a fire going. She flipped the on-switch and a flame danced. Next she fed her biggest addiction: internet.

*

The rain was unrelenting, but that didn't spoil the scenic three-hour drive down to Medford. Thick evergreens stood tall, temporarily excusing Oregon's overabundance of annual rainfall. While the rest of Eugene was slumped in front of television deities, Colette was climbing and descending mountains at seventy miles-per-hour.

When she arrived in Medford she hit the mall. Thirty minutes later, clutching three new sacks, she could smell her credit card burning. After one last store—two if you counted the kiosk—she cooled it. She needed to. Tomorrow's date lived in Portland, where skyscrapers and perfectly manicured women made it impossible to stay on budget.

Back at the car, she stowed her purchases and swapped CDs. Tapping the steering wheel, she plotted her next move. "Dinner isn't until seven. I'll grab lunch, catch a movie, get a pedicure." She applied a coat of lip balm and slid her keys into the ignition.

"On second thought..." Feeling adventurous, she fooled with the GPS. "Redding, California can't be more than a couple of hours away." Mr. GPS concurred and she was back on the interstate anticipating the mouth-watering burger, fries, and shake calling her name. When she crossed the state line she felt wildly independent. "Hello California!"

Hours later, long after the sun had gone down, she nearly sprained an ankle catapulting herself through the solid wood door of an Italian restaurant. Between the traffic jam and the cop who claimed she was going twenty-two over, she couldn't believe she made it back to Medford in time.

"Good evening," said a hostess who couldn't be older than fourteen. "How many in your party?"

Colette glanced at the dozen or so waiting to be seated. "Two. I'm meeting a Michael," she said loud enough for him to hear. "We have a reservation." Colette watched impatiently as the hostess took forever inspecting her sheet. "It might be under Mike. Michael or Mike. He's probably already seated."

"And you're sure you have a reservation?"

Her hands tensed at the thought that he had forgotten to call. "Yes, for seven o'clock." Colette did a double-take on the crowd. Half of them stared back dumbly.

"Let's see," she said slowly as she read, her front teeth clamped down on the tip of her pencil like a beaver.

Nearly all of Colette's patience had been expended on the drive over and this under-aged princess wasn't helping. "I don't know why he would have given you my name, but you might check 'Colette.'"

"Okay, I see it here. Michael. Reservation for two. Seven o'clock."

How the ditz sifted through five reservations without any help was a mystery. "Great. Yes. Thank you." She was back in the game.

"He left. You just missed him."

Blood rushed to her face as if she had scared the guy off. "What do you mean? Where did he go?"

"He didn't say. He asked me to cancel the reservation."

Colette looked at her watch. It wasn't even twenty after.

Surely he didn't hit the road after ten measly minutes. "Did he say why?"

"Again, no. He didn't."

Clenching her teeth, Colette sighed in frustration. Her entire Saturday was centered around this date, and he had stood her up. Forget Michael and his stupid alligators. Tomorrow would be a new day, a new man. *And* a mystery guest, she suddenly remembered. It was probably a moody thirteen-year-old, but still.

"Can I get you a table for one?"

Colette cinched her coat around her torso like a robe. "What do you think?" As she walked out the door, she drew a big fat "X" through Medford, Oregon. It wasn't until she merged onto the freeway that she burst into tears.

*

"I hate this place," Colette whispered to Jazmine, eyeing the inhabitants of the downtown Eugene café as if they were newly released prisoners. "I'm hungry and there's not a single thing on the menu that can change that."

The young woman behind the counter—in glossy black lipstick and skull earrings—bumped the till drawer shut with her hip. "You'd be much prettier if you smiled. What can I get you?"

Caught off guard, Colette softened her expression. "I'm not eating."

"Why am I not surprised?" Her eyes darted to Jazmine. "Are you also here to not-eat?"

Jazmine looked at Colette with an open-mouthed smile and

then back at the cashier. "I'll take a croissant, a cup of split pea soup, and bottled water." Then she paid, collected her lunch, and followed Colette to a tall table by the window.

Once seated, Colette leaned forward and whispered, "You don't think that lady heard me tell you that I hate it here, do you?"

Jazmine blew on her soup with the poise of a flutist. "Nah."

"I know, right? What was her problem?"

"Oh, I don't know. The scowl on your face could have come across as judgmental."

Colette corrected her posture. "Pardon me, Dr. Phil. You know this place gives me the heebie-jeebies. It smells like yeast and B.O."

"That would be patchouli oil and bread. Yeast doesn't have an odor."

"Yeast? Yes it does."

Jazmine grinned. "Is that what your doctor keeps telling you?"

Colette wasn't in the mood. The background music droned on, giving her the feeling they were gathered at a séance. And not that she was prejudiced, but "hippie central" wasn't her idea of a nice lunch. She fantasized about where they'd be heading next—Papa's Pizza. Colette watched in horror as Jazmine spooned green slop with curdled-like chunks into her mouth. "I'm sorry, but I have to get out of here."

"Fine. Bring me some to-go stuff, Miss Priss."

Colette obeyed and in sixty seconds they were back in Jazmine's car. Pulling into traffic, Jazmine's eyes grew. "I almost forgot. How did last weekend go?"

Colette took an antibacterial wipe from her purse and ran it along the dusty dash. "Saturday didn't show and I cancelled Sunday."

"You went a whole weekend without a date? Ladies and gentlemen, this is a first."

Colette laughed. "That's not what I said. Get this. Sunday showed up with a relationship expert to analyze his behavior around certain types of women."

"And what type are you?"

"Who knows? So I went to the ladies room and never came back. I've never done that before, but it felt good. Long story short, I met this other guy in downtown Portland, and he took me to China Town for dinner. Jaz, you would have married him on the spot."

"Why? What's wrong with him?"

"That's just it. Even *I* liked him."

"Now that's something I rarely hear coming from you. Please tell me you gave him your number."

"I actually considered it this time, but I had this feeling something wasn't right."

"No!" Jazmine slammed the palm of her hand against the steering wheel. "You are unbelievable, Colette Halbrook. It's a phone number, not your social security number. You still have that 'no second dates' rule, don't you?" Colette tried to deny it, but Jazmine knew better. "The only thing your little rule is protecting you from is a nice family of your own. At some point you're going to have to go on a second date with a guy. And then a third. And a fourth. That's how we do it on planet Earth."

Colette nodded. "I know. You're right." And she was. But Jazmine hadn't experience firsthand that a skilled liar could wreak havoc on a woman's life for years to come. Colette still cringed when she thought of her first and only serious boyfriend. He had exotic blue eyes, a contagious laugh, and four ex-wives that she hadn't known about.

"Do you want me to help you track him down? We could email him. We could tell him that your coworker is forcing you to go to a birthday party at a pool hall with ten of her drunken friends and ask if he would pretty-please come with you. You know me. I can throw together a party like nobody's business."

Jazmine could be a little blunt at times, but her intentions were sweet. "Thanks, Jaz. Really. But you know when you get the feeling something is off? With this guy, everything appears completely wonderful, but somehow I can tell it's not."

"Like he's hiding his bad qualities?"

"Exactly! It's like he's not giving me the real him. Plus, he has a beard."

Jazmine cranked up the radio. "I can't handle you right now. Please don't talk to me."

*

Dressed in sweatpants, a fitted t-shirt, and lime green headphones, Colette parked her car in the Valley River Center mall's parking lot just as the sun was coming up. After pulling her curls into a messy ponytail, she stepped onto the bike path.

Jogging solo was taking a risk, but her stomach wasn't getting any flatter in front of the computer. She was halfway across the bridge when the sight of the Willamette River stopped her. The sound of trickling rapids was soothing, though she found herself looking over her shoulder with trepidation.

Pacing herself at a speed she hoped her cardiovascular system would survive, she crossed the bridge and took in the lush paradise that surrounded her. The wide open lawn was dotted with Oregon-sized evergreens, and the clean river creased the outer edge of the park. A good ten feet lower than the concrete path was a dirt trail, with steep passageways in between.

She spotted two transients lying on benches, but they were asleep. Hopefully they would stay that way until she was safely inside her locked car. "This is unwise," she whispered between breaths. "You're like bait to these homeless guys."

Her heart pounded against her chest, but she couldn't tell if it was lack of exercise or the fear of being snatched that caused it. Instinct warned her to turn back, but she couldn't. It felt too good. The park was breathtaking, at least in comparison to where she normally spent her mornings, and her body was becoming healthier in too many ways to count.

"On your left!" said a voice from behind. She whipped her head around and watched as a cyclist passed her. She was female and she was alone. Colette grinned. It was as if she now had permission from the city of Eugene to go ahead and enjoy their park. Within seconds the woman was out of sight. It was odd that Colette hadn't heard her approaching. Paranoid, she cut the music and looked over her shoulder.

Her neck snapped forty-five degrees when she heard something in front of her. A cyclist emerged from a lower dirt trail and was about to plow into her. She gasped upon realizing that she had veered onto his side of the path. Instinctively she sprung off the pavement, lost her balance, and landed in the moist grass immediately to her left. The cyclist simultaneously veered off the trail, but chose the same side Colette had. She saw his knuckles tense as he squeezed the brakes.

"Whoa, whoa, whoa," he said quickly.

Upon impact, she grabbed her leg in agony and tried to catch her breath.

He threw down his bike, hopped over it like a ninja, and was on his knees trying to decide what to do with his hands. "Where are you hurt? Is it your leg? I can't believe I hit you. I'm so sorry."

Too ashamed to acknowledge her mistake, she avoided eye contact. "That's okay. I'm fine." Her mind processed the split second she had seen of him. He was a strong man in his twenties or thirties, he was wearing dark sunglasses on a dim morning, and he was dirty. Relying solely on peripheral vision, she noted that his Oregon Duck shirt was faded and his feet were crying out for a new pair of tennis shoes. And maybe she was overanalyzing, but his scraggly beard was chilling, given her present state of mind. "I have to go." As she stood, he steadied her awkwardly by her elbow.

"I'll walk you to your car."

"I just want to go home."

"Fine, but let me give you my number so I can take care of your medical bills." She watched as he patted himself down. "I don't have a pen on me. Do you?"

On second glance, he wasn't bad looking. Narrowing her eyes, she focused on his hip. "Is that a gun under there?" She searched his face, ironically feeling less threatened than before.

He took a step back and grinned. "I'm afraid to answer that question truthfully, so I'm going to have to go with a no. You seem a little spooked as it is." He cleared his throat. "I can't say I blame you. I almost sent you to the emergency room."

She stood to her feet, disregarding the hand offered to her. "I think you startled me more than anything. I'm fine."

"I hope you're right, but I still feel terrible. If you need to get a hold of me, I'm Bryce Ro—"

"Thank you, but I'm fine. I'm a nurse. I would know if something were wrong." Her face was already redder than lipstick. What would it hurt to add a few more shades? "Actually, I owe you an apology. Had I simply stayed on my side of the trail we wouldn't have collided." There. She said it. "Enjoy the rest of your day."

She headed toward the bridge with two realizations: first, he *did* have a gun underneath his shirt, and second, he wasn't going to use it on her.

CHAPTER 3

It was the first time she had used an alarm clock in over a year and her body was feeling the sting. Colette scooped up the clothes she had selected the afternoon before, turned on the shower, and reconsidered the morning's agenda. It was unlikely that the guy with the gun would be at the same park at the same time on two consecutive days. On the other hand, a seven a.m. bike ride could easily be part of his daily regimen.

If she was really going to stalk him, she needed to concoct a believable story in case she was caught. But this time around, she would be dressed more like herself: jewelry, makeup, and pants that didn't allow her to gain a hundred pounds and still fit.

Second guessing herself, she turned off the shower and went back to bed. Rolling onto her stomach, she slipped her hand beneath the pillow. No woman in her right mind went to all that trouble for a second look at guy she wouldn't consider dating. Closing her eyes, she meditated on the tantalizing sound of his voice. Firearms aside, he seemed like a sweet guy.

A gust of wind sent rain pounding against the window as if it were challenging her to come outside and defy it. Their kids would be tall, she thought. He was probably six-five. And combine that with *her* tall genes...

Throwing the covers off, she marched back to the bathroom.

She was sick and tired of playing it safe. Nothing new ever happened at home, and she didn't feel like waiting until Saturday night for some entertainment.

She was forty-five minutes later this time, and it was just as dark as the morning before, a result of the thick sky. If there had been any real chance of seeing him, she missed it. Nonetheless, she opened her umbrella. A gust of cold rain smacked the side of her face. Fumbling for her hood, she cinched it tightly. Logic guaranteed the park would be a ghost town, but something told her he was standing exactly where she left him.

She chose a bench with a decent view of the river, amused that even the homeless had enough sense to stay home. She squatted slowly, sliding her hands down the backside of her coat. The length would offer just enough protection for her tush, but her legs would have to fend for themselves. Reluctantly she sat, her derrière teetering on a single two-by-four.

She began flipping through a book on gardening, a subject she knew nothing about but was determined to learn. Her plot of land was a wooden balcony with a few terracotta pots. She wouldn't be harvesting corn this fall, but a tomato plant and a few herbs would be nice.

The sound of rushing water took her back to her childhood, to the one summer her mom took her camping. It was supposed to be the first of many campouts. The two of them cheered when they got the tent up, even though they had marveled at the simplicity of the design. To her mom's delight, Colette gasped when she opened the cooler. It was stocked with all kinds of goodies, including homemade blackberry cobbler. They sang songs, told stories, toured a lighthouse, and goofed off in the painfully cold ocean. If amnesia stole her childhood and she could save just one memory, that campout would be the one.

She noticed a man on roller blades stumbling onto the bike path. Her heart quickened at the thought that it might be her biker friend. He was missing the beard, but a razor could explain that. She watched him push off with his right foot before immediately coming to a stop. He reached into his pocket and studied his phone. A minute later, he surprised her by gliding down the path as if it were second nature. The closer he got, the more certain she became. *It was definitely him.*

Panic set in. She had yet to come up with answers to some obvious questions. For starters, why was she reading a book in pouring down rain? She inhaled sharply knowing this was just the kind of thrill she had hoped for. Mission accomplished, she thought. Time to go home. If she was lucky, he wouldn't recognize her. She buried her face in the book, hoping he would sail on by.

But he didn't.

Using the sleeve of his hoodie, he cleared a spot on an adjacent bench. He looked like a cross between a fidgeting little boy and a sexy firefighter. He was wearing the same slick shades on a dark morning, but a baseball cap replaced the bike helmet. He cleaned up pretty nicely, she noticed—a little *too* nice for her taste. She set out to withhold from him the satisfaction of being noticed. There was nothing more obnoxious than watching a man swoon over himself, as if his good looks made him a better catch than the next guy.

Even sitting down he looked tall. His boyish dark hair escaped out the sides of his hat, the curve of the bill overdone. As the minutes passed, he didn't offer so much as a yawn. This was her reward for stepping out of her comfort zone. She flipped to the next page, for the sake of his expectation, to some nonsense about butternut squash and floating row covers.

She could feel the heat of his gaze upon her. After rereading the same sentence a thousand times, she decided to make a break for it. She closed the book. Just as she was about to stand up, he beat her to the punch, his muscular frame towering to an unsafe height. Crossing her legs, she flipped the book onto its belly and studied the back cover.

He took the spot right next to hers as if it had been offered to him. "Hi there," he grinned, displaying a perfect set of teeth. "You're pretending you don't recognize me from yesterday."

Unprepared for anything more complex than the classic "hello," she scrambled for a clever response. Nothing was coming to her and then time ran out. "Who me?" She felt like a thirteen-year-old attempting to form words in front of a boy.

"That's okay. I was doing the same thing. I'm glad to see you're alive."

"I guess you could say I survived my first brush with death."

"No broken bones or anything?"

"Nope." She didn't mention the four-inch bruise tattooed on her shin.

"You don't mind that I'm sitting here, do you? Because I noticed the sun seems to prefer your bench."

She extended her palm from beneath the umbrella, allowing raindrops to dot her skin. "As long as you don't chase my sun away."

"You got it."

After an awkward pause, she returned to her book. It was quite the rush sitting next to him. His calves were toned, she noticed, but they were positioned too close for comfort.

Breaking the silence, he sneezed. Then he rubbed his soiled hand onto his thigh. She would have teased him for it, but the odds of it coming out smoothly were slim. His leg bounced timidly, giving her the upper hand for once.

"You mentioned you're a nurse?"

"I am a nurse, yes."

"That's not an easy career considering that people's lives are in your hands. How do you like it?"

She wasn't about to plunge into a deep conversation with the guy. They were sharing a bench, not a beer. "Every job has its days."

He nodded in agreement. "I always thought it would be cool to work in the medical field. I'd want to be the guy that yells 'clear!' and then 'zap.' What are those things called?"

She grinned. "Defibrillators."

"Have you ever used one?"

"No. I mean, I know how. I've just never had to."

"That's probably a good thing. A paramedic would be cool too. I'd be in my ambulance flying around corners. The guy in back would be like, 'Hey, I just lost an arm back here!'"

"When you're not playing hospital, what do you do?"

Something in his expression changed and he hesitated. "Right now I'm working on my pilot's license."

The question was aimed at his career, not hobby, but she ran with it. "Are you wanting to fly for a commercial airline someday?"

"Nah, too boring. Maybe I'll be a flight instructor for a while. Who knows."

And she had her answer. He was jobless and still living with his mom, a prime example of why she refused to date strangers.

In a few minutes he'd think up some bogus career, and the lies would escalate from there. Brushing her theory aside, she played along. "That would be worse than teaching Drivers Ed. If your driver pushes a wrong button, the radio comes on. But one wrong button from your flight student, and you get ejected from the plane."

"Hey, if it's your time to die, you might as well go out in style."

"I'm hoping for a boring, asleep on my couch, watching *I Love Lucy* kind of death."

He laughed, showing off those gorgeous teeth again. "Now that scares me. My obituary is going to read 'fell off the face of a mountain onto a sharp glacier; body eaten by ferocious grizzlies.'"

She'd been out with a hundred guys, but there was something unique about this one that was drawing her in. Maybe this is what they called "chemistry." If Colette had a type, which she didn't, adventurous would be hovering at the top of the list. And if this guy's DNA hadn't included "deceptively charming," he would hook her effortlessly, that is until he threw her back in exchange for the next fish. Luckily she had the brains to keep her head above water.

"By the way, I'm Bryce." His voice had a Brad Paisley richness that could keep a woman up all night just listening. When he extended his oversized hand, she took hold of it.

"Please tell me that's not the hand you sneezed all over," she grinned, impressed by her own cleverness.

"I'm pretty sure your hands have been worse places than mine. I was hospitalized once and it wasn't pretty. Those poor, poor nurses."

"I'm not even going to ask." On a whim, she went for first base. "I'm Colette." She cringed when she heard herself. It sounded rehearsed. And random. Shaking hands would lessen the awkwardness, but doing so twice was out of the question.

"Glad to meet you, Colette."

For the life of her, she couldn't remember his name. Where was her head? "You too."

He cleared his throat. "So... do you get to cut people open?"

"I'm not a doctor." Normally she wouldn't divulge information about her personal life to just anyone, but she couldn't help herself. "Actually, I take care of the tiniest patients in the hospital."

He gestured to the pencil poking out of her book. "That explains the Mickey Mouses."

"That would be Minnie Mouse. Mickey doesn't wear bows."

"Or dresses, I suppose."

Danger signs were plastered all over this guy, but she couldn't walk away. He was adorable. For the first time in her adult life, the stupidity of her friends started to make sense. Given the right circumstances, she could see how it might be worth it to be used by a guy like him every once in a blue moon. She wished he would take off his glasses so she could enjoy his eyes.

"Do you take care of preemies?"

"For the most part, yes. Every once in a while I get one who's full term. They're much more vocal than the little guys."

"I imagine you've seen some three pound babies?"

"Just a couple," she grinned. "I've taken care of several one-pounders."

"Babies that small can survive?"

"Some do." The face of one of her babies flashed in her mind.

From the very beginning she loved him. By the time he was four months old he looked like a chubby newborn. The parents were overjoyed that they weren't going home empty-handed that night. Less than two weeks later, dad got out of bed to check on him and their worst fear had happened. Colette could hardly breathe when she got the news. The memorial service was heartbreaking, to say the least.

Pulling her from her thoughts, his pants started to sing. "Woops. That's me." He slid the phone out of his pocket, just far enough to view the screen. This was it. She was about to get a morsel of insight into his personal life. After glancing at the number, he tossed Colette a quick smirk as if he knew what a privilege this must be for her. Colette raised her eyebrows curiously. He put the phone to his ear. "I'm kidding," he grinned, stuffing it back into his pocket. "I know better than that."

"I don't mind. Really."

"It can wait."

"That's ridiculous. Take the call."

"Honestly, I would have declined it anyway. This guy sent me an email ten minutes ago. To tell you the truth, I've been avoiding his calls for quite some time."

Hilarious, she thought. That was precisely what her friends liked to do, ignore her phone calls. That one statement was more telling than anything spectacular he might say thereafter. "And who exactly are you hiding from?"

"Everyone."

Gag me. So he was one of those. Mr. Popularity. It was probably his mother calling to let him know she was finished with his laundry. Or better yet, his girlfriend. Or fiancé. He wasn't wearing a ring, so that ruled out wife.

"I'm not married," he grinned. "I saw you check."

"You're full of yourself. I did not."

"And while we're on the topic, I'm single." He smiled as if he knew it would work. "I'm kind of curious if you are too so I can ask you to dinner."

She uncrossed her legs. "So why are you hiding from the world? Did you rob the Whitehouse? Is the FBI after you?"

He must have picked up on her prissy vibe because his smile was now forced. "My life got pretty hectic so I pulled the emergency brake. Screech. I'm taking it easy for a while. I'm laying low."

"Cool. Good luck with that." She loved how men didn't need good character, or even a job, to get a girl anymore. This day and age, women left no opportunity for the chase. Not that she wanted to be chased. What she wanted was her couch and a box of raisins. "I should get going. I'm cold."

"Oh, okay. Sure. Alright." He stood to see her off as if she were a guest in his home—except *this* host happened to be standing on eight wheels.

She nodded her version of goodbye and walked away. A pang of guilt followed. From the change she noticed in his demeanor, it was almost as if she had hurt his feelings. "Good luck with the pilot license," she called over her shoulder.

There. Her conscience was clear. As she crossed the bridge, she acknowledged the inevitable; a part of her, the gullible part, was going to miss him. Deceptively charming, she reminded herself. The best looking ones always were.

"Colette!"

She spun around and cocked her hip. It didn't take a sociologist to know what was coming next. He wanted her number.

He shouted as if they were children on a playground. "Can I take you to dinner tomorrow night?" He was skating toward her.

With a hand planted firmly on her hip, she narrowed her eyes. "Why?"

When he stopped in front of her, he lowered his voice to a notch above a whisper. "C'mon. Have dinner with me."

"You didn't answer the question." She doubted he was as conniving as her ex, but the way he was looking into her eyes was like déjà vu.

He exhaled as if he was gathering his thoughts. "Let's be real for a second. Why would any man pass up an opportunity to have dinner with you? You know you're gorgeous."

And there she had it. He was after the same thing as the rest of his species. "Do you ask out every female who crosses your path? Because a set bounced by a couple minutes ago. If you skate fast enough, you can probably catch her."

His face glowed like a hot stovetop.

She continued, "I'm sure your success rate with women is off the charts, but for the sake of a fresh perspective, I don't even remember your name."

"My name is Bryce," he said slowly, "Rocco."

Now *that* was a name she wouldn't forget.

Finally he removed his glasses, though she no longer cared to see his eyes. He looked at her sternly. "I wanted to buy you dinner because you *seemed* like a nice person, up until you sprouted horns."

Her jaw dropped in rage. "Forgive me for not setting myself up to be used. And here's a fun fact for you. I like to date guys with a job."

His bewildered face was no indication of the number of

women he had successfully bagged. Suddenly she regretted seeing his eyes. They were angry again. And the worst part? He didn't say a word. She felt smaller and smaller until she couldn't take it anymore. "I'm sorry. What I meant to say is, thank you for the kind offer, but I'm not looking for a relationship right now. It's been a pleasure, Bryce Rocco." *If* that was even his real name.

"A real delight," he muttered.

"Can I get your autograph before I go?" Judging from the scowl on his face, her joke was absolutely not funny. "Sorry. I bet you haven't heard that one a million times. My friend was obsessed with him when she was in college. Like really obsessed. She quoted lines from his movies all the time." When she noticed her arms had been flailing as if every word needed reinforcement, she commanded them back to her side. "I'm sorry. Take care."

After a sharp about-face, she walked away feeling rotten. For no reason at all, she had ripped him apart. In an attempt to console her worthless self, she focused on the fact she would never see him again.

Jazmine had been right all along. Something was seriously wrong with her. She unlocked the car and tossed her book onto the floor.

"Colette!"

Expending every last ounce of courage, she turned around, facing the bridge.

"Since dinner is a big fat no," he hollered, "can I at least give you my number?"

The man was insane. "Have a nice day, Bryce."

"I'll do just that. And I'll see you in three days, same bench, at noon."

CHAPTER 4

"Roxanne, this is Colette Halbrook. I've got all the baby gear, but I'm still missing one little item—or two if you're needing to place twins. I understand you're busy, but if you could please call me back, I'll know you're getting my messages. Thank you so much and I hope you're having a great day."

Colette ended the call and slammed the dryer door shut. "Return your calls, lady!" She scolded herself for not leaving her phone number. It would be counterproductive to bother Roxanne with another voicemail. Over the past six months, Colette had rattled off her number so many times the woman probably had it memorized.

She folded and shelved a load of linens, swept and mopped the floors, and headed out for work. As usual, Stuart was nestled in his chair.

"Good afternoon, Colette. The gas station down the road is going up for sale."

She transferred her computer monitor into her left hand and pulled the door shut. "You're kidding."

"No. I am dead serious. My buddy knows the owner, so that's how I know about it. According to my buddy, the owner has somewhere in the neighborhood of five children."

"What's he going to do now?"

"I don't know, but I'll let you know as soon as I find out." His eyebrows slanted toward his nose. "Hey. What are you doing with that computer screen?"

"I'm taking a one-month sabbatical from the internet. A friend of mine is going to babysit the monitor so I don't cheat."

"Would you like me to monitor the internet usage on your cell phone? I can link it directly to my computer."

She laughed. "I don't use my phone much, so I haven't upgraded to internet. I know. I'm old-school."

After a look of confusion, Stuart was back to his gas station speech. Colette's mind was elsewhere.

The memory of her altercation with Bryce was like being smacked in the head repeatedly with a stop sign. Something was off and she needed to fix it. A shrink would blame it on the trauma of losing her mother at such a tender age and having no memory of her deadbeat father. But there was no way she was still suffering from past hurts. The real problem, she pinpointed on the way home from belittling Bryce, was her dependence on internet.

*

After a little shuffling, Colette and a postpartum nurse managed to wheel a full-sized hospital bed into the private room across from Pod Four. Propped up in bed was a young woman named Julie Shelton recovering from a C-section. She had a full mouth of pink and white braces, and wore a headband with a purple flower tilted on the side. Her husband, Jeff, held a camera in one hand and a stuffed rhinoceros in the other.

Julie's eyes looked painfully heavy as she strained to get a first glimpse of her one-pound two-ounce baby boy. He was lying on his back beneath bilirubin lights like a specimen on a table. His bony limbs were lifeless as his chest rose and fell at a rate predetermined by ventilator settings. His body looked like it was coated in layers of wet red tissue paper and the skin on his shoulders was bunched up like that of a turtle.

Three wires—blue, white, and red—were pasted to his torso and a fourth thicker wire was attached to his foot by a soft Velcro wrap. His arm was splinted to protect the I.V. and a hat was pulled down over his eyes. White tape took up a good portion of his lower face, preventing the tube down his throat from being jostled.

Julie's hand went to her mouth and tears filled her eyes. "Look, Jeff. There he is. Honey, we have a son."

Nodding his head, he responded with a breath. His face was solemn.

"He's so cute," Julie smiled. "Look how tiny he is, his little toes and fingers." She turned from her back onto her side, wincing in pain. In a high-pitched voice, she told her baby how much she loved him, how perfect he was, and that she would be taking him home to his new bedroom soon. Julie's eyelids collapsed momentarily. She watched her baby for the next several minutes in silence.

"Have you guys decided on a name?"

Julie smiled. "Charlie, after Jeff's dad, Chuck. His middle name is Glenn, after my stepdad—I mean my *dad*. He's the one who raised me so Jeff wants me to refer to him as my dad now. I keep forgetting."

"I'm not forcing her to call him anything. I was just wondering if maybe it wasn't necessary to say stepdad since she's never met her real dad. She agreed with me. Didn't you, hun?"

34

"I did." Her mouth popped open as she yawned long and slow.

Colette recorded the name on the top of his chart. "Charlie Glenn," she said. "Very cute." She pressed buttons on the monitor until the word "boy" was replaced with "Charlie." She smiled. "Did I get the spelling right?"

Jeff squinted as he looked at the screen. "Looks good to me."

"Great." Colette manipulated her body around Julie's hospital bed and returned to the stool in the corner of the room. "I bet he likes hearing you call him dad."

"The first time I said it he looked like he was going to cry."

"Aw, that's sweet." Colette wondered how her own character would be different had she grown up knowing her dad. Sadly though, it was her mother who suffered in his absence, in a way that could never be undone. "By the way, I'm Colette Halbrook. I signed up to be Charlie's primary nurse. I'll be here from three in the afternoon until about eleven o'clock on weeknights."

Jeff nodded. "We're very appreciative of what everyone is doing around here for Charlie."

Julie's eyelids slid shut and she forced them back open. "I'm meeting my baby for the first time and I can't even stay awake to look at him."

Jeff touched her shoulder. "Do you want to go back?"

"I want my eyes to stay open. This is frustrating. I don't feel tired. It must be this dark room."

"I think she's ready," Jeff told Colette.

"Did I say that? Don't rush me." Julie sighed before redirecting her frustration toward Colette. "And why did they ask me if I wanted to try to save my baby? Who would say no to that? Do I look like the kind of person who would let my baby die?"

"He was born almost sixteen weeks early," Colette said delicately. "Sometimes babies that young make it and do fine." She tried to find the right words. "But a lot of times we do everything we can to save them and it's still not enough."

"Some parents actually give up on their baby before it's even born?"

Colette paused before answering. "It's not an easy decision for anyone to make. Sometimes the risk is so great, some parents choose to allow their child to pass away naturally and peacefully."

Julie paused as if she was trying to process Colette's words. "Do you think I made the wrong choice? Do you think it was selfish of us to try to save Charlie's life?"

"Not at all." There were nurses on both sides of the spectrum who felt passionately about the subject, but after nearly seven years in the NICU, Colette couldn't make up her mind what she would decide if the choice were hers.

"I could never do that. You know, give up on him like that. I would always wonder. Wouldn't we, Jeff? We'd always wonder."

His forehead wrinkled as he nodded in agreement. "I know we're young and everything, but you should know that we planned this pregnancy. Everyone likes to give me a hard time for this, but I already bought him a fishing pole."

Colette pushed back her own tears. "I'll do everything I can to help him get to where he needs to be."

Julie wiped her eyes. "I can tell you care about him. That's good, because we do too." After a few more minutes, her eyelids got the best of her and she asked to be taken back to her room.

Colette notified the nurses' station while Jeff took some pictures of Charlie. When the nurse arrived, Julie sobbed as she told her baby she was sorry for leaving him.

*

It had been several days since that morning in the park and Colette was getting to the point where she abhorred Bryce—not to mention his teeth. *Nobody* grew them that perfectly. She replayed those fifteen minutes a thousand times, analyzing his every word, movement, and intention, until she reached a point of exasperation. Bryce was an obnoxious song stuck in her head.

The intense way he studied her was unsettling. It was almost as if he had a reason to figure her out when he could have just pegged her as crazy. And when he lost his temper, disgust was written all over his face. Just thinking about it felt like poison settling in her stomach.

In hindsight, she should have graciously accepted his dinner invitation and enjoyed the evening as friends, nothing more. But each time she relived the platonic date that never happened, she found herself cocooned between his strong arms and hard chest. She was smart for walking away from a dangerously deceptive man. Her only regret was looking like an idiot in the process.

The thought of showing her face a third time to the only man who had seen her at her worst terrified her. But there she was, back on that same bench, waiting for the spider to bite.

She stretched one serving of yogurt into a ten-minute production, wishing she had packed more food. Now there was nothing left to do but sit like a bump on a log. She noticed how the wind manipulated each tree differently, causing some to gently sway and others to squirm like children. Yet they all danced to the same tune. She took in the majestic sound of the Willamette, but it heightened her anxiety more than anything. She had lived in Oregon for more than a decade of her adult life and had never once floated a river. Time was moving quickly, life was passing her by. And the thing she wanted most of all, a child of her own, was out of reach.

After checking her portable clock which doubled as a cell phone nobody ever called, she began heading to her car. It was 12:14. A feeling of rejection tormented her until finally she was honest with herself. It wasn't unanswered questions that had brought her back to the park; it was the fact that she *wanted* to see him.

She redirected her attention to the evening ahead. Baby Charlie was doing well and his parents were finally going to be able to hold him. Jeff wouldn't be in until seven or eight, after picking up Julie's mom from the airport.

As Colette approached the bridge, she took one last look over her shoulder and walked *smack* into the railing. Rubbing her torso as if it had hurt, she looked again. Bryce was standing a hundred yards away, waving. Like a robot, she waved back. Too shocked to know what to do next, she continued across the bridge until she was safely out of sight.

She took her time getting into her car and reluctantly pulled out of the parking space. Her heart worked overtime when she spotted Bryce standing on the bridge. She suspected that he ran across the park to make such good time, but it didn't show. He was walking now, with his hands in his pockets, calm as Cool Whip. She cracked her window and waited.

"You made it," he finally said, flashing his irresistible smile.

She returned the smile, noticing he was without sunglasses for a change. His eyes weren't anything special, but she loved the excitement behind them. "Only because I'm trying to figure you out."

"Oh yeah? What have you come up with?"

"I'm still confused."

His smiled widened. "Humor me by telling me why."

To question why Bryce wanted anything to do with her would be redundant, so she went with a different approach. "I think you want to be friends so I can hook you up with your dream job at the hospital—which might work out well for you since I hear they're hiring a thrill-seeking rookie ambulance driver."

"Sounds tempting, but I already have a job." He took his hands out of his pockets and clasped them together. "On second thought, seeing as how my weekends are wide open with no dinner plans, maybe I ought to apply."

"I'll put in a good word for you."

"Why don't I give you my number so you can pass it along to the boss."

"Ha-ha. Very smooth."

He reached into his pocket with a wry grin. "Oh look. My number just happens to be right here. Tell him to call me anytime, okay?" He reached into the window and handed her a green piece of paper.

"I'll do that."

"You promise?"

Through her giggling, she pretended to glare at him. "I'm not making any promises."

"If he wants to find me he'll have to call, because I won't be at the park for quite some time. It was nice seeing you again, Colette."

She felt herself relax as he walked away and out of sight. There was no question what she was going to do with that piece of paper.

CHAPTER 5

Colette dropped a stick of deodorant into the cart when it occurred to her that she had been using the same brand since the onset of puberty. She set her trusted friend back on the shelf and tried to make sense of her options. She popped off an orange cap and took a whiff. Crinkling her nose, she reached into her purse blindly. Who would be calling her at this hour? "Hey you! What's up?"

It was Summer LeCroy, her best friend since fifth grade. Back then they had passed as twins with their curly hair, rounded noses, and matching tennis shoes. Middle school was another story. Colette shot up like a beanstalk crying out to be pruned, while Summer blossomed into a shapely young woman. After their first high school football game, the two of them laughed hysterically when they discovered Colette was a full foot taller. At age sixteen when Colette finally got some meat on her bones, it was Summer's turn to be jealous. But she never really was. Summer's fun-loving personality and unstoppable confidence was impossible to compete with.

"Are you awake?" Summer giggled. "Of course you are. It's midnight. You'll never guess who just sent me a friend request. You will *never* guess."

"Who?"

"C'mon, take a whack at it."

Colette had the urge to blurt out that she had met a "Bryce

Rocco," but that would lead to another lecture about her dating life. "What's-his-face. The one with the lisp." He was the first guy that popped into her head. Actually, Gary was the first, but Colette didn't dare bring up his filthy name.

"Who, Quinn? No. Did I even tell you about his speech impediment? It didn't bother me at all. What made you think of him? We were only together for a month. Alright, alright. I'll give you a clue. Let's see. He's a guy... he's really, really smart... he got his braces off..."

"Austin?" Just saying the name out loud made her smile.

"I don't know what happened, but he is so stinkin' hot now! I have no clue how he's still on the market, but he totally is."

"So it's Austin?"

"Yes, and he just asked about you."

Her heart skipped a beat. "What did he say?" Her mind was already swarming with memories, all good ones.

"Wait, wait, wait. Hold on a sec. I'm on I.M. with him and I can't keep up. Give me two seconds."

Colette could hear typing in the background. "What's he saying?"

"Shut up, Coco. Seriously."

She tossed the same old brand of deodorant back into the shopping cart. As she walked to the register, she reminisced of moments with her first love. Austin was her badminton partner in P.E. class her freshman year of high school. After two months of flirting, he asked her out. She was ecstatic. The days that followed were awkward and uncomfortable. So one week later, she ended it. As the years went on, the flirting continued, but that was as far as it ever went.

Just as the cashier greeted her, Summer announced she was

back. "You're coming to Colorado in two weeks! Can you get it off?"

A weekend in Colorado sounded amazing. "I'll call you back in five minutes. I'm at the store about to check out."

"Okay, but heads up. I gave him your number."

Colette's jaw tightened. "Summer, you shouldn't have done that." Had she not been in public, she would have used sharper words. It was infuriating how her friends continued to force their way into her dating life as if she couldn't handle it on her own. "I have to go."

"I didn't really give it to him. You know that. I was testing your reaction to see if you'd let it slide, just this once, since the man is *your friend*!"

"I'll call you from the car."

*

Two hours into her shift, Jeff poked his head into Charlie's dim room. "Hey. Is it okay if I come in? How's he doing today?"

"Of course. Come on in. You're always welcome." She opened the door wider and stepped aside. "Charlie's hanging in there. They had to increase his oxygen this morning, but he seems to be a lot happier now. Mary said his heart rate dropped all the way down into the thirties around noon. He had some trouble coming out of that particular bradycardia, but he's doing fine right now."

"And there's no way of knowing if any of this is going to cause any sort of permanent damage?"

She pressed her lips together, shaking her head apologetically. "I wish I could give you a different answer, but sometimes we won't know until a child is two or three years old."

"It's hard to imagine him as a toddler."

"It is, isn't it? Weight gain is slow-going in the beginning." Colette skimmed the chart. "He's down just over a hundred grams from his birth weight, which is about three ounces, but that's to be expected. I'm sure you've noticed that the bilirubin lights are gone."

"I was more so noticing that the hat that was pulled down over his eyes is missing."

"Yes, that too. His jaundice appears to be cleared up. See how his skin no longer has that yellowish color to it?"

Jeff bent down and looked into the green-tinted plastic tent. "Hi there, buddy. I see you. You're looking good. I heard you had a rough time when Daddy was at work. I missed you today." He set his camcorder on the counter next to the sink. "Can I still touch him even though he's under that... thing?"

"The tent? Yes, you sure can. Just lift up the side of it and slide your hand under. If he gets too cold you can always help yourself to a fresh blanket out of the warmer." Stealing a peek out the doorway, she surveyed the hall. "Is Julie here? I heard she was here most of the morning."

"She's at home." He slid the stool closer to Charlie's bed and sat down. "She'll be by later. The house wasn't up to par and friends have been stopping by non-stop, so she's cleaning up." Looking down at the floor, he ran his fingers through his gelled hair. Startled, he looked up quickly. "Do I need to wash my hands again?"

"Nah. You're fine." She silenced the alarm that started to ding, keeping a close eye on the monitor.

"Last night when we got home, Julie fell apart pretty bad. She was sort of freaking out because she had to leave Charlie behind. Then her mom and two older sisters started running their mouths. I have no idea how it happened, but pretty soon everyone was mad at everyone. I'm not saying that Julie is an angel right now, but the least they could do is cut her some slack."

"Oh, no. Poor thing."

"She's so sad. About Charlie, I mean. Not her family."

Colette grieved for the young couple, for the treacherous journey they were only beginning. Inevitably there would be some intense weeks ahead. "It's not easy to carry a baby for five months and then go home empty handed."

"I've never seen her so upset. I left, you know, to get her something to eat. And then I came back in the house because I forgot my wallet. Julie had this stuffed giraffe on her lap and was putting one of Charlie's shirts on it. She was crying, like *really* crying, in this deep voice." He shook his head and exhaled. "It's hard for us to see him like this. He looks so uncomfortable with that tube down his throat and all the blood tests he has to get. Do you think he's got a good chance at making it home?"

"I don't know, Jeff. I hope he does. It's—" Colette noticed Julie standing in the doorway. Her eyes were red and puffy, but she looked put together in her skirt and sweater. "Hi there. You made it."

"Hi, Colette. It's good to see you." She turned to her husband. "Didn't you hear me trying to stop you? I wanted to come with you." Her eyes welled with tears, and then she lost it. "I'm not supposed to drive yet, so my mom had to drive me all the way out here. Why wasn't your phone on?"

"I must have forgotten to turn it back on when we left the NICU last night. I'm sorry. I had no idea you wanted to come. Is

45

your mom still here?"

"No, she's not still here! So you were just going to let me stay home and clean while you spent the evening with our son?" Glancing at Charlie, she gestured toward his bed. "I can't believe you were—" She stopped herself and her expression softened. Placing a hand over her heart, she smiled. "Look. His little eyes are showing. The hat is gone."

Jeff hugged Julie from behind, resting his chin on her shoulder. "I'm sorry, babe. I wasn't thinking. I'll never do that again."

Turning around, she cupped Jeff's face and kissed his cheek. "Look at him, honey. Look at our little boy. Were his eyes open earlier?"

"I don't know. I just got here."

They both looked at Colette inquisitively and she peered in the tent. "I was wondering the same thing when I got here. They're still fused shut, but they'll pop open any day now."

Jeff squeezed Julie's shoulders as if to massage them. "Did you notice how the top of his ears are still fused to his head?"

Grinning, she looked closer. "That's wild."

"Do you guys want to hold him tonight?"

Julie gasped. "I didn't know we were allowed to."

"It's actually therapeutic for preemies to be snuggled with their parents. Do you want to give it a try?"

"I would love to."

"I need to call a respiratory therapist and a nurse to help me move him. It's kind of a process when they're on the ventilator, but I don't mind at all. In fact, we encourage it." Colette handed each of them a pamphlet. "Studies have shown that preemies benefit from what's called *kangaroo care*. That's when a parent and baby have skin-to-skin contact."

Julie collected her husband's pamphlet and handed them both to Colette. "The hospital already gave us this brochure. I definitely want to do that."

"Good. We'll have an easier time keeping Charlie's body temperature up that way, and he'll be able to smell your skin."

Her eyes welled with tears. "Do you think he'll know it's his mommy that's holding him? I'm sorry. I've been really emotional lately."

"That's for sure," Jeff grinned. He intercepted Julie's fist as she playfully slugged him.

Colette returned the pamphlets to the drawer. "You tell Jeff that it's perfectly normal for a woman to be emotional after giving birth to her husband's baby," Colette winked. "And yes, Charlie will recognize that you're his mom, especially when he hears your voice."

Colette tracked down a respiratory therapist, a recliner, and Jazmine. Then they went to work untangling wires and prepping Julie. "Alrighty. Are you ready?"

"If *you're* ready, *I'm* ready," Julie grinned. "Turn on the camcorder, Jeff. I want you to get this. Colette, will you take some pictures? My camera is in my purse."

"Just as soon as we get you two settled in." After sliding her hands underneath the blanket Charlie was resting on, Colette scooped him up like a loaf of bread and pasted his moist body against Julie's skin. Jazmine and the RT carefully situated the wires and tubing. All three worked in unison until Charlie was tucked into a tiny ball, cozy against his mom's chest. They piled warm blankets on top of him and adjusted the tall heat lamp.

Julie looked down with the biggest smile. "Well hello there,

Charlie. Mommy gets to hold you tonight. Do you like that?"

Colette looked up at the monitor and was pleased by the numbers. Jazmine and the RT left the room, and Julie sat for the next two hours talking and singing to her tiny bundle of joy. Then Jeff took his turn.

By the time Colette clocked out for dinner her stomach was grouchy. The break room was vacant, a rare pleasure that undoubtedly wouldn't last long. Sweet 'n' sour pork with colorful veggies turned slowly in the microwave as she took in the aroma. One taste of this creation and Bryce would bring her home to meet his mother. The microwave beeped. After stealing a red pepper, she sat by the window and watched the rain trickle down the glass.

It was Thursday night, more than a week since she gave up her computer, and separation anxiety was at its peak. She was still kicking herself for not doing an internet search on Bryce before she dropped off her monitor at Jazmine's house with a signed promissory note. There was still no man lined up for Saturday night, and Sunday looked just as bleak. The good old fashioned way of picking up men was too much work, unless of course she was desperate enough to bat her eyelashes at a drunk in a bar, which she wasn't.

Setting her cell phone on the table, she decided to put some sizzle into her weekend. Luckily she had foreseen this moment coming and wasted no time programming Bryce's number into her phone. Typically, texting wasn't her style, but there was no way she was calling him.

Hi, Bryce. Guess who?

Her index finger hovered over the word "send." She reread the text over and over until she was sure it sounded okay. Then she exhaled sharply and sent it. She stuffed comfort food into her mouth by the truckload. What if he didn't know it was her? Her eyes were fixed on the phone as if it were a flying tarantula about to lift off. Lucky for her, she didn't have to wait long.

Just as I was starting to think I'd never hear from you again. Guess who has your number now?

Giggling, she tried to come up with a clever response. But her mind was blank. She couldn't concentrate. "Relax," she whispered to herself. "He has your number now. You're off the hook." But she couldn't relax. Her neurons were misfiring left and right.

What are you up to tonight?

She grinned, relieved by the simplicity of his question. *I'm on a dinner break at work. What about you?* She could feel her intestines twisting into knots, but nonetheless, she was having the time of her life.

It sounds like you still have a long night ahead of you. I'm at my nephew's birthday party. He's turning three. We're about to chow down on my sister's lasagna.

Just like that, his credibility went up a thousand points. She would give anything to spy on that party, to watch him interact with a toddler. *Sounds delicious. I'll let you get back to your party.*

I don't know. She put chunks of zucchini in it this time, so I might have to keep my distance from that batch. I think she's trying to poison me.

His comment made her laugh, but she was at a loss for how to respond. Writing had never been her strong point. Cowardly, she threw in the towel. *My break is almost over. I'll talk to you soon, okay?*

I'll call you tomorrow.

CHAPTER 6

"I have down that your flight arrives in Denver at 6:47 on Saturday the eighth, correct?" Summer was smacking away on chocolate, synonymous with her typical phone etiquette.

"That's only if it doesn't crash."

"Why would it do that? Planes don't just fall out of the sky. Now listen up. We're all meeting for dinner at eight, so we'll have to go straight to the restaurant from the airport. I know it's rushing it, but I told everyone to go ahead and order without us if we're late."

"How many people are going to be there?"

"One, and his name is Austin. That's all you need to know. Everyone else is just part of the venue, as far as you're concerned. If you don't mess this up, we might get a rock on your finger by Christmas."

Colette grinned. "Speaking of 'rock,' I met a guy with an interesting name."

"I thought you couldn't get online."

"I met him in person. You should be proud. He plowed into me on his bike while I was jogging." Colette laughed out loud picturing the horrified look on his face. "He hit me with his bike, and he was like, 'I can't believe I just ran you over.' I tried to get him to understand that I was fine, but he was shaken up, and when I found out his name, I was like—"

"Stop the Nascar race. You sound unusually giddy about this

guy. Not to be negative, but this isn't a ploy to take yourself off the market before next week, is it? Because I would be really sad if you didn't even give Austin a chance after all I've done to set this up for you."

Her jaw dropped like she was guilty. "Not at all."

"I hope not. Because I think you and Austin have the potential of having an exciting, healthy relationship."

"Healthy?"

"You know what I mean. Successful."

"He wouldn't still like me after all these years." She had a strong hunch Austin never stopped loving her, but she wanted to hear it from someone else, just to feel the buzz.

"What's not to like? I mean, seriously, Coco. He's always had a thing for you. That's probably why he's not married."

"Oh, I'm sure." Colette studied his graduation picture the way she used to for hours. "I like that I can trust him. His mom always seemed really nice."

"I never met her."

"Okay, this time I really have to go. I hate running late for work."

"Right. Sorry. Go brush your teeth. Wait. One more thing. This guy you met. What does he do?"

Colette said the first thing that popped into her head. "A cop. They always have good stories."

"Have you gone out with him yet?"

"No."

"I would never ask a chronic dater not to date, so I have just one request. I never thought I'd be saying this, but stay true to your rule. One date only, please. Promise me."

Colette untwisted the toothpaste cap and cranked on the

water. "Fine. I promise."

"Good. Do you think he carries a gun? Play footsies with him and check near his ankles. I bet he has one."

Colette giggled. He carried a gun alright. "Or I could just ask him straight up."

"Do you think he'd tell you? Sorry. Go to work. And have fun this weekend, but not too much fun. I don't want you falling in love days before you're reunited with Austin."

*

They were whispering when she entered the room. Three nurses left immediately, and a fourth ushered out a nurse's aide who was on her way in. Dr. Luman, thirty-five years old and nearly bald, looked at Colette with stern eyes. "You're here."

She could feel heat rise to her face as if she were found out. "What's wrong?" The flash of anger in his eyes was completely foreign to her.

Dr. Piazza, a woman in her late forties, shuffled papers in the corner of the room. She stopped momentarily to nod at Colette who stared back at her blankly. Had she said something upsetting to Julie Thursday night? Frantically she tried to recall, but came up with nothing.

Dr. Luman set down a clipboard and removed his reading glasses. "Colette. I have some bad news for you. I'm sorry. Baby Shelton had a rough weekend."

His words nearly stopped her heart. She knew what was coming, but didn't want to hear it. "His name is Charlie, not baby Shelton!" How dare he refer to Charlie as a label on a chart. A familiar image of two parents huddled together, crying, flashed before her eyes. Oftentimes she saw it coming, but not with Charlie. Not this soon. Not this unexpectedly.

"I apologize. Baby Charlie... he had a rough weekend."

"You said that. What happened? How is he?"

Dr. Piazza shook her head disapprovingly. "Colette," she sang, as if to warn her she was crossing a line.

Colette's legs weakened. Slowly, she backed out of the room and peered down the hallway. She stepped back in, dreading what was coming next.

Nervously, Dr. Luman clicked a pen over and over. "He's not doing well. Mom and Dad... uh... Jeff and..." He snatched the clipboard and fumbled for his glasses.

"Julie," said Dr. Piazza, arms crossed. She shot Colette an annoyed look.

"Jeff and Julie," he continued. "They are in there saying their goodbyes right now. They've decided to let him go."

"That's impossible. They would never. We just talked about it a few days ago and she told me how they could never give up on their baby. No. Something's not right."

Dr. Luman nodded, his forehead creased with concern. "He quit breathing for over eight minutes last night. His weight is still dropping and he's not tolerating feeds. His ventilator settings are extremely high. Everyone is in agreement that this is for the best."

"Why didn't anyone call me? I hate that. My baby is down the hall *dying*, and nobody bothered to take five seconds out of their day to let me know."

"I... I don't—"

Dr. Piazza exhaled loudly. "There is a family down the hall who could use you right now. Let's stop playing the blame game.

You're here. These things happen. You have a job to do."

Colette inhaled deeply, resolving to pull herself together. "You're right. I'm sorry. What should I do?"

"Spend some time with the family. Take some pictures. Make a set of handprints if they want you to. And when everyone's ready..."

"Okay," she nodded, understanding all too well.

*

Tears rolled down Julie's face as she held her newborn for the last time. His face was clean, and all the tubes and wires were gone. He was clothed in soft pajamas made by a neighbor neither Jeff nor Julie had ever met. Colette sat in the corner of the dark room in a trance, questioning what she had done. At the start of her shift, she held a living, breathing baby boy. And now, because of her, he was gone.

Julie rubbed his fingers and stroked his forehead, speaking to him softly. Colette suspected they had been up all night knowing they were about to lose their firstborn. Julie placed the side of his face against hers and kissed him. She whispered into his ear, too quiet for anyone to hear. When she was finished, she folded the blanket across the lower half of his body and gave him up.

As soon as he left her hands, she lost it all over again. Her whole body trembled as she sobbed. Jeff pulled her up to his side and held her tightly. They wept together, their faces buried in one another's necks. She cried Charlie's name over and over, saying she was sorry she couldn't give him the life he deserved. Beneath the sobbing Colette heard something about his painted bedroom and his grandpa.

After everything was taken care of and in order, Colette tracked down Dr. Piazza. Embarrassed by the way she had mouthed off to the doctors, she humbly asked where Dr. Piazza wanted her next.

"Take a couple of hours to compose yourself. At 8:00 tonight, I'm giving you a thirty-two weeker and a thirty-five weeker in Pod Four. They're easy babies and Jazmine will be in there with you. I understand that you girls have become good friends. Hopefully she can help take your mind off of what you've just been through."

"Okay." It was a nice gesture, but she wanted to be home. "Thank you," she added out of obligation.

"I'm proud of you, Colette. I know that wasn't easy, but you shined in there this afternoon. You're one of our best."

Fighting back tears, Colette went to her locker and grabbed her coat and purse. On her way out, she avoided eye contact with a co-worker.

"Was that a twenty-four weeker you just took downstairs?"

Colette swallowed the lump in her throat. "Yes he was."

"I'm sorry, Colette." She hugged her tightly. When she pulled away, she wiped Colette's tears with the back of her hand. "You're cute though, you know that? They say you cry over every baby that leaves here. I get why you cried over this one, but we all need to remind ourselves from time to time that at the end of the day, it's a job. These babies, they don't belong to us. They're—"

"I really wish you'd pop that whitehead off your face. It's obscene."

Her horrified expression was just what Colette needed to make it downstairs without falling apart. She pulled the car door shut, twisted the key in the ignition, and adjusted the heat setting. Her eyes welled with tears as she pulled the phone from her pocket. There was one missed call from Bryce. Screw Bryce. Life was just a big fat game to him. Bicycles and birthday parties.

As her car idled, the air was still blowing cold. She was alone. She was depressed. And baby Charlie was gone. What she needed more than anything was a friend. Not a boyfriend, not a chatterbox. Just a plain old friend.

She threw together a text message and sent it to Bryce with as much thought as a scribbled note to herself. It didn't matter if he thought she was clever or eloquent. By now he knew she was neither of those things. All she was asking for was a brief distraction from life. Tomorrow she would turn him down like the rest, and that would be that.

CHAPTER 7

Colette twisted the rearview mirror, pursed her glossy lips together, and forced a smile. Her eyes were red, but they weren't puffy like they had been at her apartment. It was going to take some serious acting to convince Bryce everything was fine. If she could just get him talking, the distraction might be enough to numb the pain of her lacerated heart. Chilling images of Charlie and his family flashed in her mind like a homicide briefing. Typically NICU tragedies didn't consume her mind beyond a few days, but this particular one, she feared, now defined her.

Alton Baker Park had been her idea when Bryce offered to meet up for dinner. Pizza and pop, she had texted him, sounded good tonight. Fine dining was more up her alley on chilly afternoons, but even if he *could* afford it, she didn't want to risk getting teary-eyed in front of a crowd.

After kicking off a pair of flip-flops, she grabbed the tall leather boots and socks from the passenger side. Guilt overwhelmed her so strongly she felt nauseous. She gulped down what was left of a bottled water and locked the door behind her. With her head held high, she crossed the lawn playing the role of a content young woman enjoying nature.

Bryce spotted her right away. "You made it," he called from a distance. His pace was faster than hers as he made his way toward her.

Colette smiled, truly glad to see him. There was a familiarity about him that was comforting. From the thigh up they were dressed the same, both in gray wool coats. Without a price tag she couldn't be sure, but his coat looked as expensive as hers, maybe more. Colette noticed he was without a hat this time. His dark hair brought out his green eyes. As less and less space separated them, she continued to feel at ease. She was doing her best not to stare, but he looked sharp. It didn't help that he was eyeing her with an intensity that made her blush.

It wasn't until he hugged her that she stiffened. Her stomach churned. Bryce had no idea what she had put a young family through just hours earlier. And what would Jeff and Julie say if they could see her now, carrying on as if she hadn't stolen their little boy's life? When Bryce released her, she glanced over her shoulder. When she looked back at him, his smile had vanished. Concern was all over his face. "Are you okay? What's wrong?"

And that was all it took. Silently, tears escaped one by one. She turned her back on him and wiped her face. What was she thinking, contacting Bryce when she knew she was emotionally fragile? How dare she put him in such an awkward position.

Bryce cursed under his breath. "Look, I don't mean to upset you. I'm sorry it's taken me this long to get the hint." When her shoulders started to shake, he put a large hand over each one and held her steadily from behind. "Colette, what's wrong? What happened?"

Humiliated, she shook her head. "I never should have texted you today. I don't know what I was thinking."

"No. Not at all. I'm glad you did." The size of his palms made her feel protected. When her crying subsided, he put his arm around her and crouched close to her face. "Come with me," he whispered.

Together they crossed the grass, their slow steps in unison. He helped her down onto a quilt. She was intrigued by the salad, breads, and many soups set before her. She wiped her eyes once more and smiled. "This isn't pizza."

He sat down next to her, one leg extended onto the grass. "Nothing gets past you, detective."

She bumped him with her shoulder. "I'm just surprised. This is a lot of food."

"This wasn't my doing. I'm just the chauffeur."

"Either way, it looks delicious." Hugging her knees against her chest, she took in Oregon's beauty as if she were seeing it for the first time. The sunset was spread across the sky in brilliant hues of oranges and reds, and the water trickling by had a peace about it.

She saw Bryce pull a bottle of wine out of a paper bag. "Oh, none for me, thank you."

"You don't drink?"

"No, but don't let that stop you. It doesn't bother me." She cringed when she saw him put it back. For some reason, with Bryce, she felt compelled to explain but she couldn't think of a single reason why he needed to know about her dark past.

"Tell you what, Colette. Why don't we postpone this meal for a few minutes and sit by the river?"

"Okay, sure."

Not ten steps away, he helped her down a five-foot embankment leading to a small rocky shoreline. She followed him until the tips of her boots were covering damp rocks. Briefly, he looked over his shoulder. "Dinner can wait. Let's sit."

The rocks were cold, but the sunset looked toasty warm. Bryce picked up five or six rocks the size of peach seeds, shook them like dice, and spread his fingers allowing them to fall through. He did that several times before he spoke again. "Do you want to talk about it?"

She knew she owed him an explanation, but how could she admit that she had taken somebody's life who didn't ask to die? Her heart was broken for the young couple who would never see their son carry out the dreams they had for him. Even simple ones like writing his name for the first time, learning how to swim in the deep end all by himself, or calling his grandpa just to say hi. It felt backwards that she did what she did, and there was no consequence, no punishment. And maybe that was the reason she finally let the words slip out. She needed to fully feel the shame of what she had done. "I took his life."

He narrowed his eyes, studying her face. "No you didn't."

"Yes I did. I barely had a chance to think about what I was doing. I just did it." Her eyes started to burn, but she refused to cry.

"Who did you kill? What happened?" He put his hand on her back. "Was it your boyfriend?"

"My boyfriend?!" Bewildered, she searched his face. There wasn't a hint of humor. After an awkward pause, she broke into laughter. "Did I kill my boyfriend?" She couldn't get over his seriousness, as if she were capable of such a thing.

He laughed too, but cautiously. "Okay, okay. I was wrong. I don't know why I said that." His smile faded quickly. He opened his mouth as if to speak and then closed it again.

She knew his perception of her was about to change. Any positive attributes he recognized would soon be overshadowed by negative ones. She repositioned her sore body and closed her eyes.

It was a full minute before he spoke again. "A baby passed away? Was it one of your patients?"

She nodded. "Charlie was his name. His parents loved him so much."

He used his thumb to stop a tear rolling down her cheek. "You can't blame yourself. Those babies, they're sick, right? It's not your fault."

In that moment, he felt like her best friend. Going against everything she knew herself to be, she opened up to him. "I went to report. The parents, the doctors, everyone. They all agreed. Everybody. They told me to do it and I did. I didn't even think about it first. Charlie was small, but he was alive. And now he's..."

Bryce put his arm around her and held her. "You have a good heart, Colette. I can tell already. A noble career and a good heart."

"Thank you." She didn't like the way it made her feel to be praised for such a despicable act. She slipped out from beneath his arm, stood, and brushed off her backside. She would finish crying later, in the privacy of her apartment. She inhaled a deep, choppy breath. It was time to change the subject. She picked up a rock and tossed it in the water. "It's pretty out here. I really like the river." To her disappointment, he only nodded. She sensed he was uncomfortable. "Do you ever float it?"

He stood too, but allowed plenty of distance between them. "It's been years. I just bought a house on the McKenzie River a few months ago. If you like this, you'd love it out there."

"You must like to swim." She saw his mouth curve into a subtle smile. Now she was getting somewhere.

He took two steps closer. "Not this time of year, but come summertime the fish will know me by name."

"Are you that popular, Brent?"

"It's Bry—" He stopped himself when he saw her eyebrows peek playfully. "You got me."

"I'm still not one-hundred percent convinced your name is Bryce Rocco. Sounds kind of suspicious to me."

He grinned from ear to ear. "Like it or not, it's the name my parents gave me. It's an attention-getter for sure."

"I bet." As she reveled in the affection radiating from his eyes, she was dying to know why he had chosen *her*. Unless he was a good actor, he was definitely one of the nicest guys she had ever met. He was forgiving and patient, available and engaging. It didn't add up that such a sweet, attractive bachelor would ever, in a million years, give her a second chance after her psychotic response when he first asked for her number. Nothing would ruin the moment faster than a trip down memory lane, but she couldn't go on another day without knowing. "Bryce, I have a question for you."

His eyes shifted. "What is it?"

"Why didn't you run the other direction when I freaked out on you the second time we saw each other? I'm glad you didn't, but I can't wrap my mind around it. Obviously I'm missing something."

"I liked you. It's as simple as that."

"Either you're extremely desperate for human conversation, or there's something you're not telling me."

"I knew you wouldn't let me off that easy." He took several steps closer, leaving a small space between them. "I can't give you specifics just yet, but I'll give you the honest, generic truth."

"At this point, I'll take whatever I can get."

His lips parted as he eyed her mysteriously. "Something you said... hooked me."

"What did I say?"

"I'll tell you when it's time."

She laughed, but it was hard to appreciate the humor. "Your cryptic answer is going to keep me up at night."

"Sorry, but that's the best I can do for now. You're going to have to trust me on this one."

They stood in silence, dusk turning to night. What she wouldn't give to have a man like Bryce by her side. In that moment, she made a deliberate decision to give up the fight. The possibility of an actual friendship, and possibly more, was worth the risk of getting hurt. "I've never floated a river in my whole life. Any river." There. He was getting to know the real Colette Halbrook, boring and lonely with no life experiences to speak of.

"Never? Alright then." He extended his arm. "I don't have a tube with me, but how about a swim?"

She tensed up until she saw his hand fall back to his side. "Oh, you were kidding. I was thinking about jumping in."

"You must really like me because that water is cold. But a little hypothermia never hurt anyone. Let's do it."

"I was joking and you know it. And even if I wanted to, I can't. I have to work tonight."

"They're making you finish out the week? I'm assuming this all happened last night."

"It's okay. They just need me for a few hours and then I'll have two days off. Plus, I'm going on a mini vacation in a week."

"Where to?"

"Colorado. My best friend lives there."

"I didn't realize you were pressed for time. We better get some food in your stomach before you hit the road."

When they got settled back on the quilt, their bodies were closer this time. Bryce got to work pulling off lids and passing out napkins. He handed her a spoon. "Try them all and tell me which ones you like. I'm assuming that you're not vegan or anything."

"You guessed right." She picked up one of the containers and inhaled the wonderful aroma. "So many choices and they all look so good."

The next hour was the happiest she had been in a long time. Bryce was kind, inquisitive, and funny. But hesitation kept creeping back in, at the reminder that Bryce was a stranger, a disheveled guy she had met in a park. It didn't help that he was new to town either. Isn't that what fugitives liked to do? Move from place to place? Alter their appearance? Pretend to be somebody they're not? And she couldn't explain why he wanted her number so badly after the way she had treated him that second day. Any other guy would move on and never look back.

Nonetheless, she tried to find the best words to express the gratitude she felt. "I'm glad you were able to meet up with me. I don't want to think about what tonight would have been like without you."

His smile warmed her. When he finally claimed his turn to speak, he seemed to choose his words carefully. "Do you think you'll have time to get together before your trip?"

She hesitated. There was an angel on one shoulder and a devil on the other, both shouting different things, but she couldn't decipher one from the other. Was it right to allow herself to fall in love, or was it right to protect herself from another horrific

64

relationship? How many times had she cursed herself for not walking away from her ex? As much as she liked Bryce, deep down she knew it was wiser to play it safe.

"Sometimes I think about how I met you. We have no mutual connections, like someone who could say, 'I've known Bryce for such and such years' or 'Colette comes across as crazy every once in a blue moon, but otherwise she's great.'" She laughed as if she were kidding. "That's my only hesitation. I don't know that I actually... know you. Please don't take offense."

His eyes darkened and he spoke in a deepened voice. "You're telling me I might be dangerous?"

She laughed. "It's possible."

"Yet you trust me in the dark, alone, next to a river?"

"I'm watching my back."

"Okay then. Let me calm your fears. I'm not dangerous, my record is squeaky clean, and I'm not packing heat today. You're welcome to search me."

She could feel herself blush. "That won't be necessary."

He cut a piece of multigrain bread, spread a dollop of butter across it, and handed it to her. "When can I see you again?"

She closed her eyes momentarily and swallowed hard. "You'll never know how difficult this is for me to say, but after tonight, we're going to have to go our separate ways."

CHAPTER 8

"You're doing it again," sang Jazmine. She tapped a pen against one of her baby's charts and eyed Colette curiously. "This is *so* not my imagination."

Jazmine's continuous scrutiny was too much for a Monday night. Colette snatched a diaper from the drawer and shot her friend a tight-lipped smile. "Would you give it up? I'm not doing anything."

"What's she doing?" asked Dusty, a second-year nursing student. "And why is her face all red?"

Jazmine threw her arms up. "That's what I want to know. I've done everything but tie her up and torture her to get her to talk."

He raised one eyebrow and laughed mischievously.

"Shut up, Dusty," Colette said with a smirk.

He put his hands in front of him as if he were negotiating with a Pit Bull. "What did I say? Did I say something? No I did not."

Jazmine put one hand on her hip and gestured with the other. "One second she's smiling, the next she's blushing. Colette's always up for hearing everyone else's business, and finally she's got a juicy story of her own and she won't say a word."

Dusty cleared his throat. "Allow me to explain. There's a new man in town who is extremely pleasing to the eye. The smiling is a natural reaction to exhibits A and B," he said, flexing his biceps. "Ain't that right, Colette?"

"Guilty. Can we drop this now?" She turned off the warm water and carried the tiny, partially-filled bathtub across the room. She stopped mid-step when the intercom buzzed.

"Colette? Are you there?"

"Yes?"

"You have a visitor. A lovely visitor. Her name is Jenn. She says she's Bryce's sister."

Colette's left hand slipped, but she caught the tub before it hit the floor. Water splashed in all directions, and her scrubs got the worst of it. Frantic, she set down the tub. "Uh... thank you. I'll be right there." It was impossible to think straight with Bryce's *sister* down the hall. Colette looked to Jazmine for support.

"Who's Bryce?"

"You're not going to help me, are you." Strapped for time, she immediately went for the blanket warmer, slipped, and landed on her side. If it hurt, she couldn't feel it.

"Ooh. Crash and burn." Dusty grabbed her by the arm and helped her up. "You okay, girl?"

Colette caught Jazmine's curious glare, but offered no explanation. "Dusty, I'll give you ten bucks if you mop that up for me."

"Twenty and it's done."

"Thank you! And Jaz, please watch my babies. I'll be two seconds."

"Fine, but who is Bryce?"

"I'll tell you later. Be right back." No sooner had she left the room than she marched back in. "Jaz, I need your shirt. I can't go out there looking like this. Switch me."

Dusty laughed. "Wow. This night just keeps getting better and better."

"Colette, you're out of your mind. That's a good way to get us both fired. I'm going to do you a ginormous favor and say no."

"I wouldn't be asking if I wasn't serious. You have to switch me." As a last ditch effort, she looked at Jazmine with desperate eyes. "Please do this for me. I need your help." When she saw the change in Jazmine's expression, she sighed in relief.

"Colette, you have to relax. That girl has no idea what just happened back here. You're good. I promise."

She ground her teeth and then sighed. "I hope you're right." Making her way down the hall, she allowed Jazmine's statement to sink in. Her panic lessened, but electricity continued to pulse through her body as if she were about to meet royalty. This was Bryce's sister! And there was no telling what she was doing there.

Then it hit her. Maybe she was about to give Colette a piece of her mind for rejecting her brother three days ago. But what sister would care? Sucking in one last good breath, she opened the door.

An adorable blonde pregnant woman with noticeable acne was beaming with excitement. "Hello. I'm Jenn, Bryce's sister." She extended her hand confidently as if she were hosting an important business meeting.

"Hello," she echoed with equal enthusiasm. "I'm Colette."

"I know. The curls," she laughed. "They're beautiful. It's so good to meet you. But you can never tell my brother we met. He will literally flip out if he finds out I asked for you."

To hear Bryce referred to as a brother was strange. That meant he was part of a family which meant *someone* knew him, and that in itself gave him almost enough credibility to be

68

datable. Colette glanced at the receptionist, a plump grandmother of twenty-five grandkids, who was smiling so wide it looked cartoonish.

"Anyway, Bryce asked me to deliver these flowers and—oh, here you go—and I knew you were somewhere on the other side of those doors. I couldn't help myself."

The massive arrangement was mesmerizing. "Thank you. Wow."

"I know, right? I was so jealous when I saw them." She fiddled with a Calla Lily. "I nearly broke my back getting them up here. I don't know what he was thinking sending a pregnant woman to do the job."

Not knowing what to say, she gestured to Jenn's belly. "Is this your first?"

"Not quite. I have a fifteen-year-old, a six-year-old, a three-year-old, and then this," she said, pointing to her abdomen. "All boys."

"You're going to be busy." She was dying to read the card peeking out of the flowers.

"Going to be? I *am* busy. Plus, when I'm watching Bryce's three kids, look out."

Colette's eyes expanded like blowfish.

"Kidding. I'm just kidding. I saw your face. You were like, 'Bryce didn't tell me he has kids.'"

The receptionist laughed along with them. Colette predicted she was enjoying the scene far too much to keep it to herself. It was bad enough that everyone knew she had been single for the past decade. Now her nosey co-workers would know there was a man in hot pursuit.

Jazmine wedged herself between the double doors. "Heads

up. Cecily's mom is on her way and she's bringing fresh milk."

Colette smiled knowing Jazmine would see right through it. "I'll alert the press."

Jazmine tucked her black hair behind her ears delicately. "Hi there. Look at you. How far along are you?"

"Two more months and he's out of there."

"A boy? How fun. By the way, I'm Colette's good friend, Jazmine Anderson."

"Anderson? Any relation to Jack Anderson? He and I used to work together."

"No, I don't think so."

"I hate to interrupt," Colette cut in, "but we should be getting back."

After saying their goodbyes, Colette walked quickly down the hall with her trophy of flowers, half embarrassed, half proud. Jazmine followed Colette into Pod Four and thanked the nurse who had stepped in.

"What was that?" Colette demanded.

"What did she end up saying about your wet shirt? No big deal, right?"

"How dare you, Jazmine. You had absolutely no right to follow me."

Dismissively, Jazmine checked over her babies and rearranged a few things that didn't necessarily need it. Colette glared in her direction, awaiting an apology that never came. Fuming mad, she prepared a bottle, retrieved a recliner, and scooped up her oldest baby. Nobody, including Dusty, said a word. Colette couldn't handle the silence any longer. "If Cecily's mom is really coming in, we need to talk before she gets here."

Jazmine continued to ignore Colette, though it should have

been the other way around. Jazmine had forced her way into a private conversation, completely disregarding Colette's feelings. Some of Jazmine's best qualities were also her worst.

Jazmine sighed. "Are we even friends, Colette? I mean, really. I share *every* detail of my personal life with you to a point where you're yelling TMI. And now you have a boyfriend or whatever, and you deliberately keep me out." She wedged a bobby-pin between her lips and gathered up loose hair. Her mouth curved like she was about to cry. "I don't want to be friends anymore if this is how you treat me."

Her words stung deeply. "You're right. I don't know why I kept it to myself. Come over after work and I'll explain who Jenn is."

"Who cares about Jenn? I want the file on her brother."

"Obviously I meant Bryce too."

"Aw. You smiled when you said his name."

Grinning, Colette shook her head. "I'll buy pizza and ice-cream, and you'll hear every detail. Not that there's a whole lot to tell. We're not dating or anything." It suddenly hit her that she'd have to provide an explanation of *why* they weren't dating.

"Consider yourself forgiven. By the way, what's Bryce's last name? Maybe I know him."

CHAPTER 9

Huddled in a fetal position, Colette rolled around on her apartment floor in agony. She checked the time. In fifteen minutes, she estimated, the torturing would stop. If she weren't due at work in half an hour, she would crawl into bed, pull the covers around her neck, and recite *While You Were Sleeping* as it played loudly in the other room.

She picked herself up off the floor, limped to the kitchen, and tossed a barbequed chicken breast, two tangerines, and a container of yogurt into a sack and left it on the counter. When she opened the front door, she was hit by a forty-five degree wind chill.

"Good afternoon, Colette," said Stuart, closing his laptop. "I sto—"

"I'm in a hurry this morning." She grabbed a winter coat out of the entryway closet and pulled the door shut. "I left something in my car and it's making me late."

"What did you leave in your car?"

The pain was so intense, she almost dropped to her knees. "Nothing."

"Are you mad at me, Colette?"

"No!"

When she got to her car, she popped the trunk. Frantically,

she unzipped her polka-dot suitcase and began the search for an item her calendar stated she wouldn't need for another six days. Of all the months to be wrong!

Her suitcase was as organized as a medical supply drawer, yet she wasn't having any luck. Did she even pack them? The frigid temperature intensified the pain and she was forced to shut down the search. That left her no choice but to ask a neighbor. The girl in the apartment next to Stuart's borrowed tweezers last year. Initially the request struck her as odd, but Colette was more than happy to help. Given their history, her neighbor would have no qualms about returning the favor.

She marched past Stuart, stopped at the door next to his, and knocked loudly, hoping the stay-at-home mom was home where she belonged. Colette knocked again. The lights were off and the blinds were shut. Maybe it was naptime. She rang the doorbell.

"They moved," said Start matter-of-factly. "Two days ago. He got a job in Hawaii."

"Of course they did," she said to herself. "Hawaii. How nice for them."

She headed to the grocery store feeling like a cheese grater was slicing her insides. The medicine, she noted, would take about five more minutes to kick in. After giving the car a couple of miles to warm up, she opened a vent and immediately shut it. The air was still ice-cold. She pounded the dashboard with her fist. "You stupid, stupid car!" By now she was shivering. Two DJ's were arguing about the public school system so she changed the station—to a car salesman screaming about a mega sale.

The grocery store was coming up on the left, but she needed three seconds of good music to straighten out her afternoon. With frostbitten fingers, she flipped down the visor and fumbled for a CD. Not missing a beat, she made the left-hand turn across two lanes of traffic while simultaneously sliding in the CD.

The sound of rubber against asphalt was so blunt it sounded fake. Seconds later, a horn was still blaring. The offended pickup truck backed up in the middle of the street and the car behind followed suit. Then the truck turned into the parking lot and pulled up next to Colette. A dark-haired man in his thirties began rolling down his window and she did the same, hoping she hadn't been the cause of the commotion. "Did I—"

"Learn how to drive, lady. You almost wrecked my truck."

Colette got out of her car and slammed the door. "Excuse me?"

"Look before you turn! Simple as that!"

"I did look first!"

He laughed. "Oh, you did? That's reassuring. Do me a favor and stay off my road."

She plunged her fist through his open passenger-side window and up went her middle finger. Then she turned around, grabbed her purse, and power-walked toward the grocery store just in time to get rained on. Not halfway to the door, she heard the truck peel out, sending chills up her spine. She walked faster, dodging rain drops as if they could be avoided. She watched in terror as the pickup circled halfway around the parking lot to the front, and turned down her aisle. Had he stopped any later, it would have been a homicide. She swallowed hard when his shoes hit the asphalt. He was a giant. Frantically she checked for witnesses. One step and he could squish her like a pop can.

He grinned maliciously. "Are you looking for a fight?"

"Please leave me alone," she said timidly, avoiding eye contact. She tried to walk past him, but he cut her off.

"It's my move. *You* almost busted up my pickup. *I* call you out on it. *You* make the mistake of flipping me off. Who has the next move? I do."

Fully extending her arm, she pointed across the parking lot. "Look out, look out!" She ducked down, stamping her hand on the pavement for balance. He spun around to the monotony of two elderly women pushing grocery carts. Colette bolted.

*

She turned off the ignition and slumped against the steering wheel wishing it was already tomorrow. After the week she'd had, Colorado couldn't come soon enough. She was still shaken up by Tuesday's incident with the crazed guy in the pickup, and baby Charlie's memorial service was in an hour.

Most of the attendees, if not all, would know she was the reason he was gone. She feared some would think of her as an abortionist, one who didn't value life if the body was underdeveloped.

Over the past several days she had remained composed, a façade to avoid unsolicited remarks from co-workers. It actually worked, perhaps too well. Nobody, it seemed, had a clue what she was going through. There were times it felt like she was attending a gathering obscenely drunk while everyone else was sober. The number of times she had cried at work was off the charts.

As she applied several coats of chap-stick, her mind flashed back to the jerk in the pickup, as if she didn't have enough to worry about. Frustrated, she pulled out her cell phone and searched her pitiful list of contacts. Scrolling down to Summer's name, she passed Roxanne's.

Something told her to call.

Today was the day.

When the call went to voicemail she could have wept. "Roxanne. It's Colette Halbrook. Since you're having trouble placing me with a baby, if a child comes up who is four or younger, that would be wonderful. Two toddlers would work as well. I love little kids and it would take me less than a day to convert the nursery into a bedroom with bunk-beds. Or a baby and a four-year-old. Siblings even. Please call me at 555-0104 and leave a message letting me know where we're at. Thank you so much. I appreciate all your hard work."

"You old fart," she added, after making sure the phone was off.

Umbrella up, she kicked the car door shut while pulling from her pocket the note Bryce had left in the bouquet of flowers, an item she now carried with her wherever she went. She read it with anticipation as though she hadn't already memorized every last smudge of ink. A smile appeared on her face as she allowed his words to carry her to a fictitious world of love and romance.

Colette,

I've been thinking about you, wondering if you're doing okay. I'm sorry your job requires so much of you. Even from a distance I can tell you're touching many lives. Hold on, here comes the mushy part. Your smile is prettier than a flower.

-Bryce

After tucking the note into her pocket, she floated away on a small wooden boat destined for a secluded beach with palm trees, warm water, and the rowboat's captain all to herself.

CHAPTER 10

"I'm upgrading you to first class. Congratulations."

It was five o'clock in the morning. Either Jazmine was hopped up on some good coffee or she still hadn't crashed for the night. The lip gloss and fake lashes told Colette it was the latter. "Shhh. I have neighbors, you know."

Making herself at home in the breakfast nook, Jazmine opened her laptop. "I need your password to do the upgrade."

"I'm not flying first class. It's not even that long of a flight." She set three avocados on the table. "Do you want these? Hopefully they're not too ripe."

"Who cares how long the flight is? I'm buying."

"Very funny, Jaz. I'll be right back." Colette went into the bathroom and began scouring the sink. In a few hours she'd be up in the clouds heading back to the good old days, making conversation with other travelers. She grinned with excitement. Her infatuation over Austin was intensifying by the day, and poor Bryce was getting the boot. What choice did she have? The odds of happily ever after were higher with Austin, and two-timing the bachelors would leave her without either one.

"Co-lette! Get out here before I have an aneurism!"

"Just a sec."

If things went well in Colorado, there was no telling how her life would change. For starters, she'd have a travel companion and someone to kiss goodnight, and she wouldn't have to get

Roxanne's permission to become a mom.

"You're *cleaning* your bathroom?" Jazmine was in the doorway, hands on her hips. "You're unstable on so many levels. C'mon. I helped you book the flight. Now it's your turn to help me."

Colette tossed the soiled nitrile gloves she was wearing. "I'm asking myself why you're being so generous."

"You haven't lived until you've flown first class."

"A week ago you were ready to write me off, and now you're offering hundreds of dollars toward my vacation? Something's up." Colette marched to the kitchen and closed the laptop. "You're trying to *purchase* Bryce's last name so you can track him down like you did that entrepreneur. Despite what you think, I've got this. I don't need your help."

Jazmine sighed, her gaze falling to the floor. "Look. I saw how upset you were when you got back from your baby's memorial service yesterday. I feel terrible about getting all prissy a couple of days after she passed away."

"He."

"I'm an idiot. *He.* Let me make things right. I didn't even call to make sure you were okay. What kind of a friend does that make me?"

"You don't have to—"

"I want to." Jazmine was on the brink of tears. "I want you to experience first class. It's better than what you're picturing."

The cousin who raised Colette was a firm believer in giving with a cheerful heart, and *accepting* with a cheerful smile. The latter, she had cautioned, was oftentimes the hardest. "If it means that much to you, thank you."

Colette felt like a spoiled child swallowed up by a seat tailored for a sumo wrestler. She rested the left side of her head against the glass and observed the runway.

Baby Charlie had been on her mind off and on all morning. She wondered how Jeff and Julie were holding up as their mourning transitioned from shock to reality. She clung to what was said at the memorial service: Jeff and Julie's decision was not made in a moment of weakness, but out of protection and love that can only be fathomed by those who have walked the same labyrinth.

When the parade of passengers ended, Colette surveyed the eight people paired up behind her, as well as the old woman, also without a seat partner, in the window seat across the aisle. The plane hadn't even started moving, and they were all reading, texting, or attempting to sleep. She had expected the flight to be like dating, a chance to get to know someone new, but from the looks of it, she'd be lucky to get seated with a hermit.

She unzipped an inner compartment of her purse where Bryce's note was tucked away. Smiling in anticipation, she unfolded it. For the thousandth time she was reading it, yet none of the magic was lost. There was no telling if it took him ten seconds or the entire weekend to write it, but it made her feel special. *Something you said hooked me,* he had told her. She wished she knew what it was so she could say it again—to Austin.

Restoring her hope for socialization, she spotted a man up front in a gray floppy hat and a black hoodie who had barely made the flight in time. Colette grinned with amusement as he hugged the cute flight attendant accompanying him. Colette's smile widened when the blonde wouldn't let go, even as a second man with a face Colette knew she'd seen before, impatiently squeezed past the huddle.

Suddenly she recognized him. It was the psychotic jerk with the truck! She burrowed her face into the window, terrified he would spot her.

"You've got to be kidding me," he said loud enough for the entire airport to hear. "You've got to be *kidding* me."

She glanced up at his cocky smirk just long enough for her peripheral vision to catch him getting backhanded by the other guy. Slithering lower in her chair, she closed her eyes and hoped he'd keep going to the back of the plane—to his kennel, with the other dogs.

Seconds passed like minutes. There was no way she was going to be trapped in a metal box thousands of feet in the air with a nutcase who had a vendetta against her.

"I know her, man. She's the babe who almost wrecked my truck. I'm positive, dude. It's her."

"Gentlemen," said the flight attendant in a soft voice. "I need you to take your seats now."

Heart pounding, Colette's eyelids were on lockdown. If she lived to tell the story, Jaz would definitely be getting her money's worth on this purchase.

When she heard the men stow their carry-ons, she knew a decision had to be made. Her sweat glands went into action as she counted down from ten to make a break for it. There were other flights to Denver, she told herself, and she wasn't about to be terrorized on this one. When she got to six, she stopped. It was too late. He chose the seat right smack next to hers.

Outraged, she opened her eyes to complain to the flight attendant... when her heart froze. *Bryce* was sitting next to her.

She couldn't breathe. He looked equally startled, and all she could do was stare. It was as if somebody read a list of winning lottery numbers and every single digit matched her ticket perfectly. Same time, same flight, same row. Never in her life had she been so lucky.

Her heart pumped harder. This meant he knew about the parking lot incident, but from his friend's perspective. She caught a glimpse of the flight attendant still giddy from the hug. The woman looked away when their eyes met.

Desperate to clear her name, she locked eyes with Bryce. "It's not what you think. I was having a horrible morning and, yes, I almost caused an accident, but your friend came unglued on me. I didn't even touch his truck." Colette's blood boiled in anger when she noticed his friend sitting across the aisle gawking as if he were enjoying an episode of Seinfeld.

Bryce lowered his voice to a notch above a whisper. "You don't have to explain. I know how my brother can be."

His brother?

Bryce removed his hat and cupped it over his knee. He looked good and smelled even better. "It's good to see you, Colette. I've been thinking about you all week."

She was still trying to process that they were brothers. There was a spark in Bryce's eyes that drew her in all over again. Here she was on her way to make things happen with Austin, and all she wanted was to go home with Bryce and have his babies and cook his dinner and live happily ever after.

"Say something, Colette. You're making me nervous."

Her heart sank at the thought that Bryce's mom probably

already hated her, thanks to his vile brother. "Which one of you was adopted?"

"Same mom, same pops. What's this?"

To her horror, she watched Bryce reach for the card *written by him* clutched in her shaking hand. As she jerked it away, his smile grew even wider. After unbuckling her seatbelt, she stuffed the note into her back pocket. "I hope this plane crashes," she groaned.

"Don't say that. I didn't see it."

"Right."

"Honestly. I have no idea what that was." He touched her leg reassuringly. "So... did you get the flowers I sent?"

She covered her hot face and closed her eyes. "They were very pretty. Thank you."

"I took a chance on the card. I'm glad you liked it."

It was too late to find an exit. The plane was already moving away from the terminal. The engines started to roar. She tried to calm herself down. So what if Bryce knew she had feelings for him? And who wouldn't be flattered to find someone reading a card written specifically to bring joy to their day? Uncovering her face, she smiled timidly. "I'm trying to recall how many times I've humiliated myself in front of you."

"Don't be embarrassed. I like that I've made an impression on you. Now, if I could just get you to answer your phone, I'd have it made."

"If I answered your calls, I wouldn't be able to walk away. I already told you why I can't be with you."

"That was before either of us knew that you were friends with my big brother. He can vouch for me."

Leaning in, she lowered her voice to a whisper. "I'd rather

take my chances in a dark alley in Chicago than to be left alone with that guy." She motioned across the aisle with her eyes to where his brother was looking out the window. She couldn't even see the tiny old woman sitting beside him. "He can't stand me, and I can't say that I blame him, but I was having a horrible morning and—"

"You don't need to explain."

"I still have no idea what I did, but I was about to apologize to him anyway because I could tell he was mad. I was caught off guard by his meanness. He wouldn't let up and I just sort of snapped." She sighed, doing her best to hold it together. "I feel like you're the guy who got chosen to see me at my worst and I hate it."

Bryce put his hand on her lower thigh and looked at her with care. "I know what it's like to have your actions misconstrued by people who don't know the real you."

Her mouth fell open a bit. "Yes, it's like you know your intentions are good and that you're not perfect, but people see what they want to see. I'm not trying to make excuses, but that incident with your brother was just that. If you knew how my morning had gone..." The concern she saw in his eyes spoke of his loyalty to her. She felt guilty for the fact that in a few short hours, she'd be flirting with Austin.

"Believe me. I can imagine. You've had a hard week. I'm sure Gage will feel terrible when he realizes what you were going through."

"I don't want any sympathy from him, but a do-over would be nice."

"I'll tell you one thing." He leaned in closer and lowered his voice. "He doesn't know you like I know you."

Her soul absorbed his voice like aloe vera as her head went limp against the back of her seat. "I like you, Bryce," she whispered. "You're the nicest person I've met."

"I know one person who would disagree with you."

"Who's that?"

"Gage."

She laughed. "Why's that? Did you accidently do some damage fighting back? I'm sorry, but he scares me. He does."

"He's definitely got a temper on him, but once you get to know him, you'll understand the sarcasm behind it. Truth be told, a lot of it is probably my fault. When we were kids, I deliberately did stuff just to get a rise out of him. He'd get so frustrated with me. One time when I was six years old, I lit his grasshoppers on fire that he was saving in a jar. He had even tried to name them and assign them different professions. Poor Gage was in tears when he found out what I had done. The way he was wailing, you'd think his dog was just murdered."

"Did you get in trouble?"

"I don't remember. I'm sure I did."

Bryce's credibility was going up. He had a sister and a brother—a psychotic brother, but a sweetheart of a sister. She pictured a distraught little boy sobbing over a jar of charred insects.

If Bryce could see the good in his brother, Colette would do the same. Perhaps she misjudged him as he had misjudged her. She reminded herself that Bryce had given her the benefit of the doubt time and time again, practically no questions asked. The world needed more people like him. Somehow, she vowed, she would make things right with Gage. "You didn't tell me you were going to Colorado. What are you guys doing there?"

"Gage loves to ski, so I'm tagging along at Loveland this weekend."

"No you're not!" She shoved him a little too hard. "That's where we're going tomorrow. I grew up in Golden, Colorado, and Loveland isn't far from there. My best friend still lives there and that's who I'm going with."

"What a coincidence," Gage said from across the aisle, his eyes locked on Colette. "That's like, totally crazy. The odds of this happening have got to be pushing one in a billion."

When she realized he was mocking her, she eyed Bryce nervously. Did they know about her plans? How could they? Bryce knew she was going to Colorado, but she never said anything about skiing or flying into Denver. Bryce looked guilty and Gage was grinning in a way that made her want to claw the sadistic look off his face. "Did you...?" It was so absurd she didn't know how to ask.

"Your friend, Jazmine..." Bryce looked afraid. "You wouldn't answer my calls and I was worried about you. I can move to coach. I bought an extra ticket in case this genius idea blew up in my face." Bryce unbuckled his seatbelt just as the plane came to a halt. "Party's over, Gage. Let's go."

Had Jazmine known about Bryce from the beginning? Using both hands, she grabbed his arm and yanked him back into his seat. "Oh no you don't. I have a very important question for you." She watched his leg bounce nervously as he offered his undivided attention. She swallowed. "How do you know Jazmine?"

His face was flaming red. "My sister told me that you're friends with a girl named Jazmine. Like I said, I was worried about you, so I called the NICU last night to make sure you were okay. I didn't want to bother you, so I asked for Jazmine."

"And she gave you my flight info?"

"She did."

Terror was flashing in Bryce's eyes and she felt terrible for him, but she didn't have time to calm him down. She needed answers. There was no way Jazmine would set her up to be stalked by someone she knew nothing about. Bryce was obviously lying, but deep down she sensed it was the kind of lie one would tell to conceal a surprise party. Maybe Jazmine and her boyfriend were one flight behind them. Or even on the same flight, back in coach. "Jazmine wouldn't have done that. There's no way."

"Well," he said gesturing with his hand. "She did. In fact, this whole thing was her brilliant plan. She's very persuasive. It only took her two hours to convince me that I wasn't going to scare you off, and that I wasn't going to wind up in prison."

His story was convincing. Clearly he had spoken to Jazmine long enough to know what she was capable of. "You could be a serial killer for all she knows." She glanced out the window as the plane started moving again.

The corner of his mouth rose. "To her credit, she considered that. That's why she insisted on meeting me in person."

"And when you didn't murder her, she assumed you were fine?"

He threw his hands up and exhaled. "I don't know anymore. I don't know what I was thinking. Tell you what. Don't be mad at Jazmine, okay? This will make more sense coming from her. Enjoy your trip. I'm going to move back to coach as soon as this plane is done doing its thing and you won't ever see me again."

Her heart beat faster. She was about to lose him for good. "I'm just trying to understand how you pulled this off." When nothing changed in his expression, her heart sank. He looked defeated.

Regardless of how it happened, she was given the chance to spend the next two-and-a-half hours next to Bryce with nothing but a hinged armrest separating them. She glanced at his distraught face and knew what she had to do.

Swallowing hard, she worked up the motivation to give it her all. "I'm glad you're here, Bryce." Her voice sounded hollow, the words rehearsed. She pulled Bryce's note from her back pocket and placed it in his hand. "You can't keep this because it's mine, but I want you to understand how much I like you. When I opened my eyes and saw *you* were my seat partner, I—"

The plane came to a stop and within seconds the engines roared louder and louder as if they were taunting the laws of gravity. "I hate this part." She clutched the arm rests. "I take back what I said about the plane crashing."

Bryce put his arm around her and squeezed her shoulder. "You can't be scared. This is the fun part."

Soon the plane was picking up speed and she could hear the strained engines wince in pain. As the plane's small wheels tripped over bump after bump, Colette hoped the plane's captain had a steady hold of the flimsy steering wheel she was picturing. She straightened her shoulders preparing for the worst. "What's wrong with the runway?"

"You're safe. Here we go."

On cue, the plane went airborne, beginning its ascent thousands of feet into radiant blue sky. She looked out the window amazed at the view. Her vacation had officially started.

"It's gorgeous, isn't it? Just think, we're the lucky ones who get to fly away."

He leaned in for a closer look out her window.

"There's Grandma's house," said Gage. "Bryce, do you see it?"

Bryce glared at Gage and shook his head subtly.

"Sorry, man." His apology was sincere, though Colette couldn't figure out what for. "Look. There's Grandpa's RV."

Bryce put his hat on and darted across the aisle. Squatting at Gage's feet, they both strained to see out the window as if they were little boys on a Ferris wheel. "See it? See the water tower?"

Bryce tapped the window. "Hey, Grandma."

Those two words made her heart melt. The affection in their voices spoke of the bond within their family. With almost no relatives to speak of, she feared it would be challenging to find a place among her future husband's kin, whoever that might be. There was no doubt that the talents of wife and mother would come naturally to her someday, but the anticipation of sister-in-law and daughter-in-law made her uneasy.

When Bryce returned to his seat, Colette caught a whiff of his seductive cologne. "Did Grandma see you?"

He clicked his seatbelt back into place and removed his hat. "Yes she did and she sends her love."

When their eyes met, electricity ripped through her body. Everything about him drew her in; the way he smiled, the tone of his voice, the way he would lessen the distance between them whenever he had something to say. "You were smart in sending your sister with the flowers. It was reassuring that somebody on this planet knows who you are."

"Because con-artists don't have sisters?"

"Exactly," she laughed.

"Colette, thanks for being such a good sport about all this. It turns out Jazmine knows you very well."

Colette rolled her eyes. "She likes to think she does."

"She told me she's holding your computer hostage for a while."

"The computer thing was my idea. I needed a break."

"That's right. She said that."

Colette eyed him suspiciously. She wanted to ask him if he went to Jazmine's house, but decided she was better off asking Jazmine herself. It was coming together now, the reason Jazmine had been so eager to upgrade her ticket to first class. Not to mention her vivacious energy at five in the morning—she had just finished entertaining Bryce! She could feel her face darken as she debated whether or not Jazmine had run her mouth to Bryce about Austin. "What else did you guys talk about?"

He blushed as he smiled. "I'll let Jazmine answer that one."

By the end of the flight, Colette couldn't wait to praise Jazmine for setting up such an amazing rendezvous with the man of her dreams. And she was even more eager to get the full scoop on how Jazmine's evening with Bryce had gone. Jazmine had a gift for details when it came to men and would be able to recount exactly what was said and how. Then she would go on to add her own interpretation of the underlying meaning, as well as assess his tone and mannerisms. At the end of the day she was an amazing friend, and it was a shame every girl couldn't have a Jazmine.

"Hey, Bryce? Tell me why you were first interested in getting to know me." The unanswered question was eating her alive.

"Everything about you got my attention."

"You told me that something I said hooked you."

"That's true."

"What did I say?" She re-crossed her legs, positioning them closer to his. A little seduction couldn't hurt.

He contemplated for a moment. "Are you going skiing tomorrow?"

"Bright and early."

They were leaning so close to each other their heads were almost touching. She glanced at his warm lips, wondering what it would be like.

"Meet me for breakfast in the lodge around eight o'clock and you'll have your answer."

"You promise?"

"I don't think I have a choice. Tomorrow is the day."

CHAPTER 11

Gage was the last person Colette expected to be stranded alone with in Colorado. The two of them stood side-by-side, awkwardly, like shy neighbors in an elevator.

Shortly after the plane had touched ground, Bryce discovered a new voicemail requiring immediate attention. He instructed Gage to help Colette with her luggage so he could run ahead and find someplace quiet to make a call. Gage didn't ask questions, which told Colette these urgent calls were a frequent occurrence.

When Bryce exited the plane, Gage hopped across the aisle to where Colette was standing and allowed a stream of passengers to go on ahead of them. She was antsy to catch up to Bryce, but at the same time, was impressed to see that Gage was putting others ahead of himself.

Crowded in front of a carousel in baggage claim, Colette scanned the airport for any sign of Bryce or Summer. Twice she tried to strike up a conversation with Gage, but his only contribution had been one-worded answers. His standoffish demeanor was puzzling given his decision to make things right halfway through the flight. When Bryce had excused himself to the lavatory, Gage politely slipped into the seat next to Colette's, and they spent the next twenty minutes chatting about old college professors, front-loader washers, and their favorite movies. By the end of the conversation it was obvious that their previous encounter had been nothing more than a bad case of road rage.

When the carousel started spitting out luggage, Colette pulled her curls into a ponytail and wiggled into her coat and backpack. An important looking businessman caught her eye as he frowned at his watch. She visualized Bryce in a suit and wondered what exactly he did for a living. During the flight it had been on the tip of her tongue to ask, but conversation had been flowing so smoothly she didn't want to defile it with a potentially sensitive subject.

Gage smiled at Colette as if to say they were in the same awkward boat together. Grateful for the kind gesture, she returned it warmly. "Maybe one of us should text your brother to let him know where we are."

"Can we be real for a second?"

Her smile faded as her guard went up. "What do you mean?"

"I'm sorry, but the Colette I saw on the plane is not the same chick who flipped me off five days ago." Superiority flickered in his eyes.

She went from shocked to angry in a matter of seconds. "Hmm," she said with her chin held high, determined not to say anything that might require an apology.

"That's it? That's all you have to say for yourself?"

"What do you want me to say? You provoked me and I reacted."

"Like a barracuda on crystal meth! It's not every day you see a princess so quick to bring out the middle finger."

"Was I supposed to bow down and beg for forgiveness for causing an accident that you dreamed up?"

His laughter was dripping with mockery. "You must really

have my brother fooled with that sweet personality of yours, because he usually leaves the chunky girls alone."

Her jaw dropped in outrage as her eyes welled with tears. Turning her back on him, she took a step forward and studied the conveyor belt for her ticket out of there. Her heart thumped around in her chest like a water-deprived fish and she could feel the sting of his glare on the back of her skull. Any fear that he might hurt her was nonexistent now. In fact, she dared him to touch her.

"You can dish it, but you can't take it?"

Livid, she turned around. "Get over yourself. It's disgusting." She bit her tongue to refrain from going any further, but it got away. "I never put a scratch on your precious truck, did I?"

"This isn't about my pickup."

"Sure it is. You're harassing me about an accident that never happened. I'll say it again and hopefully you're listening this time. Get over yourself."

"There's a lot of confidence behind that pretty face of yours." He squinted as if he were trying to get a clearer look. "I don't think you're a ditz. Nope." He tapped the side of his head. "I think you're smart."

He wasn't making any sense, but she fired back just the same. "That seems to be the consensus."

"You better keep up this charade as long as you can, because as soon as Bryce finds out, he'll find a real woman."

"Trying to protect little brother, are we?" As the potency of his words sunk it, her ability to keep fighting was extracted. She turned her back on him feeling completely inadequate. As she tried to decode the meaning, she spotted her luggage. Her lifeline.

"What's there to protect him from?" he bellowed for all to hear. "You're an attractive piece of meat. Let him have his fun for a while."

Her face burned in shame. Forcing her way to the front, she yanked her suitcase off the line and retreated.

By the time Summer showed up, Colette had pulled herself together. She'd have to be a lunatic to believe one word coming from Gage's mouth. Bryce was crazy about her and he proved it beyond a question.

Summer jogged across the crosswalk clutching her oversized purse with both hands. "Coco, sorry I'm late! You're really here!" She almost knocked Colette over with her hug. "The traffic." She was panting. "It was like the entire city knew I was late. This old lady, too short to see over her steering wheel, pulled out in front of me. I mean, of all the days to be running late. It's insane."

"Don't worry about it. You made it." Colette picked up a strand of Summer's shiny hair. "Look at you, Summer. You look great."

She shifted her purse from one shoulder to the other and took charge of Colette's suitcase. "Thanks. You too. Did you get any sleep on the plane? I bet you're exhausted after working last night. And then the drive to Portland."

"Someone kept me awake the whole flight," she grinned. "In fact, he followed me on my vacation. I've never been so surprised in my life." If black was the reaction Colette was expecting, Summer gave her white. It wasn't the fact she was speechless for the first time in her life that was surprising; it was the blank stare. No excitement, no outrage. Nothing. "His name is Bryce and he's the nicest guy ever. For the first time in a decade I'm head over heels."

"It's cold feet." Her hand went to her heart as she exhaled. "I can work with cold feet."

"I'm not engaged or anything. I'm still on board to see Austin. But this amazing guy keeps chasing me. It's like he's on a mission. He's tall. Way taller than me. I gave him my number."

"I'm really happy you found a super tall man, but do you remember who you're seeing tonight?" She released the luggage and gripped Colette's chin. "This weekend is all about Austin."

"I know but—"

"But nothing," she said sharply, dragging the suitcase through the crosswalk. "You can hate me for saying this, but I'm wondering if this man you're suddenly interested in is a temporary excuse to be unavailable all weekend."

"No, no, no. Not at all. He followed me on—"

"Good. Now that we've cleared that up, let's get this party started. Welcome home, Coco."

Colette laughed, overjoyed that their three-year separation was finally over. Powerwalking to the car, there was so much to say they were either cutting each other off or finishing each other's sentences. For once, she easily tucked Bryce into a box and embraced the familiar surroundings. There were so many places she couldn't wait to revisit, the first being high school. "We're not going to make it to the restaurant on time, are we?"

"No, but everybody's meeting at Dominique's house afterwards. We'll get something to go."

"Let's make that happen soon. I'm starving."

Summer reached for the elevator button, then paused. "Am I being mean?"

"No. Not at all. Why?"

"It's just that I know you so well and I know that you would give anything to have a family of your own. It's not fair what happened to you as a kid and I feel like you deserve a family. But I'm nervous for you, like you're going to throw away your only chance with your soul mate. Have you thought about that? Austin could be your one and only soul mate."

Colette wasn't sure she believed in soul mates, but in a way, Summer was right. What if Gage knew something Colette didn't? What if Bryce had ulterior motives? Or what if Bryce was the kind of guy who never wanted to get married? She didn't think so, but she wouldn't bet her life on it. There were no guarantees with Bryce, and this was her only chance at hitting it off with Austin. If she sabotaged it and Bryce found a new woman to woo, she'd be kicking herself forever. "If it makes you feel any better, I'll be crushed if Austin isn't interested."

"I know. It's scary to put yourself out there sometimes, but don't even think about it, okay? Just have a good time and see where that leads."

"That's what I'll do." She threw her arms around Summer and squeezed tightly. "I missed you so much."

They arrived at Dominique's place fashionably late; bathed, primped, and dressed to turn heads. Colette marveled at his outdated, but well kept, ranch-style home. It was painted a modern beige with white shutters, and had a good-sized lawn with a bed of thriving weeds. She was happy for him, that he actually grew up, a feat she once predicted too challenging for someone with his energy level.

Colette's heart pounded as they approached the front door. "This is weird."

Summer squeezed her shoulders. "Trust me, Coco. It's going to be just like old times once you get the hellos out of the way.

And you get to meet my boyfriend. You're going to love him. Last night Brad told me he feels like he already knows you."

"Wait a second. How do I look?" They examined teeth, breath, makeup, and backsides. "Okay. Let's do this."

After turning on her camera, Summer flung open the door, exposing a living room full of familiar faces. "Coco is here and she looks fabulous!"

Like a pack of wolves cornering their prey, the entire gang and their significant others surrounded them. The sound of alumni yelling over one another to get in the next hilarious story almost brought her to tears.

She was home.

CHAPTER 12

It was eleven thirty at night in Golden, Colorado, and the sub-freezing wind was not letting up. Colette melted into the Escalade's warm leather seat, smitten with the breathtaking city she once called home. Mountains frosted to perfection, litter-free streets lining an adorable downtown, and the same starry sky beneath which she enjoyed her first kiss. Her cheeks were sore from laughing all night and her voice was becoming hoarse. She poked a hole into a box of Lemon Heads and turned down the radio a few notches. "I like Brad. You guys are cute together."

Summer gripped the steering wheel tighter. "I think so too! Some friends of mine told me that we sort of look alike, but I haven't decided how I feel about that yet. He's a keeper, though. I can't believe he delivers my mail. It's so nerdy."

"I thought he was a mechanic."

Wrinkling her face, she shot Colette a look of confusion. "Oh, oh, oh. You're thinking of Duane. He's not a mechanic. He's my... what's it called?"

"If you say cousin..."

"No. Duane is my stereo guy. He's the one who installed my stereo. He never even ended up calling me. I thought he was going to, but he didn't." Summer zoned out as if she was still trying to figure it out. "Brad is my mailman. He delivers my mail in one of those little mail trucks. It's hilarious. I'll show you on Monday. We'll wait for him to do it." They looked at each other for a split second before busting up laughing. "I know, I know," Summer giggled, trying to speak. "My mailman. I don't know why I'm laughing. It's you, not him. I can't stop."

Pretending to drive, Colette deepened her voice. "There you go, ma'am. Here's your mail. Woops. I dropped one."

"Ooh, a postcard," Summer squealed.

"A manila envelope."

"A package."

They were laughing so hard, they were crying. Trying to pull herself together, Colette gripped Summer's thigh. "I'm not making fun of him. I'm feeding off of you."

Summer dabbed her eyes. "It's a good job, actually. And he has a house and everything. He bought it brand new when he was twenty."

"You told me about the brick fireplace."

"You should see it. It's in a quiet neighborhood with sidewalks and everything. I would take you over there, but we've only been together for like three-and-a-half weeks, four on Tuesday, so I can't just waltz in like I own the place."

"I still can't get over Dominique's house. He's a grownup."

"How'd that happen? He's a husband."

"That girl is his wife?"

"That's what I was told."

"Crazy." After kicking off her heels onto the floorboard, Colette crossed her legs into a pretzel. "I'm surprised you haven't interrogated me about Austin yet."

"Can you tell I'm about to explode? You're so moody all the time, I have to be careful. But since you brought him up, how did things go? I saw you guys chatting it up by the backdoor. I kept waiting for him to steal you away."

Colette dropped a Lemon Head into her mouth. "I like him. I mean, obviously I do. I've always liked him. He's just as fun as I remember, and mature at the same time."

"So things went well?"

"You saw us. We had a great time."

"You can be honest. It's okay. You don't *have* to like him. I just think it's fascinating how you're both in the medical field. You both work with newborns and you both love kids."

"I love money. He makes good money."

"Exactly. Did you guys make any plans to see each other before you have to go back to Oregon?"

Pursing her lips together, Colette sat forward in her seat. "I'm just going to say it, and you can react how you want. The man is a freaking gynecologist. He doesn't work with babies. He works with you-know-what's!"

"Stop it, Coco. He's an obstetrician."

"He looks at women all day. He does stuff to women. It's nasty." Colette didn't know if this was the right time to bring up Bryce again, but it couldn't hurt. "I'm practically dating that guy I sat with on the plane. In fact—" Colette stopped herself. If Summer knew about her plans to meet up with Bryce in the morning, she might cancel the ski trip all together.

Summer turned into her driveway and got out of the car. Neither of them spoke until they were in the condo. Summer climbed the stairs and stopped halfway. "The sheets are clean and you can help yourself to anything in the kitchen. I'm going to bed and I'm not setting the alarm. I'm exhausted."

"Are we still going skiing in the morning?"

"Of course." When Summer got to the top of the stairs, she turned around once more. "Goodnight, Coco. I still love you."

*

After sliding the lip of her boot into the ski's crevice, Colette stomped down and heard a crunchy click, a sound she hadn't heard in more than twelve years. She locked the other foot into place before regaining her balance. Summer was in position to push off. "Are you ready, Coco?"

"Let's do this." Colette stabbed her poles into the snow and plunged herself forward. "Wow. This is quite the workout."

"It sure is. Our butts will have a nice lift in a couple of days."

Crisp air blew gently across Colette's face as she struggled to keep her skis from crisscrossing over mounds of packed snow. Summer, on the other hand, floated along gracefully as if she were born and raised on a mountain.

Colette stopped long enough to wiggle her gloved fingers into her pocket to check the time on her cell. It was 7:40. Twenty minutes was not enough time to go up and down a mountain, but it was too much time to keep an eager friend penned up in a lodge. Keeping her eye out for Bryce, she tagged along behind Summer, scheming.

The line was fairly short, which didn't leave Colette much time to lasso her friend. "Please don't be mad, but I have to go to the bathroom."

Summer's mouth hung open as she exhaled. "Are you serious? What number?"

"What difference does it make?"

"How bad do you have to go? Can't you hold it?"

101

"Not for *that* long."

"You are so high-maintenance sometimes," she said with a smirk. "If you must..."

Back at the lodge, they popped off their skis and set them against the rack alongside two dozen others.

"Coco, your hands are shaking. Are you okay?"

She did a quick scan for Bryce, hoping Gage didn't sabotage their plans. "I'm just cold."

"Well I'm hot. How can you be cold?"

Colette marched up the metal steps toward the restroom. When she was finished, there was still no sign of Bryce. "Summer, I have something to tell you," she said, but something stopped her. What if Gage had gotten to Bryce and he decided not to come at all? Just the thought of it made her blush. "I'm starving." It was a pathetic last-ditch effort, but she was out of options. "Do you mind if we—"

"Yes I do mind. Eat some snow. I love you, but you're as bad as a toddler right now."

"I'm just going to grab a bagel for the ride up."

"I, on the other hand, am getting on that ski lift." Summer marched toward the door and pushed it open. "If you want to come with me, fine. If not, then I'll see you at the car at the end of the day." She let it close behind her.

In stiff boots, Colette hobbled after her quickly. Summer was waiting just outside with her eyes stubbornly fixed the other direction. "Call me crazy," Summer said slowly, "but I'm pretty sure that's Bryce Rocco."

Colette tracked Summer's stare frantically. Bryce and Gage were at the base of the stairs, not ten steps away, surrounded by five or six giddy women. "How in the world do you know Bry—"

Before she could finish the question, it clicked. Bryce Rocco was actually *Bryce Rocco.*

Summer's eyes were cemented to Bryce as she spoke. "Well, Miss Colette, for starters, I had a date with him every Monday night at 8:30 for three years straight. Oh man. It *is* him!" She dropped her coat, catapulted herself down the steps, and stopped midway. "He's looking at us! He's looking at us! Coco, my camera! It's in my coat pocket. Hurry!"

How could she not have known? Had they met on Hollywood Boulevard, then of course. But Eugene, Oregon? He certainly didn't dress like a celebrity—up until now, that is. Add a gold medal and some international news cams to the scene and he'd pass as an Olympian. The flight attendants! They must have been in on it. Who else had seen them together? Nobody, she thought. Then she remembered Jazmine. Great. The entire NICU knew by now.

Maybe it had all been a dream, but in her heart, she cherished Bryce's friendship... the connection... the first stages of intimacy. Except, the Bryce she knew, didn't actually exist. To suggest that she could compete with actresses and models was like comparing a stale bologna sandwich to sizzling fajitas.

Summer fell all over herself scaling the stairs. "What is wrong with you?" She dug for the camera. "You know how much I love Bryce Rocco. Take the picture!" After turning it on, she slapped the camera into Colette's hand.

Colette watched curiously as Bryce addressed the twenty or so that were now gathered around him. "Thanks for saying hi, but I'd like to spend some time with a few of my friends now."

Deep and confident, she thought. He was the definition of masculine. Bryce turned around and looked at Colette inquisitively before starting toward her. To her amazement, the crowd dispersed.

"Coco! Take the picture!" Summer's eyes were bugged out as if they were spring-loaded.

Positioning the camera in place, Colette did a countdown from three. "Say cheese. He's right behind you."

Summer flashed a frenzied smile while Bryce, unbeknownst to her, struck a pose chewing all ten fingernails like a crazed teenage fan. A smile escaped Colette as she snapped the photo. "I got it."

"Say hello to the cover of my next Christmas card. Let me see it." Swiping the camera, she pressed the preview button. "No way." Turning around, Summer found herself face to face with her former idol.

"Hi there. You must be Summer." He extended his hand. "I'm Bryce and this is my brother, Gage."

After shaking his hand, Summer turned to Colette with a soft smile. "Did you set this up for me?"

Laughing, Colette shook her head. People were staring, but she didn't mind the attention. In fact, she was kind of enjoying it. "You know that guy, Bryce, I told you about?" Flirtatiously, Colette's eyes darted to his. "Well, here he is."

"You're not trying to suggest that Bryce Rocco is the man you've been dating."

Alarmed, she looked at Bryce. "I never told her we're dating."

"Yes you did! You totally did!"

"That's not what I said. I told you that I met someone, but I never told you we were dating."

Bryce stole Colette's hand and looked into her eyes. "May I tell her then?"

Colette bit her bottom lip as the corners of her mouth curved upward. "I can't even think straight right now. What just happened?"

Bryce looked at Summer with a look of exasperation. "I've tried everything to get this woman to give me a chance, but she puts up a good fight. Any suggestions?"

"Don't worry. I'm on it. She's crazy about you, and that never happens with her." Summer turned on the camera. "Everyone loves a photo op!" She snapped several pictures of Colette and Bryce, still hand in hand. "Coco, I can't believe you kept this to yourself. How is that even possible?"

Gage cleared his throat. "Apparently she had no idea he's famous until just now." He tapped the side of his head like he had at Baggage Claim. "I was wrong about you, *Coco*. I never should have accused you of being smart. It won't happen again."

Bryce narrowed his eyes. "Leave her alone, Gage. Nobody's laughing."

Summer looked at Gage doubtfully. "I don't know who you are or where you're getting your facts, but trust me. Any friend of mine knows all about Bryce Rocco."

Gage folded his arms and raised an eyebrow arrogantly. "My mistake, I guess."

Colette covered her hot face, expecting third-degree burns. The one and only time she gave up internet, *this* had to happen. How could she have been so stupid? From what she understood, he played in action movies, not romantic comedies, so she couldn't blame herself for not recognizing him. But the name alone should have been her first clue. Suddenly she felt two large hands heavy on her shoulders. She swallowed.

"Colette," Bryce said softly. He waited for her to look up. When she finally did, he leaned in closer, his foggy breath brushing against her forehead. "I didn't want you to know," he whispered. "I wanted an authentic friendship with a smart, exciting, compassionate woman, and you turned out to be so much more. Now that I've gotten to know you, I need you in my life. I want you to be my girlfriend."

When he stepped back, she felt like a little kid pushed onto a stage, abandoned with a microphone. She didn't know what to say. Breaking eye contact, she looked down. His boots were humungous. "Where did you get those? They're huge."

"I used to have tiny feet. Plastic surgery changed my life."

Gage pounded his fist against his palm. "Mission complete. I say we hit the slopes."

"I second that," said Summer. "Do you two love birds want some time alone?"

Before Colette could object, Bryce spoke up. "Not at all, Summer. You and I have hardly gotten to know each other."

Summer's hand went to her heart as she giggled. "If Coco ever lets you get away, she'll never hear the end of it from me. I just want you to know that."

Colette glanced at her star-struck friend, relishing the incredible moment. As the girls followed the guys down the stairs, they gave each other a look as if to say, *wow*. There was so much to discuss, but so little time. When Colette started to comment, she was cut off by Summer. "I would give anything to trade places with you right now. Do you have any idea how lucky you are?"

"He followed me onto the flight," Colette whispered. "We met two weeks ago and I made a complete fool out of myself."

"You must have done something right. Have you seen the way he looks at you? I've always said you're a great catch, but apparently that was an understatement."

At the base of the stairs, the boys went right and the girls went left, which gave them a few more seconds to gossip. Summer popped on her skis. "You are the cutest person I know. I'm betting he loves that about you. I have just one bit of advice for you. It pays to get a last name."

"I'll remember that for next time."

"If you play your cards right, there won't be a next time. Your biggest concern will be what to name the baby. And please don't choose anything way out there like celebrities like to do. Oh man. My best friend is a celebrity!"

"You know it," Colette giggled.

It didn't take long to discover that Colette was the least-seasoned skier of the group. To relieve some of the pressure, she told the trio to go on ahead, that she preferred to be the caboose. There was a line at the ski lift which allowed Colette some time to brace herself for the chilling ride to the top.

It was hard to imagine Bryce in an action film, leaping off buildings and dodging bullets. And even more intriguing was the thought of him raising his voice and talking trash. He was too sweet for that.

The longer they stood in line, the more she noticed a trend; everyone knew that chiseled face. It wasn't long before she found herself chatting with strangers, enjoying every minute of it. Summer noticed too. "I don't get how you're so confident around Bryce Rocco, but at Dominique's house you were more on the shy side."

"Bryce and I just sort of... click. He's easy to talk to."

Bryce stopped midsentence and put his arm around Colette. "I'm glad you think so."

Suddenly she remembered. "What was it that hooked you? You said you'd tell me today."

"Yes I did," he said confidently, "and I'm a man of my word. You ready?"

CHAPTER 13

High-altitude wind fanned Colette's face, a delightful welcoming to the fabulous outdoors. The view from the top of the world was spectacular. Freshly-fallen snow sparkled as if magical clouds had showered diamonds across the mountain the night before. Icy slopes wouldn't be a problem this morning. The path before her was decorated with thick white powder which fluffed weightlessly when roused. Most of the surrounding trees had been birthed in an era of simplicity, before the stressfulness of rush-hour traffic, incompatible computer programs, and caller ID. The mountain was timeless, its guests at peace.

A tsunami of snowflakes collapsed when Summer stopped abruptly. "What was he saying to you on the way up?"

Colette eyed the guys. From what she could tell, Gage was doing most of the talking. "We were discussing food. He grills, but doesn't cook. Your typical man."

"Bor-ring. I want the juicy stuff."

Stretching strands of curls away from her forehead, Colette positioned her goggles in place. "Do you feel like I've been ignoring you?"

"Yes you were, as would I, you, if I were in your shoes. Ignore away. Of course you'll remember me when invitations to lavish star-studded parties arrive in your name."

Parties? It was as if heaps of files were dropped onto her desk, each containing a striking question. Would she be expected to recall the names and faces of everyone in the business? Were Bryce's closest friends people she had nothing in common with? What would they think of her? Did Bryce even live in Oregon? How many months at a time would he be away?

"Coco, you should see your face right now."

"Do you think Bryce even goes to those parties? He doesn't seem like the type who dresses up to eat caviar."

"I know he does. I've seen pictures. I'll show you tonight. The magazines find all kinds of dirt on him."

Suspicious, Colette turned around. His smile startled her, the way it pulled her in.

He launched a snowball her way. "After you, ladies. Don't let any trees pounce you on the way down."

Cocking her hip, Summer spoke in a snooty voice. "Please. I've been doing this since I was three. If anything, the trees fear me." Nudging Colette, she spoke quieter. "Can you believe I'm mingling with Bryce Rocco? This is so not happening."

Colette rolled her eyes. "First of all, stop calling him that. From now on his name is Bryce—period. And secondly, you're going to have to stop lusting after my man."

"Bam. Shut it off, just like that?"

"Picture you and Brad sneaking into the back of his mail truck. That should do the trick." She could feel Bryce's eyes on her, and was glad he got to see a more carefree side to her personality.

Keeping her voice a notch above a whisper, Summer put on a cute smile. "Let's not forget who loved Bryce first. But you're right. I'll stop undressing him with my eyes."

"You're too kind."

The morning flew by in no time. Of all the ski trips she had been on, this was the most frightening. She would push herself to new limits just to avoid becoming a straggler. Her diligence was paying off; Bryce didn't feel the need to keep checking on her, and Gage never once ridiculed her abilities, an opportunity he wouldn't have passed up had he noticed.

Two corners into their third run, Colette fell back from the group. Singing quietly, she danced down the mountain relishing the radiant blue sky and anticipating Bryce's next offer to make it official. Her answer was simmering on the tip of her tongue. Fail or veil, she was ready to commit.

She came around the next few corners expecting Bryce and Summer to be waiting, but apparently she hadn't been missed. Up ahead, the path forked. To the right was a continuation of the intermediate trail. To the left was more advanced. Either way, the trails would spit out at nearly the same spot, she guessed. Suddenly she spotted them at a standstill on the edge of the advanced trail. Swinging her hip forward, she made the turn smoothly.

"Coco! Over here!" Summer was waving.

With an overabundance of confidence, Colette threw herself down the slope. Her skis were angled toward Summer and Bryce, and more of Bryce's fans, she presumed, like missiles. Slicing the snow, she attempted to change course. Her right leg was all for it, but her left hesitated. They began parting in a way she hadn't seen before. Upon feeling the first pang, she did something dumb.

She sat down.

Somersaulting down the mountain, both skis flew off. When she closed her eyes it felt like an incoherent dream, the kind where you know you're about to die, but you wake up just before it happens. She knew she was heading straight toward the cliff. Her vocal chords vibrated in a panicked scream. Miraculously the tumbling stopped and her face was planted firmly in the snow. Pulling herself out of the mess, she sat up. Her forehead was throbbing, but she wasn't in pain. Bryce and Summer were by her side within seconds.

"I thought I was going to roll off the cliff," Colette said between heavy breaths.

"What cliff?" Bryce was squatting in front of her, his hand on her back.

Colette looked up. She was nowhere near the edge. In fact, in order to find a cliff, she'd have to do a great deal of searching. She noticed Gage up the hill chatting it up with three young women, completely unconcerned that she could have been beheaded. When Gage caught her eye mid-sentence, a vindictive grin crept across his face.

"I'm okay," she shouted to him. "Maybe next time."

Gage shook his head. "Why are you so combative, Coco?"

Hatred pulsed through her veins upon hearing her nickname. "I'm kidding," she smiled. "You know that." But inside she wanted to give him a nice hard push down the mountain.

Bryce combed packed snow off her hat. "That was quite the fall. Are you really okay?"

"I feel like I've been zapped with a Taser. I have no clue where my skis went."

"I'll get them." Summer began sidestepping up the incline. "You crack me up. There you were, skiing along. Next thing I know, the snow sucks you down and pummels you."

Bryce gripped Colette's upper arm as she started to stand. "How do you feel?"

"Compared to that time you ran me over, pretty good."

He wrapped his arms around her and growled like a cougar as he squeezed her. When he released her, he was looking up the mountain toward the three women Gage was entertaining. "No pictures, please," he hollered. "What's up, Gage? Why am I doing your job?"

The agitation in Bryce's eyes was unnerving. A few hours earlier, he had practically posed for a photo shoot with a mob of fans outside the lodge, but one red-head decides to snap a few pictures, and suddenly he's angry? There was only one plausible explanation—he didn't want to be photographed with *her*. And why would he? He probably had five other "I must have you" women lined up in other states. If only she knew Bryce's history. Without it, any level of trust was foolishness.

"Sorry about that, Colette. Believe it or not, Gage is my bodyguard. He's on thin ice this weekend."

"So he's not really your brother?"

"Wishful thinking?"

"Perhaps."

"Sorry to disappoint, but Gage is a Rocco." A group of skiers caught his eye as they sped past. "Do *you* have any siblings?"

Her palms started to sweat at the mention of family, but she played it cool. "Growing up, I always wanted tons of brothers and sisters, but I was an only child."

"Do you still want a big family?"

One single child to call her own was as far as her dreams stretched at the moment, but thanks to Roxanne, she was barren. "A big family would be amazing, but I'd be happy with two or three. What about you?"

"I haven't really given it much thought. My nieces and

113

nephews are a handful, so that's been a reality check for me. I'm definitely not ready to be a father tomorrow."

Speaking of reality checks. "You'd be fine never having kids?"

"Don't get me wrong. I definitely want to be a dad someday, but I realize it's a life-changing event. I just want to be sure I'm ready for it."

Summer glided down the mountain with her skis pointed into a "v" and a second pair wedged in her armpit. She motioned for Gage to follow, and when he did, the three women he was entertaining tagged along like mosquitoes. When they got to Bryce, one of them played with his goggles flirtatiously. "Do you have room for three more beauties this afternoon? I swear, we're your biggest fans."

Bryce put his arm around Colette. "Thanks, but maybe next time."

The red-headed woman waved her finger back and forth between Colette and Bryce. "Are you two together?"

Bryce looked at Colette with warm eyes. "I'd like to think so." He backed away and chuckled. "We're good friends. Really good friends."

"Actually..." Colette debated whether she should say it. Here was an opportunity to get out of her rut, no matter how unconventional the relationship. She could either play it safe and miss out on happily ever after, or take a chance with a man she was already in love with. "I would say we're more than friends."

Smiling, he bowed his head to her level and whispered, "I'm the luckiest man in the world." He started to straighten, but hesitated. Lowering his head a second time, he added, "And I'm crazy about you."

Her body melted until she could barely blink. As she exhaled butterflies, she imagined his lips covering hers. Never before had anything felt more right.

*

Dusk was fast approaching and their stomachs were full when Bryce led Colette into the forest through deep snow several yards off the beaten path. Summer and Gage had gone their separate ways. It had been amusing hearing Summer go on and on about her boyfriend before asking Gage to join her. The shocker was when Gage declined because his *wife* wouldn't like it. It was like learning the physiology behind one's ability to distinguish sound—you believe, but you can't wrap your mind around it.

Following Bryce's lead, Colette sat in the circle of packed snow they had cleared together. When their eyes met, she saw what everyone else saw—a celebrity. As much as she tried to deny it, deep down she knew she was battling the temptation of wanting to be with him for the status. All day long she had fantasized about coworkers, former classmates, and even her dentist finding out they were a couple.

"What are you thinking?" he asked.

"I'm thinking about how I hooked you. You said that when you realized I didn't recognize you, you wanted to spend more time with me. Had I known who you were, we would have parted ways as enemies, more or less."

He nodded solemnly. "You're thinking I was *only* interested in you because you didn't know who I was."

She cut in, knowing what he was about to say. "No. I'm

115

questioning my own motives. What if I'm the type of woman you were trying to avoid?"

He shook his head. "Not possible."

"Honestly, it feels pretty good to have my name linked to yours. Who wouldn't want to say they're in a relationship with a movie star, you know?"

"You're trying to tell me that you only like me because I'm famous?"

"Since we're not sugar-coating it..." She threw her arms up. "I don't know. Maybe."

Looking deep into her eyes, so deep she felt it, he smiled. He wet his lips with his tongue. "Close your eyes."

Swallowing, she did as he asked, but they popped back open.

"Don't make me come over there." It was an empty threat. If he scooted any closer he'd be in her lap.

She smiled nervously, allowing her eyelids to collapse. What if she was a bad kisser? It had been a while.

"Are they closed?"

She nodded.

"If I took your hand and walked you behind one of these big trees," he said slowly, as if he was trying to seduce her, "and I kissed you, nobody's looking, I guarantee your lips would be doing half the work."

Her heart quickened. "You might be right," she whispered, opening her eyes.

"And guess what else. I'm betting my career would be the furthest thing from your mind."

She kept looking from his eyes to his lips, desiring a taste. Whatever they were talking about was lost. He sat silently for a minute or two, like a lion waiting for the right moment to pounce. He was playing a game and it was working.

"Colette Halbrook," he said conclusively.

She raised an eyebrow and laughed. "Yes?"

"You're saying that you want your name tied to mine for the fame, I imagine. You want to be famous?"

"Sure, why not," she smirked, wondering what happened to the kiss.

"Why do you want to be famous?"

"I wouldn't say I aspire to be *famous*," she said, gesturing quotation marks. "*Fame* is relative to *accomplished*, right? Everyone wants to be known for something."

"If you could be known for one thing at the end of your life, what would it be?"

Living in a world full of suffering, it was impossible to narrow it down. "I would want to be known for something meaningful, like discovering a cure for cancer or stopping a genocide. Dating an actor is not at the top of my list, if that's what you're wondering." It wasn't the type of question that could have a wrong answer, but she could tell it wasn't the right one either.

"I'm trying to find out what makes you tick. Everyone wants world peace. Your life will end when you're, say, one-hundred. What do you hope people will say at your funeral?"

Was it safe to tell him? How could she word it without sounding too cliché? "It's hard for me to put into words, so bear with me."

It started to snow for the first time that day and she loved how she had someone to share it with. Her body trembled in response to the temperature, but beneath her skin she somehow felt warm. "Whether it's by adoption or someday down the road, you know…" She could tell he was hanging on her every word. "If I could be known or remembered for just one thing, most of all, I would want people to look back on my life and think of me as someone who truly loved her kids and knew how to show it."

He was nodding as if he wholeheartedly appreciated what she had said. "You would get along with my mom. And that's a compliment."

Opening up to him felt intimate. If she could close the door on everything else and be swept up in his arms forever, that would be living. "I bet your mom is proud of you. I'm almost afraid to ask, but is anyone else in your family famous? The only thing I know about you is what I've seen firsthand."

"That's the way it should be, right?" He held her hand and squeezed. "I'm the only Rocco who pursued acting. But it's not even accurate to say that I pursued it. Circumstances happened and *it* found *me*. I'm glad it did though. I'm not complaining."

"You hear about people trying to make it big in Hollywood and everybody knows it will never happen. How did your friends and family react when you told them about your first big break?"

He tightened his lips and paused. "Somehow the press hasn't found out yet," he said slowly, "but there's something about me I think you should know."

CHAPTER 14

Colette tore out the magazine article, crumpled it into a wad too small to grasp firmly, and stormed across the squeaky floorboards. She opened the front door to darkness, the wind howling. Aiming for Japan, she chucked Bryce's pretty face, a shot taken years ago, back when the rest of the country first learned of his true character.

"Coco, get a grip," Summer said from across the room. "What did you expect? Everyone has exes. His just happens to be Capri Saxton."

"You think I'm jealous?" Colette slammed the door and returned to her spot on the area rug. "I'm changing my return flight. I'm not going to chance a pre-arranged seat partner."

"Don't you think you're being unfair?" Summer said delicately. "We're talking five years ago."

Colette snatched a magazine from the dozens strewn throughout the living room. Front and center was the flawless Capri Saxton. Even frowning, the platinum-blonde actress was cuter than Barbie. Colette pried her eyes away from Capri's high cheekbones just long enough to read the headline:

AMERICA'S SWEETHEART DESPERATE FOR ANSWERS
Capri regards Bryce's marriage proposal as 'a cruel joke'

Leaning forward, Colette handed the magazine to Summer. "I'm guessing he never took her back."

Summer's lips moved as she read silently. "If you're looking to shock someone, I'm not that person. I know Bryce Rocco better than my own brother," she chuckled. "Granted, Bryce and I are both thirty and my nomadic brother is pushing fifty."

Thirty. So *he* made the plunge before *she* did. Not that she still cared about his age... or his shoe size—seventeen, according to his publicist. From what she could piece together, Bryce dated Capri Saxton to further his career. Then he proposed to the poor girl with no intention of marrying her. As if breaking her heart two days later via email wasn't enough, he refused to speak to her when she wanted answers.

Colette shook her head and sighed. "How did this not ruin his career? I'm not even finding an apology from him. His fans are idiots."

"Maybe we are, but you can't help but like the guy." Summer left the room and returned with a stack of crackers. "This is your classic Hollywood breakup. Two actors date. One dumps the other. Thus, the world gets something fresh to gossip about."

"It's mean."

"Who cares? Everyone gets dumped. Everyone hates their ex when it's over. She's just mad because she didn't dump him first."

"I hope someday your mailman never blindsides you with a breakup postcard."

Summer narrowed her eyes. "What you're really saying is you hope he dumps me so I'll know how it feels. That's not nice, Coco."

They studied each other for a moment before breaking into

laughter. "Give me some of those," Colette said, reaching for the crackers. "I hate how in every other shot he's either advertising alcohol or girls. And did you see this one? It says he gambled away his fortune."

"Check the year. He was a kid."

She flipped the magazine over. "I think you're wrong. If he's older than me..."

"You know guys mature later than girls."

"Ha! That's no excuse, but nice try." Colette studied a photo of Capri Saxton in a bikini. "Her stomach is so flat. Mine's pooched out and blubbery."

"You're still worried about that?" Summer glanced at the picture. "Those are fake you know."

"Her boobs?"

"Yep. And her cheeks."

"Really?" Colette looked closer. "If she'd just turn her body a little more..."

Summer laughed. "I'm talking about the cheeks on her face, goofball."

"Ew."

*

Colette heard a knock just after setting the dial to permanent press. It was probably Stuart. She flipped on the porch light, checked the peephole, and sucked in a breath. She didn't have the energy to fight. Opening the front door, she faked a smile.

"What's up, stranger?"

There was no sense in dragging it out. "Please don't hate me."

"Shut up. You know I love you. How was your flight?"

Jazmine's face was glowing as if she were newly engaged. It was no wonder. Two days prior, on the way home from skiing, Colette's account of her time with Bryce had been recklessly uncensored. Words like "perfect" and "marriage" had escaped from her lips.

Jazmine's smile went flat. "Is it just me, or are you blocking me so I can't come in?"

"Forget everything I told you. Right after I called you, I found out some horrible things about him."

"I know. I talked to Summer for three hours this morning while you were on your flight."

"Oh." The thought of her two closest friends chatting behind her back was unsettling. "And...?"

"Relax. I'm with you. Bryce Rocco is not your soul mate."

A wave of relief swept over her. "No he's not. Thank you for seeing that. Wow. I'm blown away right now."

"Summer disagrees."

"I know. I feel terrible."

"Dude, are you going to let me in? I'm dying to see those pictures."

"Now that I know you're not going to assault me."

"Don't feel guilty," Jazmine said, kicking off her shoes. "It's obviously not meant to be. But it was fun while it lasted, right?"

"For sure."

"Was it weird seeing pictures of your boyfriend in magazines?"

"It's like it wasn't even him. You know I'm not attracted to guys who party. Yuck."

"Well I am."

"Look who just dumped you."

"It's all good. I kept the jewelry."

"I looked at picture after picture of him and all I could think was *womanizer*. He was either posed with girls or thinking about them."

"Let's count how many guys you've been out with in the past year."

"That's different and you know it." Colette picked up a pillow and plopped down on the couch. "You know what I hate? Bryce isn't even going to remember me. He'll move on and never give me a second thought."

"Not true." Jazmine joined her on the couch. "He's getting out of acting. He'll be broke in a year. You watch."

Colette's eyes widened. "Where did you hear that?"

"Relax. Your secret's safe with me. Summer made me swear up and down, east and west, not to tell a soul."

"She told you? Bryce confided in me. He trusted me not to tell anyone, and now Summer's blabbing it to whoever? Why would she do that? Why would she tell you, of all people? You guys aren't even friends."

"I know you think I can't keep a secret, but watch me. The only person I told was my grandpa, but he literally lives and sleeps in front of his TV. It was nice to have something besides the weather to discuss. Hey, these are the flowers from Bryce. I bet you didn't have a clue how filthy rich he was. If you ask me, he should have at least included chocolate. Cheapskate." Her eyebrows peeked. "Who are you calling?"

"Who do you think?" Colette waited impatiently for Summer to pick up. "Jaz, listen to me. It is very important that you do not tell anyone else. Bryce hasn't made up his mind yet. His agent doesn't even know he might be getting out of the business. He's been avoiding him." Colette slapped her forehead as if she were checking for a fever. "This is getting out of hand. Why are girls so gossipy? I never should have told her."

"Relax. You're panicking for no reason. What's the big deal?"

"The big deal is, Bryce trusted me."

CHAPTER 15

The NICU was buzzing with excitement by the time Colette clocked in Tuesday afternoon. What normally would have made for an instantaneous boost on the popularity scale was inevitably going to knock her down hard. Playing the shy card, Colette did a lot of smiling and shrugging to keep from making claims that would expire by morning.

Since her arrival back in Oregon, the only voicemail she received was from the day before, when Bryce realized she wasn't on his return flight. He was mildly concerned, but mostly excited to see her again. She hadn't even broken it off yet and already guilt was overshadowing the reasons behind her decision. Each time she replayed his voicemail, the sound of his deep baritone struck the same painful chord as Elvis' lovely version of *I'll Be Home for Christmas*.

On her way to the restroom, she nearly bumped into Denise, a middle-aged lactation consultant with dark gray hair. Denise tugged her braid and set it over her left breast. She had a serious case of split ends, Colette noticed. Her hefty salary, plus whatever income that wedding ring represented, should have sufficed for a haircut, a package of Crest Whitestrips, and a bra.

"I heard you slept with Bryce Rocco." Denise adjusted her purple-framed glasses as if to get a clearer picture of the act. "How was it?"

Colette's mouth hung open in judgment. "You seriously just asked me that?" Before she could stop it, a smile began forming on Colette's face, blossoming into a perfect "don't you wish you knew."

"C'mon. We're both women. You know you're dying to kiss and tell. Was it anything like the love scene in *Split Decision*? He was so tender and sexy. I must have replayed that scene a thousand times."

"Gross, Denise. That's disgusting."

"Maybe so, but I'm only human. Give me one small detail and we'll call it a day. I promise. No more questions."

"I don't know where you heard that, but it's not true. Really. It's so not." The more defensive she became, the less she believed herself.

Dr. Piazza came around the corner and raised her eyebrows questioningly. "You're nice and cheerful this afternoon, Colette. Might Bryce Rocco have something to do with that?"

"I don't know what you heard, but we're not dating or anything."

"I'm just an old lady," she said with an air of superiority. "Very well. Keep me out of the loop. But allow me to say just one thing in regards to your little escapade. If the rumors are true about California, you'll need to put in a full two weeks' notice, in writing, if you're expecting a letter of recommendation from me or anyone else on this staff. Do you understand?"

"I'm not moving to California."

Without so much as a glance, Dr. Piazza waved her stained coffee mug. "Of course you're not." She opened the door to her office, paused, and then turned back around. "I'm not trying to get motherly with you, but you're old enough to realize things don't always work out the way we plan. I strongly suggest you take my advice. Two weeks."

"Okay, but I'm not moving."

"Great. Then you'll have no qualms about committing to the twenty-seven weeker delivered this morning. I'll tell Angela to switch with you tomorrow."

Colette's heart sank. She was still trying to cope with the loss of baby Charlie. She wasn't ready to hold the fragile life of somebody's whole world in her hands again. There was too much that could go wrong; too much pressure to do everything just right.

"They're a nice African American family. I have the feeling you and mom are going to bond right away. She'll like you. They all seem to like you for one reason or another, and I appreciate that about you."

Colette held back her tears until the door closed. "I can't do this. I just lost a patient a week and a half ago. Why is she punishing me?"

"Come now," said Denise. "She's not punishing you."

Colette couldn't stop the tears. She missed Bryce and was angry with him for not being who she wanted him to be. She needed his reassurance that everything would turn out okay. She needed to know someone cared. Her girlfriends were fickle. One minute they loved her, the next they wanted to ring her neck for not doing *life* the way it should be done. Not Bryce, though. Her relationship with Bryce, brief as it was, had been different. He was forgiving and understanding. He was irreplaceable.

"Here, take this." Denise handed her a tissue. "Everyone's already talking about you. Don't give them one more reason. Quick now. Dry your tears."

Colette nodded, dabbing and fanning her face.

"I would divorce my husband to trade places with you. Not really. Maybe I would though. I don't know. You'd have to give me more time to think about it. Anyway, you're the type of gal who will give Capri Saxton, or any one of those pretty things, a run for her money."

Like a tightened faucet, Colette's tears stopped. "You really think so?"

"Honey, I know so."

*

Colette shoved her key into the lock. Without glancing behind her, she asked Stuart a question she knew would catch him off guard. "Are you lonely?"

She could hear the hesitation in his response, which sort of amused her. "Lonely, as in...?"

"Never mind." Colette leaned against the door as she turned the knob. Seven billion people crammed onto one planet and *she* was lonely. The only two friends she had were next to impossible to get a hold of. She was in her twenties. Her prime. Aside from some online dating and her Bryce "escapade," as Dr. Piazza had put it, her life was pathetically uneventful.

Stuart cleared his throat. "If you don't mind my asking, are you okay?"

For the hundredth time she asked herself why Bryce hadn't picked up the phone to call her today. Wasn't that what boyfriends were supposed to do? It was all the more reason to break it off. She didn't need this kind of stress day in and day out. With a hand on her hip, she whirled around. "What do you think of Capri Saxton?"

Stuart's face transitioned from nervous to scholarly. "Capri Saxton is the daughter of a renowned film director named Clyde Klein, I believe."

"But you're not sure?"

"No. Yes. I know this for a fact."

"Does anything else about her stand out to you? Like, do you think she's pretty?"

"She looks magnificent in the color white."

"Okay. Have a good night."

"Wait. Do you remember what day it is?"

Leaving the door ajar, Colette turned around. "No."

"It's the eleventh of March. Do you give up? It's my birthday."

"Happy birthday."

"My buddies and I painted the town red tonight, if you know what I mean. But perhaps I could take you out to a late dinner right now."

"Thanks for the offer, but I just got my computer back this afternoon and I have some work to do."

"But it's my birthday. I was really hoping you could spare thirty minutes."

"Even if I could, I can't. I just started seeing someone recently. Thank you for the offer though. That was really sweet."

"You met someone in Colorado? Interesting. You never mentioned him."

"No. He lives here."

"In your apartment?"

"He lives in town."

"Where?"

129

"I would rather not say. But if it was my birthday, I wouldn't let this day end without swinging by Papa's Pizza. Happy birthday."

After making sure all the curtains were closed, she tore off her shoes and lunged for the computer. While it was booting up, she threw a bag of popcorn into the microwave, turned on the TV, and started up *Split Decision*. As the camera panned images of New York City, her heart soared right along with it. She was on the edge of her seat in anticipation.

Soon she was settled in on the couch with a bowl of popcorn resting on her thigh, gawking at the first image she had ever seen of Bryce in a movie. He was in a Manhattan high rise making a sandwich for a wrinkled woman with a cane. When his name appeared on the screen and then vanished, she got chills. Breaking the heart of Bryce Rocco wasn't going to be easy.

CHAPTER 16

She was already in love with baby Kisha, a princess among four older brothers, and Colette couldn't have handpicked a nicer family. From what she had been told, just hours after Kisha's unexpected birth, two loving aunts adorned the dark room with "it's a girl" wall hangings, a pair of pink Nike's, and a variety of Beanie Babies. Folded on the countertop next to the sink was an aged quilt her great-grandma dropped off, with hot pink letters stitched into the center spelling Kisha Girl.

Dr. Piazza's decision to give Colette another extreme preemie felt like an honor. Meeting the frightened family served to strengthen her spirit, reminding Colette of her unique purpose: saving lives.

The thirty-four-year-old mother, Latoya, was sitting up straight on a tall stool, gazing down at her two-and-a-half pound daughter. Her makeup was fresh, her hair was styled, and if she had gained more than fifteen pounds during her six-month pregnancy, her cute maternity jeans hid it well. "Kisha, all you do is sleep," Latoya said in a cutesy voice. "Get it in while you can, because your brothers be raising the roof right off the walls with all their crying and laughing and carrying on." She lifted the green tent just enough to slide her hand underneath. Gently, she blanketed Kisha's upper body with the warmth of her palm. "Not you though. You're sweeter than pie, just like your daddy. Sweeter than pie."

131

Colette gathered the supplies needed for a routine test and approached Latoya apologetically. "I need to get another blood gas on her."

"Do you have to? Kisha doesn't like that."

"I know. I'm sorry."

"I'm just playing," Latoya said, her expression solemn. "Do what you have to do to get her home. Try to be gentle if you can. But would it be alright if I hold her hand just a little bit while you prick her?"

"Go ahead and do whatever makes you two feel most comfortable."

Latoya squinted her eyes. "Alright, baby girl. They've got to give you another little poke on your foot. Five seconds is all. I know you're too small to understand why all this is happening to you, but..." As tears started to fall, she took in a deep breath and slid her finger against the inside of Kisha's hand. She smiled when her daughter's tiny fingers responded the same way a healthy baby's hand would. Latoya watched anxiously as Colette pressed a warm gel-pad against her newborn's left heel. "Mama's so proud of you, Kisha. The good Lord knows..." She wiped her face as she wept softly. "He knows you're braver than me."

*

Jazmine fed the pop machine a dollar and pushed one of the Pepsi buttons. After the thud, she joined Colette at the tidiest table in the break room. Colette noticed Jazmine's skin was noticeably darker than the day before. "What took you so long?"

"I'm glad you asked," Jazmine grinned in her cute way. "So I step out of the restroom, literally trip over this toddler crawling around, and the mom freaks out like it was my fault. So I apologize, you know, because I feel terrible for not seeing him."

"Was he hurt?"

"Who? The kid? No. The kid was fine. Listen. So I come around the corner and see the spitting image of Bryce. Same hair, same build, same sexy—you can close your mouth. It wasn't him."

"Are you sure? Did you see his face?"

Jazmine shot her a curious look. "Do you want it to be him?"

Of course she did. That would mean he went out of his way to see her. "Jaz, the man owns eight cars. *Eight*! You tell me if I want to waste ten seconds on a guy who is that greedy."

"It's not like he stole them. Why do you care what he does with his money?"

"Eight cars for one single guy screams dissatisfaction. It's no wonder Capri Saxton couldn't hold onto him. One gorgeous woman wasn't enough for him?" When Jazmine didn't zealously agree, Colette broke off a piece of french bread and threw it at her. "Stop smiling like that. You look like a snob."

"Back to my story. To answer your question, yes, I saw his face and, no, it wasn't Bryce. But being the ditz that I am, I waltz right up to the guy thinking it was. Long story short, *Steve* and I have a date Saturday night. He's a tech guy from New Zealand. You should come too, and bring one of your online boys."

"Thanks, but I'm staying home this weekend."

"Why? You're single again. You should get on with your life which, pre-Bryce, means two bachelors per week."

"I think it's weird when people date right after they break up. What's the rush?"

"Actually it's healthy. Otherwise you cry until you want to kill

133

yourself, and eat until you get fat. And since you don't know from personal experience, getting fat is expensive. You have to buy a whole new wardrobe each time it happens."

Colette drizzled bacon-ranch dressing on her salad. "I need to hurry up and dump him. This waiting game is making me crazy."

"You haven't told him? What is wrong with you? Even I'm not that mean."

"What am I supposed to do, call him? I haven't heard from him in three days. He's probably asking himself what he ever saw in me."

"He hasn't had time to call because he's too busy notifying his friends about his new smokin' hot nurse. Now he's going to have to un-tell them, and thanks to your cowardice, probably the press too."

"The press? C'mon. Like they care."

Jazmine snatched Colette's cell.

"What are you doing?"

"I'm using a visual aid to threaten you." Jazmine held up the phone as if it were the next item up for bid on The Price Is Right. "If he's not bawling his eyes out before the stroke of midnight, I'll break up with him for you. Fair warning." Jazmine gathered up her meal and stood up.

"Where are you going? We haven't had the same dinner break in weeks."

"You're in position to royally embarrass him. I'm giving you privacy to end it before he has more reasons to hate you."

"He's not going to hate me."

Jazmine laughed. "You know nothing about a man's ego, do you?"

CHAPTER 17

Colette sat on the edge of the bed with her phone pressed against her ear. It was ringing. Her heart was pounding. Bryce still hadn't called, so maybe he wouldn't answer either. She could smell the bacon and sausage she had fried up as a reward for going through with it.

"Colette," Bryce blurted out so quickly it was impossible to decipher the tone.

Her body was tense. Frantically, she second-guessed the urgency of the breakup. "I know what you did to Capri Saxton," she heard herself mumble. "I went through magazines. I've seen pictures."

He groaned. After a long pause, she heard the sadness in his voice. "Colette, I don't like having conversations like this over the phone."

"That explains why I haven't heard from you in a while."

"You didn't get my message?"

The innocence of his question reinforced her guilt. "Just one, but I figured you'd call again."

He let out a breath as if to laugh. "I *followed* you on your vacation. Do you get how huge of a risk that was? And that was after I begged for your phone number. Somehow, after all that, I actually got the girl. Then, post Colorado, I sat by the phone for two hours trying to convince myself the 'wait three days to call so you don't smother her' rule still applies. It doesn't, I decided, so I went for it. When you didn't pick up, I was supposed to keep calling over and over?"

"Did you really sit by the phone for two hours?"

When he lowered his voice it sounded intimate. "Of course I did. I like you."

Building trust with a human was like buying a used car—*only time will tell.* Shiny paint, clean interior, detailed maintenance records, new tires. But none of that mattered if, in the middle of Death Valley, it turned out to be a lemon. *Time* she was willing to give. Her *heart*, on the other hand, was a different story. She wished she could close her eyes, and when she opened them, she and Bryce would be snuggled up in bed, listening to the crackle of a cozy fire, living happily ever after.

"Colette, if all that garbage about me and Capri bothered you so much, why didn't you just ask me about it?"

She sighed. "I honestly thought magazines couldn't print stories unless they knew for a fact it was the truth."

"I'm not saying they got it wrong."

She narrowed her eyes. "So all that stuff about Capri Saxton really happened?" When she heard herself say the name of America's Sweetheart, it zapped her back into reality. Bryce Rocco was a Capri Saxton; rich, glamorous, mythical. She was out of her mind to believe she could someday build a family with one of Hollywood's greatest. It was a hilarious joke and Colette was the punch line.

"We need to talk in person. When can I see you?"

"You can't," she whispered.

"That's not going to work for me."

A tear rolled down Colette's cheek, but her voice didn't let on. "I need you to hear me out." She swung her legs off the side of the bed, the tips of her toes brushing the floor. "You're trying to win my heart. Naturally you're going to put your best foot forward. I'm not looking for someone who makes me feel happy." Her words were slow, providing plenty of room for interruption. "I need someone with unquestionably good character. You and I don't even have any mutual friends. You would know a co-worker's character by their reputation, or a neighbor's character by how many keg parties they throw or how much time they spend helping the widow next door, you know? Who's to say *you* should even trust *me*? I could be anybody."

"You've got a point. I mean, you save babies all week long, but on the weekends you could be chopping down swing-sets."

"Who told you?"

"Word gets around." After a long, drawn-out sigh, he chanted her name under his breath several times. "Basically what you're telling me is you're looking for the boy next door."

"Exactly," she said, unsure if he was mocking her. "You learn a man's character when you see his reaction to a dog using his front lawn as an outhouse, right? If he kicks the dog to Timbuktu, you might question his anger management abilities."

"You have a point."

"How many people have been fooled by a perfect date? There are plenty of guys out there who know how to play the game. Hypothetically speaking, a perfect date could mean you went out with a really good actor."

"If it makes you feel any better, I swear on my dead ferret's grave that I can't act."

She laughed. "That changes everything."

"Are you sure you don't want to settle for a movie star?" His voice was painfully sexy. "I hear they can be a lot of fun."

"I'm sure they are." She softened her voice. "That's how certain celebrities play out in my imagination anyway."

"I wasn't aware a nice girl like you had that sort of imagination."

"Like I said, you can't really know a person..."

"Alright, Coco. Here it is. Last try and I'll leave you alone. Give me a chance to prove myself. Obviously someone hurt you in the past, but I'm not that guy. Please."

"I'll never forget you, Bryce."

CHAPTER 18

Latoya quietly entered baby Kisha's private room dressed in a lavender skirt and a white top. "How's my baby girl?" Smiling, she lifted the tent and brushed her fingertips down the back of Kisha's hair, wet from the high humidity continuously blowing in.

"We bumped her oxygen down four percent and Kisha seems to be okay with it."

"Did you hear what she did in her diaper this morning?" Latoya winked.

"I did. That's a good sign. The doctor ordered three more cc's of milk, starting at her six o'clock feed. How is your pumping going?"

Latoya pointed to her chest. "Look who decided to join us. I woke up this morning and, bam, there they were. It was the same with all four of my boys so I was ready."

"The human body is an amazing thing."

Tilting her head, her smile lessened. "Do *you* have any kids?"

"For now, these babies are my only kids. Hopefully someday I'll have a couple of my own."

She couldn't get over the fact that any sex-crazed party animal had the right to become a parent, but people like Colette—educated, financially stable, and overflowing with love—were required to fill out an application, prepare their home for a strict inspection, and create a personality compatible with oddball caseworkers like Roxanne.

When the phone on the wall rang, Colette answered. The woman on the other end frantically asked for Latoya, so she passed the phone off without any questions. As Latoya listened to the call, her lips tightened. She kept nodding her head in understanding, as if she and the caller were speaking face-to-face. After promising to be home in twenty minutes, she handed the phone back to Colette.

"Those boys." Shaking her head, Latoya laughed. "Girl, I'm telling you. The one up from the youngest flushed his foot down the toilet and now it's stuck. He's hollering because he's scared that 911 is coming to the house. If his foot is still whole and my sitter hasn't lost her mind, I'll be back soon." She blew Kisha a dozen kisses and was gone.

Two hours later the receptionist told Colette that mom and four of her sisters were washing up. Colette found it strange that all four aunts were visiting on a Wednesday afternoon, but on second thought, figured the tight-knit family rushed to the house when they heard about their nephew's emergency. Respecting the NICU's visitation rules, Colette said it would be fine to send the aunts back two at a time.

Latoya entered the dark room carrying a wrinkled magazine and a colorful stuffed caterpillar. "Kisha, baby. Mama's back. I missed you." Love was written all over her face as she lifted the tent and cupped her hand over Kisha's round belly. "Her eyes are open," Latoya said excitedly. In a high pitched voice she chatted softly with her daughter, telling her about the hundreds who were on their knees before the face of God Almighty, petitioning for her life, and what a party it's going to be the day she comes home.

The two aunts were grinning at Colette to the point it was becoming awkward. From what she could tell, they hadn't so much as glanced at their beautiful niece. When Kisha's eyes got tired a minute or two later, Latoya stopped chattering. She kissed her own finger and touched it to her daughter's face. "How in the world am I supposed to raise my boys and Kisha all at the same time? I can't be two places at once."

"That's just it." Colette touched Latoya's arm sympathetically, all too familiar with her situation. "On the toughest days, continue to remind yourself that you're only one person. You can make up lost time with your boys in a few months, and when you can't be at the hospital, know that Kisha is getting one-on-one care around the clock."

"I know, but she needs her mama. Excuse the analogy, but this is worse than watching grass grow. I've spent an entire week staring at her, waiting for her to get bigger, and what happened? She got *smaller*. You see what I'm saying? Do you see why I feel like she'll be in this... closet, if you will, forever?"

"Time has a way of going very slowly in here."

"You're telling me. I'm not saying she's not the cutest little girl I've ever seen, but in all honesty, she hardly looks like a baby. I can't even picture her with chubby thighs." Latoya's eyes got bigger. "That thirty-two weeker across the hall, he looks healthy. If Kisha ever gets to that point, I'll have no complaints."

"When they start out as small as Kisha, those last few weeks are often the hardest."

"Why is that?"

"It's a roller coaster, which you're probably already starting to figure out. After so many weeks, many parents feel like they can't take it anymore."

141

"Is that the truth? The only reason I halfway believe you is because you're the expert. I can't imagine anything worse than seeing your child in critical condition like this. It will be interesting to see if I eat my words in a couple months."

One of the aunts cleared her throat and eyeballed Latoya with a look of "I'm still waiting."

"You hush," said Latoya. "I love you from the bottom of my heart all the way up, but you've been getting on my nerves ever since you got to town. Colette and I are having a conversation."

"Carry on."

"Don't worry. We will."

For the next minute, there was a silence nobody cared to fill, so Colette spoke up. "I take it your son's foot is still in one piece?"

Latoya laughed as if she was exhausted. "His foot is fine. It survived. But my poor toilet bowl didn't. I think those firemen enjoyed busting it up."

"Oh no. You know what they say. Boys will be boys." Colette could feel the tension ripening between Latoya and her sisters. She scanned the monitor and was happy with the numbers. "Do you mind if I step out for a few minutes? If you need anything, I'll be right outside the door."

Ignoring the question, Latoya began cooing at Kisha. Carefully, she pulled her hand away from her sleeping daughter. "Page fifty-six." Latoya picked up the magazine that had been lying face-down on her lap. "She looks absolutely nothing like you, but she's got your hair, your job, and is living in your town."

"What's this?" Flipping the magazine over, she gasped when she read the cover.

"Don't forget the name," said the aunt who had been quiet up until that moment. "Ask her if her last name is Halbrook."

142

"Tell me Bryce Rocco's lover isn't the one who's been caring for my baby every day."

Colette was more concerned with the article than answering any of their questions. "Oh no. This can't be good," she mumbled, swallowing a lump of dryness as she flipped through the magazine. Thirty pages too far, ten pages not enough. Back and forth she fumbled until she came to page fifty-six. "Oh no, no, no," she whispered. "No. That greedy little—"

When the monitor began beeping she remembered where she was. Practically slapping the magazine against the torso of one of the aunts, she went to baby Kisha. Her heart rate dropped quickly until it was officially a *brady*, but Kisha's skin color looked fine. Seconds later, the monitor caught up and the beeping stopped. "Latoya, do you think she needs a f-fresh blanket?" Colette was trying to play it cool, but she couldn't wait to get her hands back on that article.

"Do you want me to get her one?"

"Sure."

"Are you cold, sweetie? I'll be right back." Latoya opened the door to the warmer and took out a stiff blanket. "So it's you?" Latoya asked as she laid the blanket across Kisha.

Colette hadn't even had a chance to read the headline. She had been too focused on the hideous picture taking up half the page. Her mouth, wide open in mid-sentence, framed her strangely rolled tongue as if she had no control over the muscles in her face. Disproportionate didn't even begin to describe her eyes. It had taken her two decades to learn how to wink, but alas, in the photo, she looked like a pro; one eye was wide open, the other borderline shut.

The shot was taken after the ski slope had kicked her butt,

and there was no doubt who had snapped the picture. Photoshop out Colette's face, and the shot could have been cute. Bryce was kneeling beside her, grinning. It was the perfect "you're going to laugh about this later" moment.

And laugh she did. At the airport, Summer and Colette simultaneously retold the side-splitting story to Summer's bemused boyfriend. When Summer's eyes welled with tears, Colette made a mad dash to the ladies' room.

Colette looked at the three curious women. Latoya smiled sweetly, but in her expression was pity. The other two were on the edge of their seats in anticipation of the reaction. When she looked back at the article, her eyes wandered from the hideous picture to the headline that was being circulated into millions of hands. It was as if someone lit a fuse and her body imploded all at once.

DATING DOWN:
BRYCE GOES FROM CLASSY CAPRI TO CLUMSY COLETTE

The debris ricocheting in her head made it impossible to skim the article. She tried to fight it, to suppress the cascade of emotion that was already unfolding, but she couldn't. Covering her face, she cried like a baby.

CHAPTER 19

Bryce's four-week-old flowers were shriveled and dry, but Colette loved them as if they were her ninety-year-old grandma; still beautiful. After stealing the bouquet from her nightstand, Colette toted it to the breakfast bar where she scarfed down a bowl of oatmeal. When she was through, she jogged to the bedroom for a necklace and a mess of bracelets, and hit the road.

Jazmine was waving from her parked car as Colette pulled into the Fifth Street Public Market in downtown Eugene. The trendy collection of shops and galleries was just what she needed to take her mind off everything. August was the last time she had been there, for the wedding reception of a neighbor she knew about as well as her insurance agent.

The two of them walked around the historic courtyard chatting. Jazmine made no mention of Bryce which surprised her, and every time Colette was tempted to go there, she stopped herself. She knew firsthand how painful it was to listen to a girl obsess over an ex-boyfriend.

"Do you want to watch those weirdos dance?" asked Jazmine, gesturing with her eyes to the middle-aged group dressed from neck to toe in silver spandex.

"Check out those chic leotards. Where do I sign up?"

They climbed one of the many cast-iron staircases for a

balcony view. Colette moved a shuffled newspaper from one tabletop to another, hoping the anonymous reader wouldn't accuse her of stealing his spot. Then the two of them sat, sipping Italian sodas, each of them engrossed in their own thoughts. The lack of conversation attested to the deepening of their friendship. Mere acquaintances needed constant jabber in order to feel comfortable. Friends, however, were free to simply be.

It had been two weeks since the press had pointed out the obvious, that Bryce was "dating down." Ironically, Colette's popularity was rising as if she had accomplished something great. Although she would never admit it, she was basking beneath the spotlight, enjoying her fifteen minutes of fame that went on a little longer than she deserved. She laughed off the headline, acting as though she could never be lucky enough to date a hotshot actor, but hey, if that's what the rumors were saying, why not.

Jazmine rustled through her purchases. "Do you think this honey is really going to help my allergies?"

"Local bees made it, so I'm sure it will." Colette smiled at a man pushing his two sons in a stroller. He gave her body a subtle once over before they locked eyes. Then he was gone. It made her miss Bryce. *Everything* made her miss Bryce.

Jazmine looked at Colette curiously. "Really? Tell me more."

"The same pollens that are irritating your sinuses are in that honey. You're a nurse. You should know this."

"I figured you made me buy it because it's organic."

"All honey is organic."

Jazmine ran her manicured nail across the front of the jar. "See? It specifically says 'organic.'"

"Why would anyone spray pesticides on a beehive?"

"To keep those pesky bees away," she laughed. "I should have bought the smaller jar. It's just one more thing I'll have to move."

"You're moving? Did you find a house?" Colette hoped she hadn't tuned out Jazmine the first time she delivered the exciting news. Most of her brain cells were doused in Bryce, so to learn that she'd already toured the property and helped Jazmine paint the kitchen wouldn't surprise her.

"Actually, Colette, there's a reason I wanted to hang out. It didn't feel right telling you at work."

"You're not moving away, are you?"

Jazmine tucked her black hair behind her ears. "Actually, sweetie, I was atrociously jealous that your friend, Summer, is moving to San Antonio. It's so warm and sunny there."

Colette set down her Italian soda, borderline annoyed. "Summer's not moving. What in the world did I say to give you that idea?"

"You really need to get on social media. It's ridiculous that you're not. Her boyfriend got a new job. He's about to propose to her, but don't you dare say a word. Nobody knows yet, not even Summer. Anyway, she's moving and asked if I wanted to come with."

A black hole swallowed Colette and she began falling faster and faster. "Why would she ask *you* over *me*? She doesn't even know you. Oh, that's right. You're Facebook friends now. Silly me."

"I wouldn't call her and I best friends or anything, but we actually click quite well. We were emailing back and forth and then one day we started calling each other."

"Who called who?"

"Don't quote me on this, but I'm pretty sure I'm not required to answer to you. It's not like you own her."

Colette stood up and debated running away like a pigtailed school girl. The one and only thing Jazmine and Summer had in common was Colette. "If you don't mind, I would like to see those emails."

"You know what? I'm not going to finish this conversation until you're in a rational state of mind. I've caught you off guard, and because of that I'm going to cut you some slack." Jazmine shoved the jar of honey back into the bag and gathered her things. "When you're ready to be happy for me, call me." The click, click, click of Jazmine's heels echoed as she twisted her hips across the courtyard.

Colette called out after her. "Does this mean you *are* moving?"

Jazmine stopped and pressed her lips tightly into a smile. "In three weeks, babe."

*

Dark clouds taunted Colette as she walked up the sidewalk below her apartment. When her phone went off, she rearranged her purchases for a free hand and checked the caller ID. Gritting her teeth, she declined the call. Over the past couple of weeks, nearly a dozen so-called friends had suddenly remembered her number. Something told her she should respond to one or two of them since, as of an hour ago, she was officially alone in the world.

When she reached the top of the stairs and turned toward her apartment she nearly fainted. Stuart was standing like a statue, dressed in a suit and tie, holding a bundle of red roses. Colette narrowed her eyes. "Hello," she said nervously.

"C-Colette. Ahh. Colette." He cleared his throat. "Colette? I was wondering if you would like to have dinner with me tonight. That is, if you're able to."

"Wow. This is unexpected." Awkward had never felt so awkward. "You and I are friends, which is fine, but..." Using the bottom corner of her coat, she began buffing her apartment key to a shine. She struggled to come up with the nicest way to turn him down.

"Friends. Yes. Of course. We *are* friends."

Colette sighed. His expression made her realize how much he was hoping for a yes. And it wasn't like she had anything else planned for her Saturday. "Sure. Why not." When Stuart's face lit up, she felt the weight of one more problem. "Except I have this one rule. Normally I don't let my dates in on this, but I should probably tell you right off the bat. I only go out with the same guy once. I know it's dumb, but it works for me."

"You're not dumb at all. Trust me." His eyebrows were wiggling like worms. "The reservation is for 5:00. It's for Mazzi's if that's alright by you."

"I have some errands to run first. Can I meet you there?"

"Yes you may. I'll see you at 5:00 at Mazzi's. Do you need me to draw you a map?"

"I've been there before."

"So you'll actually be there?"

"I will." Colette slipped into her apartment without the roses that Stuart never got around to handing her.

Before her afternoon cry, she sat on her bed and thumbed through the mail. Sluggishly, she peeled open a credit card offer, ripped it in half, and set it aside. She was about to pick up the next one when she noticed a handwritten zip code on a beige envelope toward the bottom of the stack. She grabbed it, half expecting Bryce's name in the upper left corner. She checked.

No name.

The return address was a PO Box in McKenzie Bridge, Oregon. "Bryce, is this from you?" she whispered, wondering for the hundredth time where he was from. She tore into the envelope, pulled out a short letter, and skipped right to the bottom. There, scribbled in black ink, was *his* gorgeous name! Her mouth went dry as her eyes shot to the beginning of the letter. She didn't know whether to laugh or cry. She smiled nervously as a single tear fell onto the center of the letter, blurring the ink.

"I miss you," she whispered.

CHAPTER 20

Five hours into her shift, standing just outside Kisha's door, Colette gripped Bryce's letter inconspicuously within her pocket. Latoya and her husband were in Kisha's room making each other laugh as if they were seventeen. Heart pounding, Colette peeked into Pod Four. "Jaz, can I borrow you real quick?"

"Who's asking?"

"Please? It's important."

Flipping her hair, Jazmine exhaled long and slow. "Shelby, watch my babies for a second, will you? I'll be right back."

Relieved that Jazmine didn't blow her off, Colette returned to her post, a wobbly chair on wheels. Her moist fingers rubbed the paper as she contemplated sharing the letter. There was no doubt Jazmine would eat it up like olives, enjoying every word as if it were written to her, but Colette wasn't sure she was ready for opinions just yet.

Jazmine came around the corner, hands firmly on her hips. "I figured I would have heard from you by yesterday, but this is day three. Not good."

"Shhh. This isn't even about that. Stuart asked me out on Saturday."

Jazmine's eyes widened. "No he did not. What did you say?" She knelt down five inches from Colette's face, grinning.

"I went. I don't know what I was thinking."

"Dang it. This is a three hour conversation and I have a minute. You are so stubborn, you know that? I can't believe you didn't call me the second you got home. How was it?"

"It was awful," Colette said far quieter than Jazmine cared to keep things. "I never should have gone. It's bad. I think I should break my lease."

Jazmine slugged Colette in the arm. "Do it! Come with us to San Antonio."

"I can't."

"Why not?"

Colette's mind drifted back to eleven years old, to her last night with her mom. A deep-voiced woman named Piper held her back as Colette screamed hysterically, begging her mom not to leave her. It wasn't until Colette noticed her eyes that she knew her mom couldn't hear a thing. Their once sparkling blue-green shade had blackened like the starless sky above, and they were glazed over like glass. Colette fell to her bare knees, the pavement scraping specks of blood from her skin. Panic overtook her and she began crying out, doing everything in her power to snap her mom out of it. Gripping her arm, Piper yanked Colette to her feet. "Sweetheart," she said with reprimanding force. "This tantrum you're throwing is hurting everyone around you. This needs to stop now." For the first time in her life, she had felt alone. Abandoned. The chill of the memory had lessoned over the years, but it would always be with her.

Colette exhaled, weighing her options. "Because I can't, Jaz. I can't move away. I just... I can't."

"We'll talk soon. I need to get back in there. We got a thirty-six weeker this afternoon and mom's out front washing up. I'm stopping by tonight with artichoke dip, so give me time to pick it up and get gas. I'm on empty. I'm dying to find out what you did to poor Stuart."

"I think there's something seriously wrong with him."

"I could have told you that." The swinging door at the beginning of the hallway caught Jazmine's attention. "That must be baby mama. I have to go. Wait a second. Is that...?" Cocking her head, Jazmine squinted.

Colette's jaw dropped when she recognized the woman in the hospital gown. *It was Bryce's sister.* She needed to hide. As Colette lunged for the door to Kisha's room, she tripped over the chair, which hit the wall and then fell over with a crash. Her heart was pumping so fast she was already breaking a sweat. The "what if" scenario she dreamed up a month ago was spot-on, all the way down to Jenn's messy ponytail. Except in Colette's fantasy, *she* was the nurse, not Jazmine!

"Sorry," Colette said to the chair as she anxiously set it back on all fives. "See you tonight, Jaz."

"I think that's you-know-who's sister."

Colette shut the door most of the way and glanced over her shoulder. Kisha's parents were sardined in a recliner, flipping through a photo album. Busying herself at the desk, she let out a slow breath wishing that she was across the hall oohing and awing over Jenn's baby boy. Synonymous with the way Jazmine had stolen her best friend, she was now robbing Colette of the opportunity to bond with her would-have-been sister-in-law.

*

153

Fighting the urge to window-shop for men, Colette went to Ebay instead. By the time Jazmine barged in fifteen minutes later, a slightly used acoustic guitar along with a how-to book were in route, FedEx, from White Plains, Kentucky.

"Your door wasn't locked. I'm flabbergasted." Like a well-trained child, Jazmine removed her shoes and lined them against the wall next to Colette's.

"I was being nice."

"Weren't you scared of the boogie man?"

"These days nobody scares me like you do, you and your temper. I was playing it safe."

"I'm the one with the temper? You're delusional." Making herself at home in the living room, Jazmine tossed a handful of jelly beans into her mouth. "Consider yourself forgiven for Saturday's episode. I'd be mad too if my only friend in the whole world was moving someplace cool with my only other friend in the whole world."

Colette opened the to-go container and smelled the spinach dip. "You like yours hot, don't you?"

"Either way." Jazmine sat on the arm of the couch and tapped it like a bongo. "So tell me. What happened with Stuart?"

"Ugh. I can't even stand the sound of his name. He's a moron. That's what happened."

"Those are harsh words coming from you."

After adding baby carrots and a squirt of ranch to the plate, Colette joined Jazmine on the couch. "I told Stuart point-blank I'm not interested. It's like he wouldn't believe me. He was convinced Bryce was the only thing holding us back."

"From what?" she snorted. "He doesn't seriously think he has a chance with you."

"It's not like I'm *better* than him. I'm just, you know, not interested."

"Sure you are. You're better than ninety-five percent of the men you date. You and Stuart are on completely different charts and it's perfectly okay to acknowledge that."

"Well I disagree."

"You would." Hopping off the couch, Jazmine went to the pantry and returned with a bag of chips. "Socialist."

"How does that make me a socialist? And if you're so confident that Stuart is beneath me, how low am I hovering on Bryce's scale?"

Jazmine stuffed a chip in her mouth and plopped down on the couch. "The phrase 'dating down' came from a dweeb at a desk being paid a lot of money to make you look bad. The only thing crazy about you and Bryce is that a trillion-and-a-half other women want him and you're the lucky hottie he picked. And then you dumped him."

"You told me to!"

Jazmine sat silent for a moment, her lips pressed tightly together. After several deep breaths, she spoke calmly. "I shall not be put in position to defend myself for ruining your life. If you want him back, by all means, go get him. No one is stopping you."

The knot in Colette's stomach tightened with guilt. Why couldn't she be normal? Why were friendships so hard for her? Forget marriage and babies. She'd settle for a handful of nice friends who begged her to keep Saturdays open for pottery-painting or golfing. "I never should have told Stuart I'm still with Bryce. I thought it would deter him, but I think my plan backfired. Stuart hasn't spoken to me since our... you know."

"Your date?"

"I didn't want to say it."

"I don't blame you. Does he still camp out in his chair?"

Colette raised her eyebrows and nodded. "Religiously. But he doesn't look at me. And I can hear him breathe. I don't know if he has a cold, allergies maybe? He sounds like a bull."

"Why are you smiling like that? Gross. Please stop."

"Why do I put up with you?" Grinning, Colette went into her room and returned with Bryce's letter. "Guess who *this* is from."

"Let me see that!" Jazmine snatched the letter from Colette's grasp. "I'm going to read this once and then we're going to burn it. Gross, Colette. It's like you're enjoying the attention."

Colette nudged Jazmine as if she were flirting. "For your information, it's from Mr. Rocco."

Like darts, Jazmine's eyes pierced the letter. "I thought it was from Stuart! Colette, this is from Bryce! When did he write this?"

"I got it Saturday."

"You're smiling. It must be good. Keep smiling. I'm scared." Crisscrossing her legs, Jazmine wiggled her tush into the couch cushion and focused like she was reading the results of her latest PAP.

Colette-

Hi. How are ya? Startled I imagine. Ha ha.

The past three weeks I have been debating whether or not to let you go. Many would argue I should take your "subtle" hints and hit the road. I'm not so sure.

Everything I felt for you was intensified on that mountain. And the only reason I can admit that to you is because I know you felt it too.

I respect your decision in not wanting to be with me, however, I found a loophole. It's a stretch, but nonetheless, it's there.

In the meantime, I will orchestrate my next move and you will go about saving lives, wondering when our paths will next cross.

--Bryce

CHAPTER 21

Roxanne was cleaning her glasses with a yellow handkerchief when Colette entered the cluttered office. Roxanne's face lit up as she set the plastic frames on the tip of her nose. "Miss Halbrook, welcome. Come in, come in."

"Thank you." Colette took her seat, hopeful that good news was hidden somewhere in the file beneath Roxanne's claw-like nails.

Biting into a mostly eaten sandwich, Roxanne opened the file. "Colette," she said between chews. "Miss Colette Halbrook." Wrinkling her nose, she shuffled through several sheets of paper. Then she stuffed the file somewhere beneath her desk, mumbling under her breath as if she was annoyed.

Colette sat impatiently waiting for the magic word: baby. This was the closest she had ever come to motherhood. "I was excited to get your voicemail." Colette cleared her throat. "I'm sure you were disappointed when you couldn't get a hold of me. If there's an emergency, I can always be reached at work. I think I gave you that number too. Do you need it again?"

Roxanne laughed. "Do you hear any sirens? There's no emergency."

"Sorry. I'm just... I'm a very good home. My apartment is clean. It wasn't just for show either. I'm a very clean person."

Roxanne's thumbnail flicked against the plastic tabs on a stack of files. "Um-hmm."

The silence was making her crazy. "I was thinking about switching to organic cleaners. You know what? It's just a good idea anyway. I'm going to go ahead and make the switch. It's so much better for the environment and everything."

"You go right on ahead and do that. Aha. Here it is." She flipped through the papers like a book before closing the file abruptly. She folded her hands on her desk. "Miss Halbrook. I can't say enough good things about you and your home. From what I understand, you take care of premature babies for a living."

"That's right."

"I'm sure you do a fabulous job. And I appreciate your persistence in checking in with me. Every two weeks like clockwork, it seems to be."

Colette chuckled nervously. "I didn't want you to forget about me."

"Of course." Roxanne hesitated, and then continued slowly. "You're probably hoping I'm needing to place a baby with you."

"I have a bedroom all ready for a boy or girl. It's unisex." Suddenly she regretted using that word.

"Fabulous."

Blushing, Colette nodded.

"Perfect." Removing her glasses, Roxanne smiled as if someone were about to snap her portrait. "You see, it's the older children we often have a hard time placing. Had you been open to a wider age group, a child would have been placed with you right away. Perhaps the very same day even."

Colette's heart sank. "Yes I know. It's just... I want a baby. I'd even be open to a three-year-old."

"And you want to be a foster parent to help a child in need of

159

a safe and loving home, or are you doing this in order to fill some kind of a void in your own life?"

Colette swallowed. "To help children, of course." She could feel the room getting smaller and smaller. "Maybe I should explain my situation better. I work with babies for a living, so I feel like I can offer more to a younger child, especially an infant."

"Thus, you consider yourself inadequate to care for, say, a twelve-year-old?"

"I wouldn't say I'm inadequate."

"Good," she said as if they'd come to an agreement. "I wouldn't say so either. In fact, I would say that you're more than qualified to provide a wonderful home life to a preteen."

"Oh." This was supposed to be the final checkup before delivery. What was so hard about placing an infant in her arms? Whose homes were they going to anyway? Doctors? Lawyers? Stay-at-home soap-opera-watching women who camp out in their pajamas all day because they're too lazy to put on a pair of jeans and make something of their day?

"I love how you don't have any children of your own. When we're mixing biological with foster children, sometimes there are issues with jealousy or safety and whatnot."

"Exactly." She was doing her best to mask the anger brewing beneath her polite disposition. Anyone with an ounce of compassion would have warned a hopeful mother-to-be that this meeting had nothing to do with a baby. "I completely agree with you, Roxanne. I don't have three kids of my own bouncing off the walls, risking the safety of someone too small to defend him or herself. It's just me. I don't even have a roommate. Or a dog."

Roxanne pulled a photo out of the file and handed it to

160

Colette. The little girl looked to be about eight years old with dark stringy hair and empty eyes. "This is Callie. She turned twelve on Christmas day, actually. She has two little brothers, both four years old, and a sister who's six. Callie and her siblings have been in foster care for nine months and, as of one week ago, the mother voluntarily relinquished rights. We're looking at two families in town who are interested in adopting the younger ones, but Callie won't be so lucky."

"They don't want her?"

"No. She has some learning and behavioral issues, but she's a unique little girl. Very sweet. I know her well. She's amazing. Her teacher describes her as a people-pleaser. From previous visits, I learned that Callie wants to be a marine biologist when she grows up and she dreams about going to Sea World. She's never been there."

Callie had an awkwardness about her, but Colette thought she couldn't be more beautiful. "What happened to her skin?"

"It's a sad story," Roxanne said delicately, shaking her head. She then went into detail about the horrendous life that young Callie had been enduring for years. The abuse caused by the little girl's own family, by the people who conceived her, brought Colette to tears. As she wiped her eyes, Roxanne kept talking. She spoke of the cruelty her siblings had been subjected to as well as the guilt Callie felt for not being able to protect them.

Roxanne sighed. "She wants to be with her siblings. She loves them dearly. They've got a decent foster home, but of course she worries about them. Placing all four of them together is not a situation we're able to provide at this time. But we're trying to offer her the very next best thing. We're trying to secure a safe, loving home which, in turn, will hopefully lessen the anxiety she feels in regards to her younger sister and brothers."

Roxanne closed the file. "Colette, this little girl needs a home. She needs a woman in her life who can help her reach her full potential. Callie needs a childhood and she needs a whole lot of love."

The tears wouldn't stop. Colette's heart told her to swap the crib for a bed and keep little Callie safe forever. "Are you trying to offer her to me?"

"I can't make any promises that this will be a permanent placement, but it looks like a match made in Heaven to me. She'd like to visit her sister and brothers as often as possible. They live in town, so it wouldn't be too much trouble to set up. Colette, if you had any idea how many kids there are."

Roxanne shook her head. "You see, this is a problem. We need families. These kids, they need families. And they don't have to be perfect ones either. You can pick her up today. She's yours. Just say the word and Callie will have it all; a warm bed for years to come, three plus meals a day, several clean shirts to choose from each morning." Roxanne looked at Colette with pleading eyes. "And if she's really lucky, perhaps a girls' outing at Sea World for her thirteenth birthday."

As tears rolled down her face, Colette studied the picture. She longed to save her, to prove to Callie that she's loved. And a trip to Sea World would be pocket change in the grand scheme of things. She could imagine Callie's sad eyes full of life upon stepping into a sunny marine-filled theme park for the first time in her life, her dream come true. The two of them could feed the dolphins and have their pictures taken side-by-side barreling down the tracks of a rollercoaster. Colette would frame the memory and display it next to Callie's bed on her very own nightstand, so she would always remember that someone cherishes her.

"Colette. Today is your day. It's Callie's day."

"And if I take Callie, would my home still be an option for placing a baby?"

Roxanne breathed out slowly, her face full of empathy. "We'll try, but I can't make any promises."

CHAPTER 22

"She's gone."

Colette narrowed her eyes. "Who's gone?"

"Bryce's sister." Jazmine was in the hallway hiding behind the door to baby Kisha's room as if she were nude from the neck down. "Mason was discharged this morning. Strong little guy. Didn't hardly need oxygen at all." Jazmine's smile faded. "You're mad at me."

"You could say I'm jealous that you were the one who got to take care of Bryce's nephew for the past week, but I'm not *mad*."

"You look like you've been up all night fuming. I know you, Colette."

"Not very well, apparently."

"Fine. Have it your way. Have you bumped into Bryce yet?"

Colette grinned. "I'm still on the lookout." It had been twelve days since he sent the letter, yet she was fully confident he would fulfill his promise. "Did Jenn drop any hints?"

"Not one. And frankly, I'm disappointed Bryce didn't see his premature nephew the whole week." Jazmine started to walk away and then peeked her head back in. "Summer thinks she might be pregnant, so my moving plans are on hold. That should boost your sour mood a degree or two."

"Nice. I find out from *you* that my best friend is pregnant."

"I said might. She *might* be pregnant. She probably just ate too much Taco Bell and she's feeling bloated. She eats there practically every day."

Colette's jaw tightened. "Thank you, Jaz, for filling me in on Summer's eating habits, but I'm well aware of her obsession with Taco Bell."

Growling like an angry cat, Jazmine gently shut the door behind her.

Walking to Kisha's bedside, Colette steadied herself from the spinning room. "Hi, Kisha girl," she whispered. "Are you feeling okay today? Probably not so good, huh? Me either."

She took in the sound of the ventilator, something she unintentionally tuned out most of the time. It was amazing how it took such a massive machine to pump just the right amount of oxygen into the tiniest lungs. "I'm sorry we had to put that tube back down your throat. Hopefully in a couple of days you'll be off the vent for good." Kisha's fingers were curled around the tubing as if she were holding her brother's pinkie.

"Just between us, Kisha, I did something terrible last night. There's this girl, Callie." Colette hung her head in shame. "I've never met her, but I abandoned her to the system. I orphaned her." Her throat tightened when the words came out. "I can only imagine who the family is that I sent her to. I have this feeling in my gut, this strong feeling, that they're not good people."

Colette's bottom lip quivered as she inhaled. "You'd think I'd have more compassion, considering I lost my mom at about that same age. I orphaned the little girl so I could hoard the spare bedroom for a baby I may never have. And do you want to know the worst part?" Colette looked over her shoulder and then back at the sleeping baby. She looked so peaceful. "I don't even regret it."

*

A husky FedEx delivery man handed Colette a package before bolting down the staircase. Chuckling, Colette stepped back into her apartment.

"Do you know what's in that box?"

"Oh. Stuart. You're speaking to me again." A gust of wind carried drops of water to her bare arms. She hugged the box as if it would keep her warm. "It's an acoustic guitar."

Stuart eyed her suspiciously. "I didn't know you played the guitar."

"I don't, actually, but I—"

"Whatever you do, don't let that instrument out of your sight. I'm serious." He stood up. "I would like to talk to you about something, but you look cold. May I please come in for a moment?"

"I don't think that's a good idea."

Stuart swayed back and forth. "We have a situation. I understand you're somewhat famous now, though I do not wish to say how." His fists tightened. "I have reason to believe you are in danger. I had an altercation with my new neighbor, so if something happens to you, he will be the prime suspect."

Colette looked at the window catty-corner to hers. The blinds were closed and the lights were off. "What happened?"

"You don't want to know. Please don't make me go into detail. I have a new part time job which requires me to leave from time to time. I'm sorry, but I can no longer protect you."

Chills crawled down her spine. Why hadn't she been more cautious with Stuart? Was he really capable of hurting her? "Do you work days or nights?"

166

"It's my choice."

"What do you do?"

"I would rather not say."

"Are you working tonight?"

"I don't know. But if you don't see me, you should be scared."

"That sounds like a threat."

He swallowed. "I'll try to protect you."

CHAPTER 23

The pounding rain was soft music on a lazy Saturday morning. Engrossed in a romance novel, she fumbled with the hand-knit blanket draped across her legs.

Her peripheral vision caught movement outside the front window. Dressed in black leather was a huge man wearing a motorcycle helmet and a red backpack. In one smooth motion the faceless giant turned his head in her direction, threw his arm up in a wave, and was gone. Heart pounding, she scrambled to the window and closed the curtains, leaving just enough of an opening to see out. He unlocked the apartment next to Stuart's and closed the door.

Unless that was the hired hit man, Stuart wasn't a threat.

She turned off the light, tugged the curtains back open, and returned to her spot on the couch. Like a cat stalking a bird—or in this case, a bird stalking a cat—she waited. With the exception of the ticking clock in the kitchen, it was quieter than a morgue.

After a few minutes of letting her imagination get the best of her, she ended the stakeout. As she surfed through the limited number of stations her TV picked up, she felt like she was living a double life. At work she was smart, attentive, and valuable. It was easy to smile, and the smallest things brightened her day. Parents showered her with praise, and her co-workers seemed to respect her. But at home in her apartment, she was lonely.

When it finally sunk in that professional golf was the best she could do, she turned to her slim collection of movies. The decision was a no brainer. Colette put in *Center of Darkness*, the first movie Bryce had ever starred in. Violence was something she typically avoided, but this one she could now recite by heart, inflections and all. Each time she watched it she fell harder for the deep-voiced murderer.

She skipped to the fifth scene, her favorite. The camera focused on a chipped blue bathtub before panning out to a dingy bathroom. That's when Bryce entered, badly beaten. He pulled off his torn t-shirt stained with the blood of three good guys. Her body responded to his firm chest, the very reason she had watched the scene more times than she could count.

Now she had the pleasure of seeing him from behind. The metal squeaked as he turned on the faucet, the water spewing out like a high-volume waterfall. Cupping his hands together, he splashed his face. His back was chiseled with more perfection than the statue of Discobolus, but it was his rock-hard biceps that did her in. She longed to feel the weight of his body lying on hers, his rough hands following paths of her bare skin. She envisioned warm open-mouthed kisses straying from her lips to places that had never been kissed before.

Her heart pounded with excitement as Bryce stormed into the living room of the rundown apartment and sliced open a chair. Hidden in the stuffing was a computer chip. He put on a clean shirt and concealed his gun. Before leaving the apartment he made a phone call. "Six minutes," he said in a grating voice.

Grinning, Colette hugged herself beneath the blanket. The inconsistent rhythm of his breathing, the language spoken with his eyes, the hesitations. It was all so convincing and it amused her. Had she not seen it for herself, she never could have dreamed up the level of intensity she was witnessing from Bryce. In real life he was just so... nice.

Colette skipped ahead three scenes. Bryce's character didn't scare her, but everyone else did, so she muted the volume. Knowing what was coming next, she cringed as a sixteen-year-old killer-for-hire got closer and closer to his victim. The wife of a wealthy drug dealer was moving a load of laundry from the washer to the dryer, and her baby was in the other room, asleep in a swing. He took a knife from the kitchen and slowly made his way to the back of the house.

Colette's doorbell rang. Her hand shot to her chest. Nobody used the doorbell. They knocked.

Arming herself with a cell phone, she crawled on all fours. Her eyes burned at the thought of being shot through the peephole, so she sacrificed her left eye as if the right was more valuable. Her jaw dropped before her lips formed into a smile.

The biker was Bryce!

This was it. This was the moment Bryce had been planning. It was really happening. Hands shaking, she made an appearance.

Still dressed in leather, Bryce looked agitated as if he were about to deliver bad news. "Hello. I... uh..." He shifted his weight from one foot to the other.

Every detail captivated her. When he didn't return the smile, her heart sank. He was struggling.

He tried again, his eyes shifting in every direction. "Hi. I was..." When he looked into her apartment, the wrinkles in his forehead became defined. Then his lips curled at the edges. "That's my movie."

"Is it?" Oh how she had missed that smile. Colette took a step back. "Would you like to come in?"

"Eggs," he grinned. "My sister, Jenn…" He cleared his throat. "Jenn had her baby and it's my turn to bring her food. The only thing I know how to cook is meatloaf and, you guessed it, that's what she wants."

A drop of perspiration fell between her breasts before being absorbed by her bra. "So you're here because…?" Was she really that lucky? Was the love of her life the new tenant living a skip away from her front door?

"I'm out of eggs. I'm pressed for time and was hoping I could bum a couple off you."

"You've come to the right place." As she crossed the floor, she defined her hips with every step.

"I just need two. Thank you so much. You're a life-saver."

"It's what I do," she said, closing the refrigerator.

Without warning, he stepped into her apartment, cracking the door. "I'm letting all this cold air in. Sorry about that."

"It feels good," she said, before realizing what she was admitting. "Here you go." Electricity shot to her stomach as she felt the warmth of his hand. "Nice outfit, by the way."

"Thanks."

There was an awkward pause, but clearly he had something more to say. Shifting his weight from side to side, he replanted his feet and exhaled. His eyes became less friendly, as if he were being forced to apologize for something he didn't do.

He glanced over her shoulder, stealing another glimpse of her apartment. Colette did the same and found it to be tidy as always. But she swallowed hard after noticing Bryce's dead bouquet of flowers still displayed on the coffee table. "I'll walk you out."

Loitering around the welcome mat, she looked him up and

down. "So that apartment I saw you go into." Already he was nodding, so she continued. "Did a friend of yours move in? Because last I heard, the people that lived there moved to Hawaii."

He pressed his lips together as though her question had stumped him. "That's a safe assumption, but give me your best *honest* guess what you think is going on."

She laughed nervously. "Call me crazy, because I know you will, but it looks like you moved in."

He cleared his throat twice as if he were about to address the nation. When he opened his mouth to speak, he paused, searching for the right words. "Temporarily, yes."

Her heart leapt. "You're messing with me."

"Didn't you get my letter? You might want to read it again. It explains everything." He held up both eggs. "I wish I could stick around and chat, but I better get started on this meatloaf. It's been a while since I've used an oven. If you smell smoke, ignore it. If you see flames, call 911."

"And if I hear an explosion?"

"Call my plastic surgeon."

She was still laughing when he disappeared inside his apartment. She didn't waste any time revisiting the letter.

CHAPTER 24

Alone in her apartment, Colette shook her head and sighed. "Bryce, I've read this letter a thousand times and I don't see anything about an apartment. Unless 'loophole' is code for 'meatloaf,' there's nothing here." She folded the letter along the crease and reopened it. "But you sure know how to make a girl melt."

His handwriting was smaller than hers, but not bad for a guy, and the pen strokes were neat, each mark written with care. "You knew this letter wouldn't tell me why you leased that apartment. A clue would have been nice." She reread the last half knowing she wouldn't discover anything new:

I respect your decision in not wanting to be with me, however I found a loophole. It's a stretch, but nonetheless, it's there.

In the meantime, I will orchestrate my next move and you will go about saving lives, wondering when our paths will next cross.

"That's it. I'm coming over and making you tell me what you're up to."

The first knock was faint. The second, a little louder. After the fifth knock she checked the wood for dents that her knuckles might have left behind. Cleary he wasn't baking meatloaf for his sister. He was gone. She wondered if he would take it so far as to sleep at the apartment. The blinds were shut so there was no telling if he moved in furniture. She sighed, knowing it could be days before she saw him again.

Back in her apartment, she paced the floor excitedly. *Bryce was her neighbor*! Tapping at the back of her phone, she contemplated which friend to call first. Unfortunately, she was mad at both of them. She ended up choosing Summer since she was dying to know if she was actually pregnant.

"Hey, Coco! I was just about to call you. Guess what?"

Suppressing a combative "sure you were," Colette tried to be happy for her. "You're pregnant." The thought of a miniature Summer skipping around, licking an orange sherbet ice-cream cone with a kitten under her arm made Colette yearn for the rumor to be true. There was no doubt Summer's little girl or boy would be good-natured and absolutely adorable.

"I hate that Jazmine blabbed it. You were right about her not being able to keep a secret. Not that I was keeping secrets from you. Brad wanted to tell our parents first and we didn't want Jazmine moving in with us if we were going to be a real family and everything. You know? So I had to warn her. You understand. Anyway, I finally took a pregnancy test a few days ago. I was scared I was pregnant and I was scared I wasn't. Isn't that weird?"

"What did it say?"

"We're pregnant!"

"You are! I'm so happy for you! You're going to be the best mom. Your baby is lucky already. Do you have names?"

"Not yet."

"Do you want a boy or girl?"

"Brad wants a boy. I want a boy because he wants a boy. I would do the whole football theme and everything."

"I'm throwing you a shower. Just give me a guest list and the date. We should wait until we find out what you're having."

"For sure. Do you think Brad will marry me? I'm trying to have happy thoughts, but what if he runs out on us? What if my baby doesn't have a dad?"

"He's not going to leave you," she said, though she hardly knew the guy.

"I hope you're right. I don't know what I would do. I was telling Jazmine how you were raised without a dad and what happened with your mom, and look how amazing you turned out. I never would have known."

Colette could tell Summer was stumbling over her words and she knew why. "You told Jazmine about my mom?"

"*Barely*. I didn't realize she didn't know. I thought you guys were super close. It wasn't even a question in my mind whether or not she knew."

"Do you think I want that stigma attached to me wherever I go? That was my mother's stupid choice, not mine. Everyone treated me like I did it. How much did you tell her?"

"Coco, I'm sorry. I shouldn't have said anything."

"It's okay. I'm not mad." Colette's eyes welled with tears and her voice was shaking. "I'm going to hang up, but I swear to you I'm not mad. Congratulations on the baby. I'll talk to you soon, okay?"

"Coco..." Summer paused for a few seconds and Colette waited. "I'm sorry, honey," Summer said finally. "I'll call you soon. Good-bye."

For the next hour Colette cried off and on, reliving that horrible night eighteen years ago. Details were seared into her mind, unusual ones, like the scuffed up shoes of the female police officer, the burnt-out streetlight down the road, and of course the hysteria every bystander would never forget. The news stations were loving it, and within twenty-four hours, the entire middle school knew—according to Summer's frantic phone call.

It wasn't until Colette returned to school that she truly hated her mother. She was used to being stared at, as was every student who strolled the halls with the beautiful Summer LeCroy. But it was the subtle pointing of fingers and the not-so-subtle whispering that was eating her alive. Not wanting to lose the only people left in her life, she stuck it out. When her peers started treating her normally again, she stopped hating her mom, and for years, would beg God to bring her back.

Colette showered, reapplied her makeup, and called in a to-go order of drunken clams and linguini from The Vintage. After dinner, she made her rounds closing blinds and curtains. From the kitchen window, she could see Bryce's light on. She smiled. Two shots of mouthwash and a teeth-brushing later, she slipped out the front door, pining for answers.

CHAPTER 25

She knocked on Bryce's door softly. Feeling like a mummy, she wondered what to do with her hands. She crossed her arms before letting them hang loosely in front, then in back. She even tried a hand on the hip. Nothing felt natural. When she glanced at Stuart, he immediately stood up.

"Colette? Can I use your bathroom for literally two seconds? Mine is broken."

She was surprised she didn't get a lecture about the "dangerous" new neighbor. "I'm sorry, Stuart, but this isn't the best timing." Eyeing the peephole, she hoped Bryce wasn't on the other side watching her fidget. "Can you ask somebody else?"

"I will literally be two seconds."

"I'm sorry to be so blunt, but the answer is no." She had spoken softly, but there was no guarantee Bryce was out of earshot.

"Yes, but is it okay if I just go quickly? I see that you left your door unlocked."

This was getting ridiculous. "Please don't ask me again."

"But I—"

"Fine. Whatever. Go. Just make it quick." If it was a true emergency, her bathroom was the last place she wanted him. And just by looking at him, she could guess he wasn't very skilled at aiming. "Don't touch anything."

The way he dashed into her apartment made her uneasy.

And to top it off, his filthy shoes were undoubtedly smearing disease all over the floor. An image of Stuart fiddling with a tampon flashed in her mind. Momentarily closing her eyes, she wished she could have inventoried the cabinets before letting him in.

Suspicion continued to taunt her until finally she tiptoed across the concrete and snuck into her apartment. Start was stopped in his tracks five feet from the door, staring at her. She could hear the toilet hissing, evidence he was finished. Colette narrowed her eyes. "What?"

"Thank you. I feel much better." He hopped from foot to foot outside, back to his chair. Disgusted, she swung the door shut. Then she went to the bathroom to assess the damage. As far as she could tell, nothing was amiss. As she scrubbed the linoleum, it occurred to her that she no longer liked her quirky neighbor, not even as a distant acquaintance. She couldn't quite put her finger on it, but ever since Stuart's stupid dinner date, something had changed.

Sucking her patience dry, she heard a light tapping on the door. She threw the soiled rag into the bathtub before scrubbing her hands raw. As she marched to the door, she acknowledged two choices: cordial or belligerent. Given that Bryce was in the vicinity, it was a no brainer. Softening her expression, she opened the door.

Bryce lifted his eyebrows. "You rang?"

"No."

"You stopped by?"

"Yes."

He was standing close enough to catch her if she fainted. She recognized the floppy hat from the airplane, a sign he was still in disguise. His tennis shoes were stained, but his jeans were sexy enough to stop her heart.

Bryce eyed her intently. "I'd like to introduce myself, but doing so out here for all to see would complicate things. Do you mind if I come in?"

She still had no idea what he was doing there, but it wasn't important. The only thing that mattered was finding a way to make him stay. "Do you have time to sit down?"

"I was hoping you'd ask."

The intimacy in his eyes took her breath away. Once inside, Bryce slipped off his shoes without being asked, just one more reason she adored him. As she led him to the couch, she couldn't help but notice it was after dark. Who would have thought that the privacy of her apartment could make her so hot?

"That's a good disguise, Bryce. The hat, I mean." When she sunk into the couch, her nerves relaxed. To her surprise, Bryce took the loveseat instead. She could only hope they were on the same page.

After removing his hat and jacket, he intertwined his fingers loosely. "I don't think it's a good idea for people to know I'm here. Would you mind keeping this under wraps for a while?"

"Of course." She wondered if he was upset about the magazine article. Remembering her manners, she stood up. "What would you like to drink? I don't have a ton of options."

"I'll take some ice-water."

Making her way to the kitchen, she tried to evaluate his mood. Something was on his mind. "I have milk and orange juice, but that's it, I'm sorry to say. What do you usually drink so I'll know for next time?" The bold assumption there would be a next time was no accident.

"Water's good. I'm easy to please."

Colette laughed as if he had told a joke. "One ice-water coming right up. I think I'll have one too." In a mad rush, she arranged some pre-sliced veggies and a dollop of ranch onto a plate she was proud of. After a little maneuvering, she was able to get everything to the coffee table in one smooth trip. As she handed Bryce his glass, she was well aware of the eyeful he was getting. "I have a question for you, Mr. Rocco, and you can't run out on me after I ask it."

He laughed out loud. "I made it all the way to your living room. Trust me. There's not going to be any running."

"Good. Here's my question." Crossing her legs, she put on a cute smile. "I'm dying to know why you're in that apartment. And please don't mention the letter. I've read it so many times my eyes are bloodshot."

"Colette, let me ask you something."

She widened her eyes playfully. "Are we changing the subject?"

"I'm not. Don't worry. What did the letter say?"

"That you found a loophole."

"A loophole for what? Did you ask yourself that?"

The way he was grinning made it hard to concentrate. "Not directly, but let me see. The loophole had to do with why I couldn't date you."

"Do me a favor and refresh your memory. What was your reason?"

What *was* her reason? If his eyes were any indication of his soul, he had the kind of joy she lost as a child. He was confident in who he was, but shy when it came to love. He was funny, yet mature, and had amazing talent in front of the camera. "I couldn't trust you. And again, you can't blame me. You're an actor. A good one."

He nodded. "Now ask yourself who you *can* trust."

"My friends?" But even that was a joke.

"You listed off the types of men you can trust."

"Co-workers?"

"You're getting warmer. Keep going."

"You better let me win this little game of yours." Suddenly it clicked. With an open-mouthed smile, Colette reached over and shoved him flirtatiously. "The boy next door! Is that it? You're trying to be the boy next door."

"I warned you it's a stretch."

"I don't think stalkers qualify as the boy next door. I think stalkers are just called stalkers."

"Maybe so, but it seems to be working."

She could feel her face glowing. "I want to see this apartment you supposedly moved into."

He scooped up his coat and hat. "Let's do it."

As she trailed behind him, she kept asking herself how she had gotten so lucky. "By the way. How did your sister like the meatloaf?"

"I don't know. She didn't invite me to stay."

"So you really baked it and brought it to her and everything."

"Sure did."

When they stepped outside, Stuart's jaw dropped. He shut his laptop, shoved it into the chair's crevice, and leaned forward.

"Hey. How's it going? I'm Bryce." Extending his right hand, Bryce flashed his million dollar smile. When Stuart wouldn't budge, Bryce winked at Colette. "It's a good thing you asked to see my apartment, because it looks like I'll be moving out tonight. Promise me you'll be a good neighbor and keep in touch."

"Seeing as how we've cooked eggs from the same carton, it would be a crime not to keep this relationship going."

"My thoughts exactly." Bryce unlocked the door and paused before opening it. Leaning in close, he whispered in her ear. "People are funny. Thank you for not treating me like a celebrity."

When the lights came on, she laughed. "This apartment is vacant."

"Packing will be a cinch."

Deliberately brushing shoulders with him, she went into the kitchen for a better look. "Look who *didn't* make dinner for his sister. This kitchen is spotless."

"I never said where I did the cooking."

"Yes you did."

"Did I?"

"I don't know. Maybe you did." Fighting the urge to wrap her arms around him, she looked the other direction. She loved that he was feeling like a friend again. "Where do you really live?"

"I just bought a house in McKenzie Bridge a few months ago. It's near Belknap Hot Springs."

"Can I see it?"

"My house?"

"I just want to drive by."

"It's an hour away. How do you feel about motorcycles?"

When their eyes locked, she felt it in her stomach. "I haven't given it much thought." Up until that moment, her dating life had been wrapped in caution tape—*danger, keep away, may cause broken heart.* If she was ever going to get what she wanted out of life, she needed to break through the barrier once and for all. "Why not. Everyone has to die at some point."

"That's the spirit." He put his arm around her, playing with her curls. "I'll drive like a ninety-year-old man with arthritis."

"Is that supposed to make me feel safer?"

"I'll keep you safe, babe. In all seriousness, I will."

She grinned. "My neighbor, Stuart, says otherwise. He told me you're dangerous. What happened?"

He looked at her with a puzzled expression before grinning. "He called me dangerous?"

"He said you guys got into it."

"Not entirely accurate, but okay. I was wearing my helmet to hide my identity, and he tried to introduce himself several times. I ignored him for obvious reasons, and that was that."

"That's it?"

"Ask him."

"I'll take your word for it," she grinned.

When they got to the parking lot Colette was fired up. She tapped on the shell of the helmet he was holding. "I'm only seeing one here, but there's two of us."

"I'll buy another one tomorrow. You can pick it out."

"You can't ride without a helmet. It's against the law."

"You don't really think I'm going to get us killed."

"And what happens when we get pulled over? Are you going to wish me luck before I drive this beast home?"

"Would you rather we take your car?"

"I think that's a better idea."

Next, Bryce said something so intimate, she felt like she was standing face to face with her husband. "The keys, please. I'll drive."

CHAPTER 26

The McKenzie Highway led them around thick forested mountains, the trees smiling down on them as if they knew what Bryce and Colette were up to. From the passenger seat, she took it all in—thousands of stars twinkling in the same spot since the beginning of time, the McKenzie River flowing unobstructed all the way to the Pacific Ocean, and mountains so magnificent it made you wonder how they came to be.

Bryce placed his hand on her thigh and smiled. "We're almost there. Are you excited?"

Feeling more sure of herself, she took her time answering. "Right now I'm just living in the moment, trying to take it all in." Hugging herself tightly, she grinned. "I feel like you're stealing me away."

"Next time we'll come up here during the day and stop at Belknap Springs. It's a few miles further up the road. Have you been?"

"A co-worker got married there, but I didn't make it to the wedding."

"Good. That means *I* get to show it you. You'll like it."

She could tell he was in his element. "Did you grow up around here?"

"Do you know where Camp Creek is?"

"Kind of."

"It's not far from town. I lived out there my entire childhood. It was great. We used to have a bunch of horses and would ride around the property all the time. My parents ended up selling the horses a few years ago. All four of us kids were so mad at them. I say kids, but we were grown adults by then."

"It's too bad they didn't keep them around for the grandkids."

Trying to contain his smile, he looked at her momentarily before returning his attention to the winding road. "Who knows. Maybe someday you'll charm them into changing their minds. I have the feeling you can be persuasive when you want to be."

"There's not a lot of negotiating going on when you live alone."

"That's true. Are you pretty independent?"

"I don't know. I don't think so."

"If I'm by myself for too long, I start going crazy."

"Same here." It was a good thing it was dark, because she couldn't take her eyes off him. She loved the way his Adam's apple shifted in response to his deep voice.

"I know you enjoy nature," he said, "but do you consider yourself outdoorsy? Sorry if I'm asking too many questions. There's just so much about you I don't know yet."

"That's okay. Ask away. I like that you're curious." Tucking her curls behind her ears, she uncrossed her legs to get more comfortable. "I don't spend a lot of time outside, but I definitely appreciate a good road trip every now and then. Going for drives is my favorite thing to do on the weekends. Oregon is so beautiful."

"But you're from Colorado, right?"

"That's where I was born and raised. I moved here to go to college." A huge part of her wanted to tell him the full story, but she wasn't ready to go there. Her focus was on growing their relationship, not introducing new drama. June was still a couple of months away, and if things between them progressed, the opportunity would present itself all on its own. "You know how some people like to make plans for the future several years out? Well, I'm one of those people. I'm a planner. This is the year I sort of planned on reevaluating things, like where I'd be living."

"Do you miss Colorado?"

"I think everyone holds a special place in their heart for their hometown, but I'm not set on Colorado, per se. I just figured I'd be making some sort of a change this year." She could see the wrinkles forming on his forehead as if he was trying to figure it out. "How many acres do your parents own?"

"Fourteen." He tapped the wheel. "If you're not busy tomorrow afternoon, you should come to our family barbeque. You'll get to meet everyone, and more importantly, everyone will get to meet the girl who's been trying to get rid of me for the past month. They love you for that, by the way."

Her heart swelled at the thought of being accepted by his family. "How many people is *everyone*?"

"One shy of a party. Can we count you in?"

"It sounds fun, but I'm not sure if that's the best idea. Is Gage going to be there?"

"I haven't heard."

"He hates me."

"No he doesn't. He hates everyone. He hates me and I'm his own brother."

She laughed sarcastically. "Not true. I saw you two in Colorado. It's obvious that he thinks highly of you."

"He didn't have a choice. I was his boss that weekend,

remember? His wife threatens to sell his boat if he ever gets fired, so he has to stay on my good side. And when that woman makes a threat, she always follows through."

Turning off the highway, Bryce rolled down his window, made a second turn, and continued on slowly. Finally they arrived at a tall iron gate. After entering his security code, the gate parted from the center. "This is it."

As he followed the paved driveway to the top of the hill, she could see pride written all over his face. When they came around the corner she saw a gorgeous two story home showcasing a combination of brick and stone. It wasn't the mansion she was picturing, but it was definitely big. The property was lit up like a golf course, revealing an elegantly landscaped front yard with paved walkways going into the surrounding forest. Angled to the left was a detached four car garage. And the best part? It had mountain views!

"Do you want to come in?"

"Can I please? This is stunning. I can't wait to see the rest. I love how the lights were done on the house. And the windows. This is really beautiful."

"I'm glad you like it." He took the keys from the ignition, laid his head against the back of the seat, and gazed in her direction, just watching. His eyes were relaxed and even though he wasn't smiling, he looked euphoric. Placing the keys in her hand, he lingered. "Thanks for letting me drive."

"I enjoyed being chauffeured," she said with an accent.

His gaze fell to her lips. "I can't believe you're really here with me."

She exhaled loud enough for him to hear and then giggled. "If you only knew what you're doing to me right now."

"Believe me, I know. I see it in your eyes." He crawled halfway into the back seat and returned with their coats. "You're going to need this." When he opened the door, she did the same, and together they walked to the front porch. "I have to be honest," he said, reaching into his pocket. "Compared to you, I'm kind of a slob."

"I'll keep in mind that this is a bachelor pad."

Bryce opened the door, all fifteen feet of it, and deactivated the alarm. The architecture was amazing. The ceiling went two stories up to where a modern chandelier was sparkling as if the sun was shining on it. There were two staircases, one on each side, following the curvature of the room. A hallway balcony overlooking the downstairs joined the two staircases together. The back wall was nothing but floor to ceiling windows which presumably overlooked the McKenzie River.

"Are these marble floors? They're shiny."

"I'm more of a carpet guy, but the house had marble when I bought it. It's growing on me though." Taking her hand, he led her into the living room. "I know you were probably picturing a ten-thousand square foot estate, but this is it. It's just me." He opened the French doors leading to the patio. "I want to show you something. Hey, what did you do with your shoes?"

Her face burned with embarrassment. "I left them by the door."

He swung his arm up and pointed to the entryway. "Go get your shoes, young lady. And keep that coat on. We're going outside."

"I didn't want to track mud everywhere."

"This is a bachelor pad, remember? Men love mud."

"Well you wouldn't know it." She slipped her shoes on and

quickly made her way to the back of the house. "I was picturing dirty socks flung on lampshades and greasy pizza boxes everywhere."

"Don't speak too soon. You haven't seen the kitchen."

Once outside, Bryce opened a wooden chest. From there, he pulled out a flashlight, a box of matches, and a few sheets of newspaper. The backyard lights were off with the exception of a blue halo illuminating a small exotic pool. Three waterfalls cascaded from massive flat rocks mimicking the venue of a Venice Beach resort. Four separate lawns tiered down to the dock. A dust of snow covered the tip of a distant mountain.

Bryce clicked on the flashlight. "Last weekend was pretty warm, so the whole clan was up here. The older kids waited on the dock with their water guns and harassed everyone who floated by. Everyone except the fishermen. The kids aren't allowed to mess with them. Anyway, they shot up this raft and when the raft returned fire, the kids ran for cover. Gage was ticked off that they weren't playing fair, so he made his kids jump in. That water is ice-cold."

"Your brother forced them to do that in April? That's cruel."

He shrugged his shoulders. "They dished it out. It was fair. Gage tried to make Jenn's oldest boy jump too, but he went running to his mama and she said he didn't have to."

"She seems nice."

"Growing up not so much, but yeah, now she is. That girl has character. You'll see it when you get to know her a little better. You two will get along great. She really likes you. She's always asking about you."

"Is she going to the barbeque tomorrow?"

"I didn't hear one way or the other, but she never misses. She loves family junk. Family get-togethers, I mean."

"But not as much as you, I can see," she laughed.

"Nah, I like to go. Once you move away you realize how much you actually like the people who drive you crazy." He shined the flashlight onto the stamped concrete. "I'll show you around. You're going to fall in love with this place." When they started walking, he overstepped in her direction and their shoulders bumped. "Are you listening to the river?"

She nodded, enjoying so much the sound of his voice. "This is beautiful, Bryce. I love it out here."

As they passed by the pool, Bryce's fingers brushed hers twice, and then he held her hand. She could feel the roughness of his skin, the warmth. She looked up at him and smiled. The river wasn't the only thing she was falling in love with.

"Are you going to be okay in those shoes? They look complicated."

"Watch and be amazed."

Bryce's laugh was more of a grunt. "That's what I've been doing since I met you."

Their first kiss was coming soon. He was prepping her. She wondered if it would be the kind where their lips barely touched or if it would go on for hours. They came to a fire pit surrounded by five logs positioned like a pentagon. It wasn't long before the two of them were listening to the crackle of a blazing fire, side by side, pulling chunks of bark off the log they were sitting on.

Trust was no longer an issue, but there was still the burning question that never got answered. "Is it too soon to ask about Capri Saxton?" she said in a small voice.

"For you I'll answer anything." He let out a long sigh. "I'm going to give you the shortened version. You won't have trouble filling in the rest." He folded his hands and looked down. "I don't want this to sound like a compliment, but as you've probably noticed, Capri's a cute girl."

It wasn't starting off like she'd hoped, but she couldn't argue. Capri Saxton was adorable, all the way down to her voice. "Yes. Continue."

"I met her shortly after high school. I was in New York trying to wiggle my way into the business when I accidently plowed into the back of Capri's limo. Whoops, right? It was my fault. Her driver called me every name in the book, but Capri seemed almost giddy about it. We got to talking, and when I tried to impress her with my acting aspirations, she told me that her father, Clyde Klein, the movie producer, would put me in his next movie. She was just sure of it. I didn't know it at the time, but she had Klein wrapped around her little finger. They gave me an audition and, just like she promised, I was given a speaking role. I played a—"

"Owner of a country club," she cut in. "I saw it. You were hilarious."

He looked at her with a funny smile. "What did you do, watch all my movies?"

"And the sitcom. I own every episode. Now I see why Summer had such a big crush on you."

He moved closer so their knees were touching. "I was sure everyone had seen that show."

"Now everyone has."

"Anyway, so Capri and I ended up dating, and that was what really launched my career. We barely saw each other the first two years because we were working in different locations.

Eventually, though, we both got some time off, and that's when I got to know the real Capri Saxton. And let me tell you, she is *not* the angel you see on TV. And if I go any further, I'm going to sound like a jerk, so I'll just leave it at that." He shook his head. "And she's not a nice person," he added. "She's spoiled rotten."

"And the breakup? Did you really email her?"

"I never even asked that woman to marry me. She kept pressuring me to buy this ring she had tried on, until one day she paid one of my guys to pick it up. *She* bought the ring, not me. Then she planned this last minute getaway to get me to propose. She wore the new rock out in public and, you guessed it, they got a picture. The next thing you know, we're engaged. But not really, of course. When her publicist confirmed the rumors, I sent the email. I was angry."

"You were justified."

"Well, regardless, I'm not proud of what I did." He pressed his lips together and then clapped once. "So that's the story. What's the verdict?"

"That I'm glad you're mine and not hers."

"Me too." He got up and added a log to the fire. "It's getting cold. Are you still okay?"

"I like it out here. It's peaceful."

"It is, isn't it? It's nice to have someone to share it with." When he returned to his spot, he slipped his arm around her, resting his hand along her waist. Immediately Colette corrected her posture to flatten out her stomach. To her disappointment, he let go. "Tell me about your parents. Do they live around here?"

This was not a conversation she was prepared to have. Keeping her composure, she started off slowly. "I never knew my dad. I'm the consequence of a one-night-stand," she said lightheartedly. "My step-dad was like a father to me. The way I remember it, we were pretty close, but he left me and my mom when I was six. I haven't seen him since. He was really into the party scene, drugs and alcohol, and I guess he wasn't ready to be a dad."

"That's sad."

"I'm not attached to him anymore, but I think that's where some of my trust issues stem from. I was determined not to make the same mistakes my mom did. I don't want to put my kids through that."

"Does your mom still live in Colorado?"

Her heart pounded harder. Keeping secrets from Bryce didn't feel right, but she couldn't bring herself to be completely honest. Besides, it wasn't as if she was obligated to spill out her mother's baggage from eighteen years ago. "Actually my mom lives south of Portland."

"That's two hours away. We might have to make a road trip one of these days. What do you say?"

When he looked up from the fire and into her eyes, she swallowed. Eyes don't lie. Not amateur ones anyway. She did her best to act natural, but feared Bryce wasn't fooled by her performance. "Actually, my mom's getting ready to move. We should give her time to get settled into her new house, you know, before we just drop by."

He didn't say anything for several minutes and neither did she. Using a stick, he jabbed the fire until a block of wood fell apart, sparks floating up like fireflies. "You know, Colette..." He slipped his arm around her, keeping his hand conservatively along her forearm. "I already know everything I need to know about you to know that I like you. Nothing you say can change that. I have a bad habit of asking too many questions."

She leaned into him shyly. "At least you're not grilling me about how I broke up with my ex." When he squeezed her arm, she melted like butter. His cologne smelled good.

"Are your curls natural?" He picked up a few strands and let them fall down her back.

She nodded. "When I was little I couldn't go anywhere without someone commenting on my hair. Literally, it was everywhere I went."

"It's pretty."

She looked at him mischievously. "So those teeth that make me jealous every time you smile. Are *they* real?"

"Oh man. You had to ask that, didn't you?"

"I'm kidding."

He shook his head and smiled sheepishly. "I like to joke, but I'll be honest with you. My teeth weren't rotting off my face or anything, but I was pretty self-conscious about them. Right out of high school, me and my credit card visited one of those cosmetic dentists, and he changed things up. So yes, these teeth belong to me, but no, not honestly and truly."

"You're full of it," she grinned.

"My mom's got old pictures hung all the way down the hall. If you come tomorrow, you can see for yourself."

"Maybe I will." Tightening her lips, she studied his eyes. "If I go to your family reunion—"

"Barbeque," he interrupted. "A lazy Sunday barbeque."

"Okay, whatever. If I go, you can't leave me alone with all those people or put me on the spot or force me to taste something that I specifically avoided."

"Never."

"And you can't make fun of me, like tell everyone how horrible I was when you met me or how I was worried about Capri Saxton. No embarrassing stories. I know you have a whole library of them already."

"Nah."

She gave him a look like she was contemplating. "Fine, I'll go. Only because it's an excuse to see you. And Mason."

"Who's Mason?"

She wasn't one-hundred percent sure she got the name right, but she ran with it anyway. "Hello, he's your new nephew!"

"Mason! Yes. I knew that." He smacked his forehead, laughing. "Don't look at me like that. Just because a guy forgets his sister had a baby..."

"If she ever asks you to babysit, you might want to count the kids first."

"When babysitting involves diapers, I'm out. No way. Mama made it, Mama can change it."

She backhanded him in the chest. "Why is it that men can crawl under houses and skin cute little deer, but they put their foot down when it comes to diapers? It makes no sense to me."

"Because we're men," he said in a deep voice.

When the smoke shifted all at once, Colette leapt up, covering her face. Bryce, on the other hand, waited it out. She circled the campfire tossing in twigs and pinecones. "You're going to pass out inhaling all that smoke and I won't know what to do with you."

When he stood up, his tall stature startled her all over again. "Is that right?"

She tossed him a closed mouth smile, enjoying the playfulness in his eyes. "I sure like you. Thanks for chasing me down."

As he started toward her, she swallowed hard. Never before had she wanted something with such urgency. Stopping in front of her, he rested his forearms on her shoulders and began playing with her curls. "You're so pretty, Colette."

She took a step closer, inhaling the scent of his cologne. "I like hearing you say that. Man, you smell good." When he pulled her closer, she rested her face on his chest.

"Do you want to know a secret?" he whispered. "You're in my head all day long. I wonder what you're doing, how you're doing. And I imagine being right here with you."

"What else do you imagine?"

He laughed. "Wouldn't you like to know." Applying more pressure, he moved his palms lower on her hips. Then he bent down, whispering softly. "I'm going to kiss you, Colette, like we talked about on the mountain."

Closing her eyes, she met him halfway. As soon as she felt the warmth of his lips against hers, she was paralyzed. He pulled back just enough to look her in the eyes. Passion was written all over his face as he studied her. Colette nodded ever so slightly, and that was all it took. When their lips met a second time, his mouth opened wider, allowing her to fully taste what she had been craving so badly.

CHAPTER 27

Colette's shoe hovered over the gas pedal as she inched along the gravel road like a stalker in a windowless van. She was debating whether to suck it up and make an appearance or book it. When she spotted a broken down orange truck on the side of the road, she knew it was just around the corner to the left. After one more turn she spotted it. "Blue siding, yellow shutters," she said under her breath. "This is it. I hate today."

She could see three teens kicking a soccer ball, but Bryce was MIA. One of the boys spotted her, and in unison, the other two heads whipped around. Clenching her teeth, she started to panic. "You can do this," she said like a ventriloquist. "They're just people." When she felt herself perspire, she cranked the a/c full blast.

The whole Rocco clan had parked on the manicured grass like a bunch of hillbillies. Horrified at what her future mother-in-law was going to think, she did the same anyway. A glance in her rearview mirror told her the coast was clear. She applied a fresh coat of lip gloss, slid her purse under the passenger seat, and grabbed the avocado salad she had prepared that morning. Jenn was on the front porch, waving. It was beyond intimidating, but exciting at the same time.

Colette hadn't even made it halfway to the door when Jenn threw one arm around her neck, squeezing tightly. "You made it! I'm so happy!"

Right then and there, Colette knew they would hit it off. "It's great to see you again. How have you been?"

"Exhausted, but loving every minute. Bryce is inside holding Mason. I think he's using the baby to impress you. He's so funny." Bypassing the curious stares, Jenn flung open the front door. "Bry-yce! Your girlfriend's here!" Then she turned to the teenagers, motioning with her arm. "Boys, get over here and meet Colette."

The three of them strolled over like it was a drag, communicating secret comments to each other with their eyes.

Jenn smiled with pride. "This is Matt, my oldest, and these two handsome brothers are his friends from just down the road. They can smell food from a mile away. Isn't that right, boys? Okay. You're done. Carry on."

Grinning, Colette followed Jenn inside. The living room was small and tidy with a wood-burning stove in the corner. Straight back was a good-sized dining room with vaulted ceilings and a lot of windows. Clearly there had been some remodeling done, but this was still Bryce's childhood home. There were so many memories packed under one single roof, and she had missed them all.

Colette's heart leapt when Bryce emerged from the hallway with a newborn cradled in one arm. When their eyes met, his cheeks went from tan to red, and she wondered if he was remembering the night before as she was. "Look at you," Colette grinned. His little game was working. She loved seeing him with a baby.

"Look at *you*," he said, gesturing with his free hand. "I like the way you look in that skirt."

"Save it," Jenn said, pretending to sensor her eyes. "Big sister in the room."

Bryce looked down at Mason, bouncing him a little. "I take it you've met my nephew?" He took careful steps toward Colette as if there were landmines hidden in the carpet.

She lifted the blanket and saw the cutest little face, sound asleep. "Actually, we haven't met, have we Mason? I'm Colette, Uncle Bryce's—" She glanced at Bryce and hesitated. She couldn't say it, not right in front of his sister. "Friend," she continued.

Bryce cleared his throat and raised his eyebrows. "Friend?"

"You know what I mean."

Jenn slapped her hands on her hips. "Leave her alone, Bryce. You're embarrassing her. C'mon, Colette." Taking her by the arm, Jenn led her away. "Most of the food's out back. I'll introduce you to everyone." She tugged on the sliding screen door forcefully until it opened just wide enough to allow them through. "Everybody," she announced, "this is Bryce's friend, Colette."

A plump older woman squealed before hugging her delicately. "Sweetheart, you came. Bryce wasn't so sure, poor thing. I told him he had nothing to worry about. Mother's intuition, I suppose. I'm Gladys Rocco, Bryce's mom. It's so nice to meet you." She barely took a breath before swinging her arm back, hitting an elderly man smack in the face. "Oh, honey," she scolded, "watch where you're going." The smile returned to her face as quickly as it had left. "This is Ted Rocco, Bryce's father, and you may call him Teddy. We all do."

Teddy was tall and slender. His face sagged with wrinkles, but his eyes were youthfully bright. "Pleased to meet you, darlin'. You're a pretty little thing, isn't she Gladys? You have a beautiful smile, Miss Colette. Bryce tells me your friends call you Cocoa, just like the chocolate."

"That was my nickname growing up. A few friends still call me that."

"Well then, Cocoa." Teddy wrapped his arms around her in a full-contact hug. "If it's good enough for your friends, then it's good enough for me."

As she returned the gesture, she saw a twinkle in Bryce's eyes. "Thanks for having me over, Teddy. It's nice to meet you."

When he released her, Gage seemed to appear out of thin air. "Hello there, Coco. We meet again."

She saw no need to overdo her smile, assuming most everyone knew how they felt about each other. "Indeed. How are you?"

Like a guardian angel, Jenn pulled her away and introduced her to many more faces. To her surprise, everyone was kind and engaging, and she found herself absorbing every ounce of attention blissfully. When it was time, she loaded her paper plate with a sample of everything except the beets, while the men and boys huddled near the food waiting for the women and girls to dish up. After tossing Bryce a cheerful wave that told him she was doing fine on her own, she joined Bryce's other sister, Ella, at a picnic table.

"Hey, girl. Have a seat." Ella scooted over as if there wasn't enough room already. Stabbing the potato salad like she meant it, she exhaled loudly. "This is awkward. Extremely awkward."

Colette chuckled politely under her breath.

Ella set down her fork and spread a napkin across her lap. "My husband is late and my *ex-husband* is right over there, chatting it up with the family like he didn't disappear off the face of the planet for five months straight when the kids were little. The kids were the ones who invited him, which is fine. It's just awkward. I wish my husband would hurry up and get here."

"Is he working today?"

"He's fixing a busted pipe in the yard. He'll be here soon."

Colette looked across the lawn. "Which one is your...?"

"My ex? He's the one in the khakis. Look at him. Do you see what he's doing? You probably can't tell. I don't know. Maybe I'm overreacting."

"He just looked over here," Colette said, proud to have something useful to contribute to the conversation.

"Did he? See? I told you. He's doing this on purpose."

Bryce's mother circled the bench, taking the seat across from Colette. "What's he doing on purpose?"

Ella pointed with her eyes and Gladys nodded. "Just remember, sweet Ella, you're putting up with him for the sake of the kids. Keep reminding yourself that."

"I'm sick of it."

"You have to let it go," Gladys said firmly. "You must. It's not worth holding onto. He does pretty well with the children now. They're happy."

"I know. I should let it go."

"That's right. You should." Gladys took a sip of Diet Pepsi, shifting her eyes from Ella to Colette. "So, Miss Colette, you let my son catch you after all that chasing, hmm?"

Ella's eyes grew. "He really likes you. We all teased him relentlessly when you turned him down. You can tell how proud he is to show off his prize today."

When all three of them giggled, Bryce looked at them curiously from across the yard. Gladys shooed him away as if he were eavesdropping. "That boy never gave up, did he?"

"I'm glad he didn't," Colette said, feeling very much like one of the girls. "He's a great guy." When both women agreed, that was all the confirmation she needed.

Two little girls in matching outfits squeezed in on either side of Gladys chattering away. "Have you met Chloe and Kara?"

"Not yet. They're adorable."

Gladys' right hand went to her chest as she reached with her left for Kara's elbow. "Sweetheart, did you just swallow your gum?"

Kara looked back at her with round eyes. "Yes."

"You shouldn't do that. It's not good for your body. Next time, just give it to Grammy and I'll throw it in the garbage for you, okay?"

"But it was dead."

"Valid point," Ella smirked. "They're Gage and Ginger's kids. Chloe's five and Kara's three. Lately they've been inseparable. It's so cute."

"I can tell they're sisters."

"They don't look a thing like their brothers."

Ella tucked Chloe's hair behind her ears. "Sweetie, don't use your hair as a napkin."

"I wasn't."

"Well, you were."

Kara grabbed her big sister's hair. "Auntie Ella thinks you are a napkin head." The identical belly laughs coming from the round-faced toddlers was contagious.

"Someone's quite the comedian," Colette grinned. "That's hysterical."

Jenn popped a cucumber in her mouth. "It's non-stop with those two. And I thought boys were rambunctious."

A sense of loss came over Colette as she saw firsthand the joy of a traditional family. As she watched Gladys interact with the children, she couldn't help believing someday that would be her. The seats filled up quickly, and by the time Bryce came around to check on her, she waved him off, suggesting he spend time with the men. Two hours later Bryce stole her away, her heart so full she thought it would burst.

Bryce led her across the open field. "Are you okay?"

She laughed. "You have a big family."

"They can be a little much sometimes. Sorry."

"Don't be sorry. I like that they're friendly. This is so much better than what I was picturing." She reached for his hand despite the audience that might be watching. After all she'd put him through, he deserved to *show off his prize*. When their fingers locked, she felt it in her stomach. "My birthday is in a couple of months," she started, hoping she would have the courage to say what she needed to. "I'd like to spend it with you."

"Of course. When is it?"

"June sixteenth." She took a deep breath. "I was thinking the weekend after, if my mom is settled, you could meet her." There. She said it. There was no way to back out now, even if she wanted to.

He squeezed her hand. "I would love to meet your mom."

She forced a smile knowing he could see right through it. "Great. This will be good." A disappointment was more like it, but he could make that observation on his own.

Bryce led her behind a tree and released her hand. "Can we sit?"

Creepy crawly things, namely spiders, was her first thought. "I'm not going to ask how many insects are waiting for me to get comfortable."

Not giving her a choice, he pulled her down. "Let your man do the fighting. I'll protect you."

"I know you will."

For the next two hours they talked in a smooth cadence, completely immersed in what the other was saying. They relived the events of the afternoon, laughed about childhood stories, and guessed what their friends would say if asked to list their personality quirks. Eventually their laughter faded, and they began opening up on a deeper level.

Bryce talked about the struggles of the movie business, the itching to take the money and run, but the fear in taking for granted the opportunity of a lifetime. Colette told him how she was raised by her mother's second cousin in Colorado from ages eleven to seventeen, and how she hadn't realized it at the time, but their constant bickering mirrored many mother-teen relationships. Colette was prepared to tell him the whole story if he asked, but to her relief, he was a gentleman.

Shades of orange and pink brushed the sky, becoming more and more vibrant with each passing minute. They were sitting across from each other, barefoot, eyes fixed on the magnificent sunset overtaking the sky.

The lull in conversation was filled with fantasies as Bryce stepped on her bare toes gently. Enjoying the electricity of his touch, she began playing the game too, caressing his skin. When the last ray of sunlight slipped away, Bryce pulled her in close. Her eyelids collapsed and their lips met.

CHAPTER 28

Over the weekend baby Kisha weighed in at a whopping two pounds, three ounces, which earned her a coveted certificate into the *kilo-club*, and more importantly, a ticket into Pod Four. Balloons, congratulatory cards, and a zoo of stuffed animals surrounded her incubator, and a painting that read *perseverance* was displayed next to the monitor.

At the start of her shift, two additional babies were assigned to Colette, and all three were doing beautifully. It was nice to work in a room with windows again, just as flowers were beginning to blossom on leafy trees in the park below.

Latoya was reclined with Kisha on her chest, humming a tune and flipping through a magazine. Jacoby, her seven-year-old, had taken a short break from whining to color a picture for his daddy. Latoya set the magazine on her lap and rested her manicured hands on Kisha. "Colette, forgive me for asking, but I heard an interesting rumor this morning. Is my baby's nurse actually *dating* who I think she's dating?"

Colette glanced at Jazmine who was grinning from ear to ear. Reluctantly, Colette studied Latoya, hoping the answer to her question wasn't printed on one of those glossy pages in her lap. "Where did you hear that?"

Latoya shrugged her shoulders. "It's just something I overheard."

Jazmine wrinkled her nose. "She met his family last night, but you didn't hear it from me."

Latoya's eyes widened. "So it's true?"

Colette couldn't help but smile. What difference did it make if the world knew she had snagged the best guy on the planet? As long as the pictures were halfway flattering, the media could buzz about their romance all they wanted. Pulling up a chair, Colette leaned forward, her elbows resting on her lap. "He's the sweetest guy I've ever met. And you would love his family. They're so vibrant, kind of like your family."

When Latoya squealed, wrinkles creased Kisha's forehead as her eyelids parted. "Did you hear that, Kisha girl? Bryce Rocco is in love with your nurse."

*

It was Wednesday before Bryce made any attempt to contact her again, and by then, Colette had convinced herself she would never see him again. When Bryce's name appeared on the caller ID, she leapt onto the couch, sucking in a full breath of air to calm herself down. "Hello," she sang cheerfully.

"Hey, babe. I was thinking about you, wondering what you were up to, and then I thought, 'why not ask her'"?

To be on somebody's mind for no particular reason felt good. "I'm watching plants grow," she laughed. "I planted these microscopic blueberry seeds and two dozen actually sprouted. Have you ever grown anything? It's amazing when you see it for yourself."

"Third grade science, but mine didn't go so well. To this day, I still don't know where I went wrong."

"Aw."

"Your name popped up in the newspaper yesterday. They quoted you."

Colette sat up. "Someone from the paper called me, but the lady was so sweet I couldn't blow her off. Are you mad at me? What does it say?"

He laughed. "Maybe I'm starving for attention, but it was nice seeing our names together."

It was too soon to talk marriage, but she was dying to point out that if they ever took the plunge, her new name would be Coco Rocco. It had a nice ring to it. "I'll have to pick up a copy on the way to work."

"It's already taken care of. Your copy is right here in my hands. I want to take you to lunch today. Do you like sushi?"

Her nose wrinkled at the sound of it. "About as much as a baggy Speedo."

"That much, huh? Then let's go get you some. Can I pick you up in an hour? It's a nice day for a motorcycle ride."

Giggling, her hand went to her heart. "Don't forget both helmets."

"Will do, babe. Get ready to hold on tight."

*

The next two months flew by like a fairy tale. Bryce was there to pick her up every Saturday, and the fun hardly let up until Monday morning brunch. Date nights were over-the-top romantic, and more Sundays than not were spent goofing off with his family in Camp Creek.

Three movie nights and a pedicure later, Colette now considered Bryce's sisters, and even gage's wife, some of her closest friends. Gage was still a jerk, but she was learning how to handle him and it seemed to be working. Gladys, the ditz that she was, quickly won Colette's heart. Every time that woman opened her mouth, Colette felt nothing but genuine love for her.

It was June sixteenth, and the sunshine was already celebrating on the other side of her curtains. After silencing the alarm, she fell back on her pillow remembering that she would get to enjoy an entire Friday away from the hospital.

Looking around her bedroom, she sighed. "I'm thirty. Blah." There were four walls surrounding her, each highlighting prime years she could never get back. Her college diploma hung in place of an all-night graduation party she never attended, a framed print of the Eifel Tower symbolized places she could afford to visit but never did, on the third wall was a picture of her young mother in windy San Francisco posing with her curly-haired daughter, and then of course there was the clock next to the door that never stopped ticking.

Technically, according to her birth certificate, she was twenty-nine for four more hours which gave her just enough time to change history. Sitting up in bed, she made a decision that she had been secretly contemplating for weeks—there was no way she was going to exit her twenties still a virgin.

It wasn't that she had lacked opportunity over the years, there were plenty, but she respected herself enough to say no. If there was one main value her mom tried to instill in her, it was to not be fooled by men who only wanted one thing. Her junior year of high school, her mom's words started to sink in.

Rather than being flattered by what was expected of her by a good number of guys who bought her dinner, she felt degraded. There was nothing special about being noticed by someone who wanted the same thing from a dozen other girls. It was that realization that strengthened her values and encouraged her to continue waiting. Because someday, she knew, a man would make vows that would last forever, and that's who she would give herself to.

When she opened her front door that morning, Bryce kissed her cheek, handed her a maple donut, and rushed her to the car, completely oblivious to the lacy black pushup bra and matching thong beneath her summer attire. Tapping her manicured feet on the floorboard, she stole another peek at Bryce, his hands wrapped around the steering wheel like it was alive.

Had she had all evening to do it, luring him to bed would be a cinch. But three hours? Clearly he had their day planned to a tee, and she doubted "take Colette's virginity" was on the schedule for 9:00 a.m. Communication was the easy answer, but what fun would that be?

Bryce placed his hand firmly on her knee. "Colette, you're not listening to a word I'm saying, are you?"

"I changed my mind. Turn around." She had no regrets about the past, but it was time to trust somebody with her heart.

He shook his head. "Sorry, birthday girl, but I'm the driver." After letting go of her knee, he turned down the radio a notch. "Think of the lifejacket as a seatbelt. You'll never need it, but it's nice to know it's there."

She slammed her right foot onto the dash. "We'll go tomorrow. I promise. Quick, take this exit."

He put on his blinker and slowed down, but just before the

turn he accelerated. "How many times have you whined that you've never floated the river?" Keeping his eyes on the road, he leaned into her. "Here's my sleeve. Cry on it one last time, because after today, you won't have a reason to. Like it or not, we're floating this river. And you'll like it. I promise."

"Bryce, I—"

"No more excuses, not today. There's not a twenty-percent chance of rain, you're not too tired after the week you've had, a meth-head in a canoe didn't drown three nights ago. We're doing this today, babe." He puckered his lips and kissed the air. "I love you, Coco."

Crossing her legs, she looked out the window. "Fine. Have it your way. But I thought the birthday girl gets to make a wish."

"Her boyfriend blew out the candles and stole her wish. Mwah-ha-ha."

She backhanded him on his chest and checked the time. If they were going to do this right, they needed time to get out to Bryce's house. It certainly wasn't going to happen in her apartment with Stuart peeking in the windows.

Pouting wasn't working and she didn't want to spell it out for him, but what choice did she have? It was several minutes before she worked up the courage to say anything. When she finally did, her words were laced with seduction. "If it was *your* birthday and you could do anything you wanted with *me*, what would you do?"

He laughed in a way she hadn't heard before. Blushing, his eyes met hers. "I would take you home with me and ask you to stay."

"And if I said no?" she grinned.

"I'd keep waiting." He picked up a strand of her hair and let it fall. "Forever, if that's how long it took."

"And if I said yes?"

His eyes said it all. He inhaled deeply and let it out. "Well, then we would..." he cleared his throat as if to fill in the blank, and they both laughed.

She reached up and began massaging his neck, hard and slow. Next she moved to his bicep, one of her favorite places to touch. It wasn't long before his body responded the way she knew it would. When he told her it felt good, she worked her hand lower, manipulating the muscles in his back. There was intensity in his expression, like he was struggling. When she got to his lower back, just above the belt, she snuck under his shirt and worked her way back up, slowly, against his flushed skin.

"You're going to make me veer off the road. I'm not kidding."

"Am I?" Leaning in, she brushed her lips against his neck. Then she whispered in his ear, ever so softly. "Take me home with you."

He exhaled long and slow. When they locked eyes, she nodded. He put pressure on the brakes as if they were coming to another exit. "Your place is closer."

"I want to go to your house."

His eyes were relaxed as he touched her cheek tenderly. "Whatever you say, Coco. You're the birthday girl."

CHAPTER 29

Barefoot on a plush bathroom rug, Colette slipped a cluster of high-end diamonds in each ear, her heart fluttering as if they were brand new. Taking a step back, she tested out several seductive poses. Never before had she felt so womanly, so powerful. Her smoky eyes spoke of desire, and her glossy smile looked dazzling next to the jewels.

Lust saturated her entire being as she removed a pair of flashy, four-inch heels from her bag. As she slipped them on, she imagined the kinds of things Bryce was about to do to her. He would take his time, she knew, exploring every inch of her body, caressing places that had been crying out to be touched.

Stripped down to a lacy black bra and panties, the pumps made her look trashier than a hooker. It was time. After turning off the bathroom light, Colette opened the door ever so slightly. Placed throughout Bryce's bedroom were the same candles she had set up, poolside, for their two month anniversary. The flames were incredibly romantic, and the background music set the tone. The curtains did a fabulous job blocking out any sign of daylight, and her favorite cologne combed the air, tempting her all the more. The French doors to his room were shut tight, a pleasing reminder that she was about to have him all to herself.

"Bryce?" She opened the door wider and peered out. Where

was he? Colette's silhouette danced on the wall as her Michael Kors clinked against marble with every step. When she touched the doorknob, she heard Bryce whistle like men love to do when a good looking girl walks by. She spun around, hands on her hips, and watched with satisfaction as his mouth gaped open. Flesh spilled out of her lingerie, begging him to take it off. "I was hoping I'd bump into you," she grinned.

Bryce was wearing the same pair of shorts well below his abs, his shirt tossed to the side as if he had just ripped it off. He was built like a warrior, every muscle defined with precision. The edge of his mouth curved into a smile, and passion burned in his eyes as he waited for her.

Crossing the floor, she accentuated her hips with every step. The moment she was within reach, his lips went to her neck, his hands slowly making their way down her back. As she fought to get his shorts unbuttoned, she questioned if she was being true to herself, her values. But the clock was ticking and there was no turning back. When his shorts dropped to the floor, her gaze dropped too, taking her breath away. He led her to the bed as longing pulsed through her veins.

Wrapping her in his arms, Bryce focused deep into her eyes, his breath intimate against her skin. Gripping his shoulder blades, she moved her lips in perfect unison with his. The hardness against her lower abdomen was making her hot. Moving her tongue, she slowed down the pace in a way that made him groan. Breathless, he stopped just long enough to get the words out. "Happy birthday, beautiful."

She kicked off her shoes, each one hitting the floor with a thud. Pulling back, she watched as Bryce's gaze fell down to her lips, then lower and lower. She could feel his stare caressing her body the same way his lips would soon be doing. "Sing to me," she whispered. "I've never heard you sing."

"There's a reason you haven't," he smiled. "But I'll do it for you."

She traced his calf up and down with her toes, anticipating her love song. His eyes didn't miss the parting of her legs, and like a reflex, he pulled her closer. "You want me to sing to you."

"Yes please."

"Any special requests?"

She shook her head, grinning.

He slipped a finger beneath her strap and let it fall down over her shoulder. His eyes darted to her unveiled breast and then back to her face. As he went down for a kiss, she stopped him. "Where's my song?"

He laughed. "You're killing me, Coco."

"I want to hear you. Just once."

"Okay, but it's going to be a short song. Two lines is all I have time for." When she nodded in agreement, he cleared his throat. "I can't think of a single song. Forgive me, but I'm distracted."

"Take your time. I'll wait."

"Okay, I got one." His lips parted, long before any words came out. "Baby..." his voice cracked, almost too soft to be heard.

A giggle escaped her. The Grammys were not in his future, but his stage presence was unparalleled. "Keep going. I love it."

"Baby love, my baby love, I need you, how I—" he stopped abruptly, fear flooding his face. "What's wrong?"

Narrowing her eyes, she snapped her bra strap back in place. "Where did you hear that song?"

Distancing himself from her, he sat up. "You're scaring me a little. Actually a lot."

214

She got off the bed. "Tell me where you heard that song. Where's my phone?" She stormed into the bathroom and searched her bag. "I asked you a question. Where is my phone?" After tugging her clothes back on, she returned to the bedroom in a panic. "My phone, please," she said, holding out her hand like a bellhop.

"Calm down. I'll get it."

"Did you put it somewhere?"

"It's downstairs where you left it."

She pointed a finger at his chest. "I didn't leave it anywhere. It was in my purse."

His jaw tightened. "Or not."

"Bryce, don't tell me I left it downstairs when I know I haven't touched it all morning." Barefoot, she couldn't get to the first floor fast enough. Running from room to room, she spotted her cell on the kitchen counter. There were two missed calls and one received call. All three were from Roxanne.

"I see you answered my phone," she hollered over her shoulder. Clenching her cell, she took a deep breath. "Please be good news," she whispered. "I need you to have good news. Please, God, please."

She listened to the first voicemail. It was a hang-up. "What's wrong with you, Roxanne? Did they not have answering machines back in your day?" The next voicemail was left one minute later. This time she heard Roxanne's voice:

"Colette, happy birthday. I have some great news. I found you a baby boy. He's nine months old, but hasn't learned to crawl yet. I'm sure that's something you will enjoy helping him with. Listen, I'm taking an early weekend, so unless I hear from you in the next twenty minutes or so, I'll catch up with you on Monday.

I know you work evenings, so this will give you a chance to arrange childcare for next week. He's in a temporary foster home right now, so we still have some time. I look forward to hearing from you. He's a cute little boy, by the way. Big blue eyes. Thanks, Colette. Call me soon."

Tears filled her eyes as the smile on her face widened. "I don't believe this," she whispered. "It's really happening." She saw movement in the doorway and looked up. "Babe, I'm so sorry. I'm sorry I flipped out, but I just got some amazing news." She held the phone high like a first-place trophy. "That was my case worker. I've been trying to become a foster parent for so long and that was Roxanne, the case worker I've been dealing with. She's going to place me with a nine-month old baby boy! I know I owe you a bigger apology than what you just got, but I just need to call her back real quick and see if it's too late to pick him up. Otherwise I have to wait all the way until Monday, and I don't feel comfortable leaving him with a stranger all weekend."

He was squinting as if the lighting were too bright. "So on Monday, or possibly right now..."

"I know this is a lot to take in, but if you knew how long I've been waiting for this. That's what that extra room in my apartment is for. I didn't want you to see the crib and everything since I didn't even have a baby, so that's why I kept it locked. To be honest, I thought Roxanne would never give me a baby."

"Am I supposed to be happy about this?"

"Bryce Rocco, you're not listening to me. If you had any idea how long I've wanted this, *needed* this, you'd be jumping for joy right now. I have always supported you and your career choices. You could decide to do that movie in L.A. and I would be the happiest, most supportive girlfriend to you. Because it's not all about me and I understand that. This is a big deal. This is huge for me. I need you to be happy."

"My opinion means nothing? You're considering toting around a baby—"

"No, I'm not *considering*," she said, trying to loosen the pound of rocks wedged between his ears. "This is something I decided long before I met you. Maybe I should have told you about it at some point, but I honestly didn't believe I'd ever get this call. Believe me when I tell you, Roxanne refused to give me a baby."

"It sounds to me like you're choosing that kid over me."

She felt the wind being knocked out of her chest. "Excuse me?"

He was yelling now, his fist raised in anger. "You just ended our most intimate moment with pure disgust. Excuse me for answering your phone, but the woman called three times in five minutes. You and I are not ready for a baby. Take a deep breath, get a grip, and do this in the right order."

"He's an orphan! He needs a home!"

"He doesn't need a home. C'mon. Do you really think they're going to put him on the streets with a bottle of milk and an 'I need a home' sign? No."

"There's a shortage of homes. Everybody knows that."

"Then why did they make you wait so long for a kid, huh? Why? Answer me that."

"I didn't want a kid! I wanted a baby!" She burst into tears. "What is wrong with you that you can't see that? My friends can see it clear as day, and I don't have to say a word."

She wanted to keep yelling until she was blue in the face, until he understood everything she had gone through to get to this day, but he was too narrow-minded to listen. Maybe she needed

Roxanne's permission to become a mom, but she certainly didn't need Bryce's consent.

Monday night she would be reading a nine-month old baby boy a bedtime story, feeding him a bottle, and tucking him into bed. At the grocery store, she would be one of the lucky ones hushing her child, telling him not to grab things off the shelves. There would be trips to the pediatrician, photo albums and home movies. They would go to the park for walks in his stroller. Strangers would tickle his toes and tell her how cute he is. Coworkers would be in awe at how quickly he's growing up. She was on the verge of becoming a mom and Bryce was trying to ruin it.

Huffing and puffing, Bryce left the room. Seconds later, he returned with his phone to his ear. "Let's see you put your money where your mouth is. You say you're infinitely supportive of whatever I choose. Watch this." His face was tense, his eyebrows sharp.

"What are you doing?"

He put his hand up and paused as if he was telling her to wait and see for herself. "Hey man. I give. I'm going to do the film if I still can. Am I too late?"

Anger seeped from her eyes as she witnessed his cruel retaliation. If he wanted to do the movie, fine. But to spite her just because she wanted to be a mom was downright hurtful.

"Awesome. Thank you. And I'm sorry for the way I've been avoiding you ... Yes, I still have it ... Correct. It's going in the mail today ... I appreciate you, man. I just needed to clear my head ... Ha! You got it ... Exactly ... I don't want to eat up your weekend, so I'll catch you Monday." His eyes darted to hers, gloating. "Thanks again, man. You're the best."

CHAPTER 30

In one shiny piece, she parked Bryce's car in the parking lot of her apartment complex sensing someone would ding the paint, or worse, hotwire it for a joy ride. She pulled the keys from the ignition, the same ones she had demanded from Bryce an hour ago, feeling as though she had lost.

The moment she shut her apartment door she fell apart. This wasn't a sour exchange of words or a lovers' quarrel. She and Bryce were in the midst of a full-blown fight, and there was no history to gauge if their relationship would recover.

It was six hours before she heard from Bryce, and by then she was ready to talk. He told her he wasn't going to discuss it over the phone, so an hour later she was back at his house feeling just as lousy as when she had left. He was waiting outside in a suit when she pulled up. He didn't look happy.

"Keys?" He didn't bother with eye contact, nor did he compliment Colette on her new halter-top dress.

"In the ignition," she said with the same courtesy.

"We can talk in the car. If we're going to make it on time, we need to hit the road." When he pulled onto the highway, he gunned it. "So this... baby," he sputtered. "Do you still want it?"

She wondered if his reaction would be similar if he had accidently gotten her pregnant. Why couldn't he get it through his thick skull they were talking about a human being, not a puppy? The way he was zipping around corners, heightened aggravation was the last thing he needed, so she dealt him a question. "If I asked for your permission, would you give it?" His jaw tightened, but he didn't answer. All of a sudden he slammed his fist against the wheel and cursed. "I feel like you stabbed me in the heart, but you don't seem the least bit sorry."

"I'm sorry," she blurted out, scared he would go off the road. "I am. I overreacted." She searched his face for the slightest change, but it was stone hard. Crossing her arms, she stared out the window wondering how in the world she was going to fix this. Her desire to be a mom was growing so deep within her soul, a baby was the only way to eradicate it. Her phone went off and she declined the call.

"Who was that?"

"Nobody."

"Don't tell me 'nobody' when I ask you who called."

She stuffed the phone back in her bag. "I didn't recognize the number. Is that okay with you, or do you want to call it back?"

"If that's really the truth."

"Why would I lie to you?"

"Why do you do a lot of the stuff you do?"

Now it was getting personal. She clamped down on the insides of her cheeks to keep from crying, and concentrated on the serene clouds dotted across the sky. "Take me home."

He exhaled a drawn out breath until eventually his shoulders relaxed. He kept glancing at her as if she had something to say. "Babe, I'm sorry." He ran his fingers through his hair, a habit he probably picked up in front of the camera. "I love you. You know I love you." He turned on the radio and clicked his tongue with the beat. "Let's not fight on your birthday."

Did he expect her to drop everything at his command? Lucky for her, he kept his eyes fixed on the road which meant she was off the hook for a response. Her phone went off again. It was the same number. She accepted the call, but handed the phone to Bryce. "You don't trust me? You take it," she whispered.

"What? No."

"I already answered. Say hello."

"Colette." He fumbled the phone as if it were a hamster. When it was securely against his ear, he shot her a look that said he was annoyed, but slightly amused. "Hello, Bryce speaking."

She crossed her arms.

"Yes, the birthday girl is sulking, I mean sitting, right next to me. Would you like to talk to her?" He widened his eyes and looked at Colette as if she heard what the caller had said. "You're kidding me. It's so good to finally talk to you." His eyes were tender as he looked at her. "Colette, it's your mom. Do you want to say hi?"

Before she knew what was happening, tears were flowing down her face in steady streams. Trying to compose herself, she shook her head, waving him away. How many years had it been? At least fifteen since she had heard her mom's voice.

"Colette can't talk at the moment. Is this a good number to call you back ... Yes ... Alright ... Tonight?" Frantically he looked at her for an answer. "We're on our way to dinner, and I've got something special planned for her birthday all day tomorrow, but I can go ahead and cancel if you need me to ... Okay ... Probably two hours, three at the most ... Of course ... She's been looking forward to seeing you too."

There was a long pause on Bryce's end and she could imagine

the earful he was getting. Perfect timing, she thought. He listened intently, offering an "um-hmm" every ten seconds or so. The lines in his forehead deepened into crevices, and several times he looked at Colette questioningly. She shrugged it off accepting her fate. He would never look at her the same again.

CHAPTER 31

Bryce handed the phone back to Colette, looking at her with what she perceived to be pity. "Your mom said she wants to see you tonight."

"Where is she?"

"I don't know."

The timing was bizarre. According to the last two letters, she wasn't supposed to get out of prison until the following week. And by Oregon law, she was required to serve the entire sentence.

Rubbing her forehead, Colette tried to make sense of it. Ever since Christmas, Colette had been counting down the weeks until her mom was free, in hopes that their two-person family could be restored. In the letters she claimed that she had changed, that the toddler's family had forgiven her in Jesus' name, and how it was their forgiveness that led her to a relationship with God. Colette doubted her religion would last ten steps outside her cell, but at least she was trying to be a good person.

Silence hung in the air like burning sulfur. Sniffling, she patted her eyes dry, salvaging as much makeup as she could. Bryce was deep in thought, probably conjuring up the gentlest way to dump her. Shoving Bryce and his opinions to the back seat, she pondered the thought of seeing her mom again.

The bitterness had ended years ago, sometime in her late teens, but by that point their relationship had deteriorated into a guilt-ridden mother and an emotionally scarred daughter who no longer recognized each other.

"You usually work on Fridays, so I made plans for tomorrow instead." His voice was heavy and his eyes weren't much better. "My folks asked me to bring you by tonight. They have something for you. Thanks for dressing up."

"What did you have in mind for tomorrow?"

"You'll see." He turned on the air conditioner and adjusted the vents. "I know you want to go home, but it will mean a lot to them if you make an appearance. And after that, you can meet up with your mom... if you feel comfortable going alone."

"She's not dangerous."

He narrowed his eyes. "Did I imply that she is?"

"What exactly did my mom tell you? You're keeping it to yourself like it's none of my business, but it *is* my business. I shouldn't even have to ask."

He pressed his lips together and hesitated. "She told me she's been in prison since you were a kid, and that you haven't been by to see her. Ever."

"And you think that makes me a bad person."

"I'll pretend I didn't hear that." He sighed with strained calmness. "She said she got released at the beginning of the month, but wanted to surprise you for your birthday."

"Why would she do that? Why would she wait until my birthday to rattle my life?" Her head fell into her lap in shame. Gone was the sweet nurse Bryce had fallen in love with. He was seeing firsthand an instability Colette thought she had outgrown years ago. This whole fiasco should have unfolded in private, not right smack in front of the guy who was still trying to decide if he wanted her.

"We both need to relax." He twisted his arm for a better angle of his watch. "I know it's easier said than done, but try to enjoy your birthday. Life usually has a way of working itself out in the end."

Her heart skipped a beat as she sat taller. "Do you really think so?" She clung to his words like a five-year-old on the leg of her war-bound father.

"Baby, I do." He studied her momentarily, his tense expression making him appear ten years older. "Your mom is really looking forward to seeing you. She misses you."

Maybe he was right. Her mom was hardly in position to chew her out for destroying their relationship. And Colette wouldn't dare point an accusatory finger so many years later.

When they arrived at the Rocco's, Bryce slipped an arm around her at the last possible second before swinging the door open. Colette's hand went to her mouth when she saw a living room full of glowing faces, several of them people she had never met before. They looked from Colette to Gladys, who was flailing her arms like a caffeinated symphony conductor. Then, in unison, they shouted, "Happy Birthday!"

It was uncomfortable being the center of attention, especially on an evening when she didn't feel like smiling, but she thanked everyone with a hearty laugh. After untangling herself from Bryce's arm, she picked up Jenn's little boy. "I didn't see any cars. Where did you guys park?"

Teddy adjusted his tie and pointed toward the ceiling. "Bryce had his chopper drop them off. There's a helipad on the roof."

"They're parked out back," Jenn grinned.

Jumping up and down, the kids pulled her into the kitchen for a glimpse of the birthday cake. She oohed and awed as was expected of her, but smiling was difficult. As the evening wore on, it didn't get easier.

Jenn patted the couch cushion and asked her to sit. Squeezing in between Jenn and Ginger, Colette savored the closeness of her new relationships. Over time Colette had wiggled her way into the family without even trying. If Bryce ever changed his mind about her, the loss would be catastrophic. Even Gage didn't seem to hate her as much as he used to. Lately their interaction fell somewhere between harassment and teasing, a baby step forward in the right direction.

Gladys was glowing like a proud grandma. "We wanted to do something special for you, Colette, but don't think we're going to keep you here all night. I may look like an old lady on the outside, but I still remember what it's like to be young and in love. Listen, I've got cake and ice cream in the other room, and then you two can be on your way." Her voice trailed off as she headed on a well-intentioned mission to get the party over with. She returned with a decorated sheet cake and a single lit candle.

Giving Gladys a tight squeeze, Colette smiled. "Thanks again for the party. It was definitely a surprise. We can stay for a little bit longer, but I was thinking we should head out around eight. My mom and I are getting together tonight."

There wasn't a soul in the room who understood the significance of what she had just said, except the boyfriend who had been avoiding her all evening. She wondered if the Roccos would extend the same open arms to her mom, or if they'd forever think of her as a prisoner. Anticipating their meeting, Colette had already set aside a thousand dollars for a new wardrobe, a hair appointment, and a manicure. There was no way she was going to allow her mom to make a disgraceful first impression, which reminded her; she needed to tell Bryce to keep his mouth shut about her mom's past, for the time being anyway.

Gladys balanced a slice of cake on the bread knife and dumped it onto a paper plate. "Does she live in town?"

With all her being, Colette hoped that no one spotted the uncertainty in her expression. "She's in the process of moving."

"Oh dear. We forgot to light the candle. Would you look at this? I've made a mess of your cake."

A half a dozen voices assured Gladys it was fine. True to her word, Gladys moved things right along. "Don't spoil your dinner, kids," she said, her eyes darting between Colette and Bryce. "Make a wish."

By the time Colette realized she wasn't getting a happy birthday song, there was no time for a wish. She blew out the candle as Chloe tugged on her dress. "How old are you, Coco?"

"I'm thirty," Colette said with dramatic eyes. Thirty and still a virgin, she suddenly remembered.

Gladys and her daughters got busy cutting, pouring, and serving. The men retreated to the furniture, and Colette excused herself to the restroom. Bryce stopped her in the hallway. "Don't feel obligated to stay."

"I'm okay."

"Whenever you're ready."

She was disappointed that he turned away without a touch. "Bryce," she whispered. "I feel like you and I are still in a funk."

"We are."

Her chest caved in like a punctured balloon. "Why?" The answer was obvious, but she wished he would be the forgiving, supportive, lovable boyfriend he always was.

"You had me," he whispered with intensity. "Do you understand? This morning you had *all* of me. And then, without warning, *smack*. He clapped centimeters from her face.

Her eyes welled with tears. "Bryce, I—"

"No," he pleaded, bracing her shoulders. "Not here." He backed her up just inside the bathroom and put his hands on her hips. The anger in his eyes was gone. "All couples fight. Don't cry."

"Are you going to break up with me?"

"No," he said soothingly. "Of course not. You can't cry in front of my parents, okay? Please." Taking a tissue, he dabbed her face.

"I'm not going to take that baby on Monday."

He shook his head. "Let's not talk about that right now. Let's get you cheered up. You're going to go back in there and eat cake, without hitting on my brother, if you don't mind," he smirked, "and then you're going to go see your mom. We have the whole weekend to talk."

"Will you come with me to meet her?"

He hesitated. "You don't want me there. You haven't seen her in years." Kissing her on the forehead, he left her standing in the bathroom.

After cake, the kids ran out back and the women joined the men in the living room. "How about Taboo?" someone suggested. Soon the room was bursting with noise as the girls' team dominated the guys.

Bryce's little nephew came inside and nestled onto his lap. Fifteen minutes later, his identical twin joined him. Seeing the three of them together made her feel like an outsider, like he cared for his family more than her. She held out for the tiniest

228

fraction of attention, but Bryce seemed to look at everyone except her.

Jenn's turn had just ended when Colette's phone rang. The men were already yelling by the time she answered. "Hello?" Why was the hospital calling her?

"Colette?" It was Jazmine. "Colette, can you hear me?"

"Just a sec. I'm going to the other room." Colette tiptoed around legs trying to keep her balance.

"You need to get down here." Jazmine's voice was almost too quiet to hear. "They've been *bagging* your baby Kisha for about five minutes, but she's shut down."

Colette's stomach dropped. "Who's the nurse? Call an RT!"

"An RT and three nurses are working on her. It doesn't look good."

"I'll be right there." Hanging up, she pictured pudgy little Kisha lying lifeless in her crib.

When Colette came around the corner, everyone froze. Tears were streaming down her face. "The hospital called. I have to go."

Bryce jumped to his feet and met her at the front door. "What happened?"

"Forget it." She slammed the door harder than she intended and dug the keys from her purse. Where was her car? Suddenly she remembered. Gasping, she stomped her foot. She waited for what felt like an eternity for Bryce to come out, but he didn't. Swallowing her pride, she cracked the door. "Can I please borrow your keys?"

Gone was the concern in his eyes, and in its place was anger. "I'll take you."

"Just let me borrow your car." She pictured Latoya wailing

over the loss of her only daughter. It wasn't fair! Why did some make it and others not? Her knees felt weak as she held out her shaking hand, waiting for her stubborn boyfriend to comply. She felt his hands heavy on her shoulders.

"I said I'll take you. Let's go."

A second ago, he couldn't even look at her, and now he was trying to be a hero? "Stop it!" Gripping his wrists, she threw his arms down. "One of my babies is about to die, on my shift, and you're holding your keys hostage until I ask nicely? This is their only daughter, Bryce, their *only* daughter, and I'm just trying to get there fast enough to help."

Like a zombie, he dropped the keys into her palm.

Stunned, she closed her fingers. "Thank you. Please call my mom and tell her I won't be able to make it tonight." She gave him her phone and ran out the door.

CHAPTER 32

Colette's legs were wobbly as she forced her way through the door of the NICU. Here was a tiny human being, the definition of innocence, who had overcome so much, only to lose her life weeks before going home to her family.

The receptionist took off her reading glasses and stood up. "Colette, nobody could get a hold of you." Her mouth hung open as if there were no words. She placed her hands on the desk, her nails clinking against the Formica. "She's okay. The baby is fine."

Colette's hand went to her chest. "She's alive? I thought she..."

"I didn't want you to worry."

Holding back tears, she took off her coat and turned on the faucet. "I'm going to stop back there for a minute. I just want to see her."

When she got to Pod Four, Kisha was wrapped loosely in a blanket dressed in butterfly pajamas in her daddy's arms. All was calm. The scene was surreal, as if time had been turned back, Kisha's death undone.

When Jazmine spotted her, her eyes grew. "I tried calling," she said frantically. "Bryce has your phone. I'm so sorry for taking you away from your party. It was a false alarm. I feel awful."

"Don't be sorry. I would have been upset if you didn't call. Thank you for thinking of me."

She saw Latoya nudge her husband, pointing out Colette's

arrival. Russell looked up and waved. As Colette crossed the floor, her heart swelled with adoration. Kisha was looking around, bright-eyed and fully alert, as she chomped away on her little fist.

"Hey guys, how is she doing? She looks wonderful."

Latoya stood up, pressed her lips into a pout, and hugged Colette. "It's your day off and you're here. Thank you for coming. This means so much to us." She fanned her eyes, laughing. "You look so different in a dress. Your feet must be miserable, poor thing."

"I wasn't expecting Kisha to pull a stunt like that. She's a big girl now. I thought we were past all this."

"She choked on her milk. I think it might have been my fault."

The nurse on duty shook her head. "You did everything just right. You didn't do a thing wrong." She motioned for Colette to look at the chart. "See this? We tried for over five minutes to get her to breathe. Her heart-rate went all the way down to zero."

Colette shook her head. "Kisha girl, no more of this, okay? You scared us."

Latoya lowered her voice. "I've already asked a million people, but is Kisha going to be okay? Her brain, I mean."

"She looks great to me, but there's really no way of knowing how her prematurity will affect things long term. If there are any delays, you may not notice until she's two or three years old."

"But she could be okay?"

"She could."

Kisha was staring up at her daddy. Russell stroked her forehead as he looked back at her. It was powerful, like he had been given a second chance. Colette could see it all over his face, the way his eyes would become glossy until he blinked.

Latoya gestured across the room. "She said it's your birthday. Don't let us keep you any longer."

Carefully cradling Kisha, Russell replanted his feet and sat forward in the recliner. "I figured Bryce Rocco would have something grander than Eugene, Oregon planned for his girlfriend's thirtieth."

She could feel the blood rush to her face. For starters, she wasn't positive she still held the title, *girlfriend*. "I'm almost out of vacation days. Bryce is taking me somewhere tomorrow, but he hasn't told me where."

Russell laughed. "The fact that you're on a first name basis with Bryce Rocco still cracks me up every time."

Latoya nudged Colette. "If you marry him, are you going to take his name? It seems like no one in Hollywood does. I think you should so we can tell everyone that Mrs. Rocco took care of our baby."

"It's a little soon to be talking marriage."

"I know. I mean in the future."

Yes, she would take his name, in a heartbeat. As an adolescent, she legally changed her last name to Halbrook, her cousin's last name. It always felt phony, but she didn't want to draw attention by changing it back. Colette held up her left hand. "If someone ever puts a ring on it, I'll definitely take his name."

A nurse, seemingly off in her own world, looked up from the computer. "Does he have any brothers? I'm single."

"Yes he does, but his brother is extremely... married." She stopped herself before saying something she'd read about in the checkout line of the grocery store. So far, the paparazzi hadn't taken much interest in her, but Bryce kept warning her that they wouldn't stay away forever.

"Colette hates his brother," Jazmine said matter-of-factly. "He's been awful to her since day one."

"That's not true. He and I like to banter back and forth, but it's more of a running joke than anything."

"Was he there tonight?"

"Yes he was, which reminds me. I should be getting back." She lowered her voice. "I think I freaked everyone out the way I left in such a hurry." After one last look at baby Kisha, Colette left the room as if she knew where she was headed.

CHAPTER 33

The sun was just starting to go down when Colette arrived at the Rocco's house. With the curtains drawn, there was no sign anybody was home. Going through the motion of knocking, Colette's knuckles bumped against the door a few times before inching it open for a peek.

Her initial fear was that the party had ended, and that Teddy and Gladys were in the bathroom soaking their dentures and emptying their bladders, but that didn't explain the handful of children looking at her like she was crazy. "Where is everybody?"

Several pointed silently toward the hallway. When Bryce appeared from around the corner, his eyes were sunken with worry. "Back so soon?"

His question caught her off guard. She gave him time to expound, to ask how the baby was doing, but he didn't. Instead Bryce's mouth hung open, waiting for an explanation as if she were somewhere she didn't belong. "I came back to return your car." She handed him the keys. "Where is everyone?"

"Down the hall in the office." The uneasy way he was looking at her made her sick to her stomach. The longer he gawked, the more she sensed it. *Bryce was guilty.*

The adults filed back into the living room like accountants returning from a fire drill. Following Teddy's orders, the children hopped off the furniture and ran outside. Gage was glaring at her so hard he looked evil, and everyone else clearly wanted nothing to do with her. She knew she had mistreated Bryce, but never in her worst nightmare could she have imagined that every last one of them would turn on her. Even Gladys was avoiding eye-contact. She felt so out of place she was shaking.

"Is the baby okay?" Bryce finally asked.

She couldn't admit that Kisha was fine, not after the way she flipped out on everyone, yet she found herself nodding. Several women had puffy eyes from crying, and that's when it hit her; yes, something had happened, but it had nothing to do with her. The epiphany was a gigantic weight off her shoulders, but it brought zero comfort to her throbbing heart. Up until that moment the Rocco's had welcomed her as family. But when it came down to it, because a certain finger on her left hand was missing a diamond, they ostracized her.

Gage put his arm around Jenn, but she swung it off with force. "Don't you dare. Don't touch me."

The room was thick with tension, and she wanted out. "I'm sorry for losing my temper," Colette said nervously. "I've seen a lot of babies pass away, but I couldn't fathom the thought of losing this particular little girl." As much as she fought it, she couldn't leash her emotions. She hated that quality about herself. The first set of tears hadn't done her any favors, and here she was blubbering again.

The front door was right behind her, coaxing her to open it and run all the way home. She inhaled snippets of air while wiping her tear-stained face. "I honestly believed she was dying and I took it out on Bryce. I hope each of you can remember a time you overacted so you can forgive me."

Her lip quivered when she paused, awaiting a response. Nobody said a word. Nobody offered an understanding smile. Bryce was too busy monitoring his family's well-being to stand by her side the way he was supposed to.

Something snapped, and she found their holier-than-thou attitudes appalling. Careful to keep her temper in check, she steadied her voice. "Obviously something happened that you're not willing to share with me, and I respect that. I really do." She was blowing smoke. There was no excuse for the way they were treating her. "So, Bryce, if you don't mind, I brought your car back. Will you please drive me home?"

Never before had she felt so hurt and humiliated all at the same time. She pined for seclusion, for her car, her bed, and ironically, for her mother.

Bryce mouthed *I'm sorry* to his family and met her at the door. "Here's your phone back. I'll take you home."

When the door finally shut, she exhaled. She was done fighting. "Did you get a hold of my mom?"

He placed his hand on the small of her back and guided her to the driveway. They were halfway to the car when he answered. "Yes, I talked to her."

"And?"

"I didn't mean for everyone to find out like this. Nobody is angry with you. We're just trying to process everything."

"I'm not mad that you guys talked about me. Obviously I deserve it, but what did you say? Did you tell them about my foster baby? Is that why no one will look me in the eye? Your brother is ready to skin me alive."

"Don't worry about Gage."

"I feel like your family is so perfect and they want me to be perfect too. You know I'm a good person, Bryce. I'm just going through a lot right now."

Bryce stared dumbly as if there was nothing to say. As much as she wanted to ring his neck, she wasn't going to beg for information, not for another few minutes at least.

She stormed off and waited in the passenger seat with her arms locked together in frustration. She jumped when her door swung open. Bryce's eyebrows were slanted so far inward they were practically vertical. He opened his mouth to let her have it, but then looked away sharply. "No, Dad," he hollered. "Don't worry about it. I'm not upset."

"Liar," she muttered.

Swinging her door shut, he took the driver seat. "Keys?"

Without looking, she dangled them in her left hand. He snatched them away and shoved them into the ignition. He waved to his dad as he circled the driveway. Just before the road, he put the car in park and stared off into the distance. From the rearview mirror she could see Teddy disappear into the house.

Gently Bryce took hold of her shoulders and looked into her eyes with genuine concern. "So that baby," he said, "she's okay now?"

A surge of hope went through her, like the clearing after a storm. "She's good." When he rubbed her back, she lost it. She wanted everything to be okay, for them to move on like nothing had happened. And maybe, by the grace of God, he did too. Wiping her eyes, she took a moment to pull herself together. "You have no idea what it felt like to walk into that room and see Kisha still alive. It blew me away."

"I can imagine." He cupped his hand along her jaw and neck.

When she looked up, she noticed he was crying too. "I'm sorry," he said. "I'm so sorry."

"Too much is happening all at once," she hiccupped. "I need you to give me a few days to get it together. I know I can. I'm overwhelmed. I'm tired."

When he hugged her, his chest smelled like the Bryce she knew yesterday, the Bryce she had learned to trust. In that moment she realized that no matter what he did or said, nothing in the world mattered more than being with him. He wasn't perfect and neither was she. The worst mistake of her life would be to harbor a grudge against the one man she truly loved.

During the drive to her apartment she let Bryce do all the talking, which amounted to less than a sentence. He walked her to her door, and out of habit she invited him in. To her surprise he followed her to the couch. "We need to talk."

"You're breaking up with me."

When he opened his mouth, and then closed it, a part of her spirit died. Silent tears rolled down her face as she nodded. The mess she caused was too catastrophic. Exhausted, she looked at him through blurred eyes and stood up. "I need to go to bed."

"I know you do." He took her hand and led her back to her spot on the couch. "I've gone back and forth trying to decide if you're better off hearing this from me or your mom. Either way you're not going to like it."

Her heart pounded with fear.

He squeezed her hands. "If my family would have been given more than twenty minutes to absorb all of this, things would be much, much different. Nobody is judging you, except for maybe Gage. But again, he's in shock too, so he's not being rational."

She wanted to reach into his throat, snatch the words he was trying to get out, and lay them in front of her as a single blunt sentence. "Does everyone know my mom just got out of prison?"

"Yes."

"Did my mom tell you why she was there?"

"I asked her."

Her eyes widened. "You haven't even met her, and you asked her why she got locked up?" She stopped herself when she saw him cringe. If she wanted details, she needed to pretend she could handle it. "What was her answer?"

"She wouldn't tell me."

"Not at first?"

"Not ever." He released her hands. "Like I said, I shouldn't have said anything to my family, at least not before you and I talked it over. It just sort of came out before I knew what was happening."

"Are you aware that she killed two people in a drunk-driving accident?"

"Yes."

"And one of them was a toddler?"

He winced, and then nodded.

"And you told your family," she concluded. "They all know."

"I'm sorry, Coco."

She narrowed her eyes. "If my mom didn't tell you, then who did?"

He backed off the couch and onto the loveseat as if he was afraid of her. He opened his mouth a half-a-dozen times before any words came out. Tears welled up in Bryce's eyes, but he kept blinking them away. "Colette," he said with tightly clasped hands. "The toddler killed in that car accident was Jenn's firstborn. They had a daughter."

Colette's hand went to her mouth as her whole body trembled uncontrollably. She felt like she was going to pass out. Her mom killed Jenn's baby girl? Colette searched his eyes to see if it was some kind of a sick joke. It wasn't.

"When I called your mom, she reintroduced herself by her full name. When I hung up, I asked my uncle why that name sounded so familiar. I was a kid when it happened, but most everyone else knew right off. We panicked. When you showed up, we were still in the office trying to piece it together."

Without warning, vomit exploded from the pit of her stomach. Her hands, her dress, the floor. Coughing, she stared at Bryce who was frozen in fear. "Get out."

"Colette, this was a—"

"GET OUT!" Her hands were still cupped in front of her throat like a beggar.

With his head hung low, he left.

CHAPTER 34

Colette snatched the newly-charged camera battery off the wall, took one last look in the mirror, and headed out. As she crossed the Ferry Street Bridge, her heart rattled in her chest. She was getting close. Exiting toward Autzen Stadium, she took the curve down Country Club Road.

Alton Baker Park was hopping with kite-flyers, sun-bathers, and shirtless Frisbee players. The pavilion was crammed with Asians, which she prejudicially assumed to be U of O students studying abroad, and the duck pond was surrounded by young families. The trees along the bike-path provided shade for lovebirds and readers, both of which were sprawled out on blankets atop the plush grass.

The wind attempted to lift her dress, something she hadn't considered before leaving the house, but it was too late to do anything about it now. The walk to the other end of the park was anything but serene. There was goose poo and feathers she was avoiding with little success, but far worse was the feeling of being watched. Thanks to her crazy head of curls, her mom would have no trouble spotting Colette from a mile away.

As she neared the footbridge, the designated meeting spot per her mom's text message, she scanned bodies, hair-types, and what she could see of faces, hoping for a heads-up rather than a startling tap on the shoulder.

As she started up the spiral staircase, she opted out of touching the germ-infested railing, but changed her mind when two teenage boys came barreling around the corner, the ringleader plowing into her shoulder. He made a sound which she accepted as an apology, and the hyper duo continued on their way. Colette couldn't help but chuckle as the nearly full-grown boys sprinted down the bike path, enjoying summer the way kids used to. Kind of like Bryce, she thought. Outdoorsy and playful.

On the far end of the bridge were an elderly couple, a family of four, and a single woman off to the right who might very well be her mom. There was a quickening in her spirit at the possibility. Apprehension, excitement, curiosity, sadness; every emotion under the sun took its turn striking her.

The woman's back was turned, thus her face hidden, as she leaned over the railing for a better look at the current. She was heavy-set with shoulder-length highlighted hair, and her frame was neither short nor tall. Colette made her way up the bridge allowing ample time for the woman to take notice, but she never did.

Anger started to emerge as she imagined her mom smiling as if everything was okay, like she had the right to pick up right where they left off. Colette glanced over her shoulder to make sure her mom hadn't come up the steps, and then let out a quiet breath as she fixed her eyes back on the woman. Too timid to approach her, Colette looked across the river and mumbled her name, "Patty," as if she were merely thinking out loud.

Startled, the woman spun around. Her face said it all. "Coco," she gasped. Tears welled up in her eyes as she reached forward, cupping Colette's frightened face.

"Momma?" her lips quivered. It was like stepping back in time to when everything was good; chocolate chip cookies baking in the oven, the two of them huddled around the coffee table, coloring.

"Baby girl, don't cry." Patty embraced her tightly, burrowing the side of her face against her daughter's neck. "Don't be sad, sweetheart." But even as she said it, tears were streaming down her own cheeks.

Frantically Colette wiped her eyes, but she couldn't manage to get it together. How many times had she pictured that irreplaceable face, those vibrant blue-green eyes, that quirky smile? She looked exactly the same... but different. Deep wrinkles lined the puffy skin beneath her eyes and her face was plump in a grandmotherly sort of way, but she still looked pretty. Her hair was professionally colored, and her wardrobe wasn't from the eighties. It was hysterical, really, but for no good reason. Colette started to laugh.

"I know," Patty grinned crookedly. "I got fat eating prison food. Who would have thought?"

"I'm not laughing at *you*. I'm laughing because you look so different."

Patty took a step back. "Thanks. I feel much better."

By one sarcastic remark, Colette allowed herself to believe the impossible. *She had her family back.*

"You look good, Mom." With rounded eyes, Colette gestured with the palm of her hand. "Like really good." As a thirty-year-old professional, it felt juvenile calling her "mom" as if they were still pretending, but lucky for her, she had plenty of time to get used to it. "Guess what. I'm an RN at the hospital. I work with preemies."

"Do you?" Patty's face was beaming with pride. "I always knew you would make something of yourself. You were so... focused."

"Was I?"

"Oh yes. Determined. Even as a little girl." She raised her eyebrows. "You learned to ride your bike without training wheels at three."

"I remember you telling me that."

Patty tilted her head. "You do? Good." Taking a deep breath, she gazed up at the sky and smiled. "You wouldn't get off that thing the day I bought it for you. When it got dark I told you it was time to go inside, and you threw one of your famous temper tantrums. There was no calming you down. It was that way every night of the week, if I remember right. Eventually, just before you turned four, you figured it out. You marched those training wheels next door and told Tabitha to keep them for her baby. She was still pregnant at the time."

Colette loved the passion her mom felt for her, even in something as mundane as riding a bike. She didn't doubt her mom would be equally excited to hear that she had her own apartment at an age when everyone else seemed to have a house, a spouse, and kids.

It was a great feeling being genuinely delighted in, and by someone who expected nothing in return. Sadly that was exactly what Colette had given her thus far. Nothing. Even after moving to Oregon, Colette couldn't bring herself to make that hour-and-a-half drive to Wilsonville to make amends. "I have a really cute apartment," she said for the heck of it.

"I'd love to see it. Do you mind? I don't have any plans all weekend."

Laughing, Colette repositioned her purse. "Right now?"

"Yesterday, if you can arrange it."

The shimmer of Patty's blonde highlights didn't stop Colette from wondering if she had a safe place to sleep at night. It wouldn't surprise her if her mom was living out of an old car or in a shelter. "Did you drive here?"

"Why don't we take your car."

"Okay. Sure." She didn't realize her hands were shaking until she fumbled in her purse for the keys. If her mom was trying to hide any harbored resentment, it didn't show. When Colette searched her eyes, Patty winked.

"Do I have any grandbabies I should know about? You're so slender, I would never be able to tell."

Colette's stomach dropped, but she hid her shame with a smile. "Not yet. Hopefully someday though." She swallowed the lump in her throat, terrified she wouldn't be able to keep it together.

Patty sighed sympathetically before taking her by the hand and stroking her arm like a kitten. "I'm sorry. I shouldn't have asked like that. You're still so young. Good for you for establishing a career first." Without warning, Patty's face turned to stone, her gaze darting sharply past Colette. "What do you think you're doing, you little twerp?"

When Colette saw it too, her hand went to her heart. "Stuart! Why are you here? Were you following me?" She noticed a long-lensed camera draped around his neck, thrusting her into a familiar state of paranoia.

"Hello, Colette," Stuart's voice quaked nervously. "Mrs.

Halbrook," he nodded with the disposition of a butler.

Patty relaxed her mouth into a pleasant smile, but her eyes were still intense. "It's Ms. Rosenfeld, for your information," she said with an air of humor. "Forgive me as I start again. Hello. I'm Patty. May I ask how you know my daughter?"

"We were neighbors until Colette exponentially increased my earnings. And would you look at the time. It's almost payday again." He swung a leg over his bike. "Know this. You could have had me, *Coco*, but you chose Hollywood instead. You'll soon see the trouble it's caused you. I regret to inform you that you're about to get what you deserve." He looked over his shoulder grinning as he pedaled away.

Colette grasped Patty's arm. "Tell me he didn't take our picture."

"Why? What's he going to do?"

Colette grabbed fistfuls of curls, bowing her head. "He's going to sell those pictures, that's what. He's going to sell them to the press and the whole world is going to see them."

"The press, honey? I think you're overreacting. What would anybody want with a picture of the two of us?"

"A lot. Trust me."

"I know I've made some mistakes, but in a world of sex scandals and politics, he'll never find a buyer. You'll see."

Before she knew what she was saying, Colette lowered her voice to a whisper. "You hurt Bryce's niece. Trust me. The world cares."

Patty swallowed hard as the wrinkles between her brows became more defined. "Wait a minute." She shook her head sporadically as if she were trying to jiggle her thoughts into place.

When Colette felt the trembling in her mom's fingers, she immediately regretted her bluntness. "Mom, I'm—"

"Wait a minute." She waved her index finger in Colette's face like she had years ago. "Bryce. You're not talking about your boyfriend, Bryce."

"Yes. No. I mean, we broke up, but the media doesn't know that." Colette could see the headlines, could see her tear-stained face displayed at the start of every checkout line in the country. Everyone would know her shameful secret; coworkers, the families of her patients, old classmates and their parents. "I was dating Bryce Rocco," she said delicately. "Mom, do you know who that is?"

"The actor?"

Taken aback, Colette nodded. "Yes."

"Are you sure it's the same..." Patty's eyes fell to the ground. "...the same little girl? Because you'd think I would have heard something, and I haven't."

Every person on the bridge was staring. Even when Colette challenged them with glares, few looked away. "We have to go." She grabbed Patty's arm and walked her briskly down the stairs.

Patty shook her head, as she stumbled with every step. "I know her parents now, Philip and Jenn, and they know me. They don't hate me anymore. They even said so."

"Did it ever occur to you they were lying? Because they hate me and I'm not even the one who did it. I was *eleven*."

"I'm going to fix this," Patty said with urgency. "Don't you worry, okay? Your mom is going to fix this. I'm begging you not to shut me out of your life again. I need you more than you'll ever understand."

CHAPTER 35

Jazmine handed Colette the magazine she had purchased on the way over. "I'm sorry to be the bearer of bad news. Have you been crying this whole time?"

Colette wiped her eyes with a dampened washcloth. "I hate my life."

"I'm sorry, sweetie." Guiding Colette to the couch, Jazmine propped two pillows under her legs. "At least you never have to see Stuart again."

"Just because he moved out doesn't mean he's not following me."

"True. But you got to see baby Kisha go home safe and sound. That counts for something."

"Did you mark the page?"

"I'll find it for you." When Jazmine extended her arm, Colette pulled the magazine back. Tears rolled down her face as she read the headline. It couldn't be more blunt:

BRYCE'S NIECE KILLED BY HIS GIRLFRIEND'S MOTHER
Colette Halbrook's attachment to Bryce Rocco was cut short when her dirty little secret came back to haunt her

Colette's lower lip quivered. "Now the whole world knows. I'm never going to be able to fix this." She clutched the magazine. "Jaz, help me. I don't know what to do."

"Colette, this is no reflection of who you are. Think of all the lives you've saved, the parents and siblings you've comforted along the way. Half of them think of you as family now. How many people can say that?"

Jazmine continued to ramble praises, but it didn't offer an iota of help toward her reputation.

Starting from the middle, Colette flipped through page after page, dreading what she was about to find. When she got to the article, she exhaled.

Having feared the worst, the first three pictures were no surprise: Colette and her mom hugging, a close-up of Colette's tear-stained face, and a disturbing shot of her mom grinning from ear to ear. The other three were of Colette and Bryce, candid, but they were actually pretty cute. In one they were out and about holding hands, another was taken at a restaurant along the river, and the largest picture was of the two of them at the lake in their swimsuits. She wondered if Stuart was the photographer of all six, and if so, how jolly his bank account was feeling right about now.

As Colette read the article, she kept shaking her head in disbelief, so sorry for the lives that were cut short by, as the headline viciously put it, her own mother. The article was packed with information about the accident, well beyond the norm for a celebrity gossip magazine, and some of it was even news to Colette.

Jazmine set down a container of mixed nuts and slapped the magazine with the back of her hand. "You look so hot in that one. I bet Bryce was dying to get a peek."

For the first time that morning Colette smiled. "He tried."

"How far did he get?"

"Do you see a ring on this finger?"

"If it were me, I never would have passed up an opportunity to take a tumble with that man. I still have my fantasies."

With an open-mouthed smile, Colette shoved her so hard she toppled off the couch. Laughing uncontrollably, Jazmine pulled herself up. "If he rebounds, I'm all over that."

"Go for it. Did you read this? He's doing a movie in August. I guess he wasn't bluffing. So much for getting out of the business." She looked at Jazmine inquisitively. "We would have broken up anyway, don't you think?"

"Nobody walks away from millions. He was probably going through a pre-midlife crisis when he told you that."

"Well apparently he's fine now. He doesn't seem to miss me. I love how he's looking forward to California surfing."

"Honey, I'm sorry. Men are jerks. It's part of their DNA."

"No, not him." Tossing the magazine on the floor, Colette groaned. "He's just better off without me."

"Not true," Jazmine smirked. "So, you and your mom. Are you guys good now?"

"I think so. It's crazy. She's such a sweet person. She always was."

"Tell me if I'm out of line, but was it a one-time deal, your mom drinking and driving with you in the car?"

"No. Something bad happened, she never said what, and she spiraled into a different person. I remember being really scared for her."

"So when they took her away, you never saw her again?"

"We were on vacation in Oregon when it happened. They sent me back to Colorado to live with her second cousin's family. My mom would call the house, but I refused to talk. Eventually she gave up calling and just wrote letters. I would write her back, but not about anything meaningful."

"How did you end up in Oregon?"

"I moved up here for college, and of course to get to know my mom again. That's why I couldn't move away with you and Summer. I knew she was getting out this year. I never went to visit, but I was hoping for a miracle when she got out."

"Where does she live now?"

"She followed me to Eugene. She has an apartment."

"Is she working?"

"She's a receptionist for a mechanic here in town."

"Good for her." Jazmine tossed Colette a bag of candy. "You're going to be okay, kid. I had my doubts about you."

Colette's mind went back to the magazine, then to Bryce. Out of nowhere, the tears started flowing again. "No I'm not. My life is over." Burying her face in her hands, she sobbed.

After letting out a small laugh, Jazmine wrapped Colette in a bear hug and held her.

*

The lid on the pot of boiling red potatoes wiggled, the burner hissed. Colette snatched two oven mitts from the counter, lifted the pot from the heat, and blew a strand of curls away from her face. By now she was sweating. Balancing on one foot, she grabbed a spatula for the fresh asparagus simmering in a splash of balsamic vinegar, Bryce's favorite.

When she heard the front door rattle, Colette gasped. She dropped the spatula onto the counter and hurried across the room. The pounding on the door intensified as she got closer.

"I'm coming!"

Seconds later, Patty was standing in the entryway, grinning. "I called you from the parking lot, missy." She wrinkled her nose like a preschool teacher. "You really should anticipate the arrival of your guests."

Colette gestured to the kitchen. "But I have dinner on the stove."

Patty threw her hands up. "It's a hopeless cause. I give up."

In the three months since her mom had been back in her life, Colette had not taken a single day for granted. It continued to amaze her how her mom had this way of giving her heart everything it needed to feel okay, for the moment at least. It didn't matter if it was noon or midnight, her mom answered her calls every time, and with enthusiasm.

"I'm trying out a new recipe for rolls," Colette said, returning to the kitchen. "They got good reviews online."

"Smells delicious."

"It calls for twice as much butter as my old recipe. We'll see if it's worth it."

"I don't know how you stay so thin, Coco. Clearly you got your father's genes."

Colette's heart skipped a beat. As a kid, conversation about her biological dad had been taboo. "Have you talked to him recently?"

"Who? Your father? No. Of course not." Patty was still scowling as she let out a one-syllable laugh. "Why?"

"No reason. I thought maybe you found him online or something."

"Ha! You must be confusing me with yourself. I've never been very good with computers. You know that." When the timer went off, Patty jumped up. "That must be the rolls. I'll get them."

Colette lifted the colander from the sink and dumped the potatoes into a glass bowl. "Perfect timing. Dinner's just about ready."

Patty hit Colette's upper arm with an oven mitt and shot her a sly smile. "Speaking of, have you gotten back on that internet dating service?"

"I've given up on guys for a while."

Patty smiled knowingly. "With the exception of one."

"What's that supposed to mean?"

"If you truly don't know, then you've got your own self fooled."

"Then I give up because I have no idea what you're talking about."

"Bryce, honey. You still talk about him like he's your better half."

Colette stared into the bowl of steaming potatoes, embarrassed that her weakness was so obvious.

Patty draped a cloth napkin over a basket and began filling it with rolls. "There you go, begging for my opinion again. I'm left with no choice but to give it. I think you should write him a letter."

"A letter, Mom? Really?"

"When *he* wrote to *you*, didn't it make you weak in the knees?"

Colette dropped a chunk of butter into the bowl. "The situation was slightly different when *he* wrote *me*. Honestly, I hope I never see him again. I'm sure he and his family feel the same. Some things just aren't worth the heartache."

"You know his family misses you. Especially Ella. It's unfair to talk about them as though they resent you. That's just dreaming up a reason to feel sorry for yourself."

"That was sweet of Ella to stop by, but the whole situation is still uncomfortable."

"I hear you."

After dinner, they were back in the kitchen scrubbing and sanitizing like mad. They had twenty-five minutes until the 7:15 showing of a chick-flick they'd already seen together once before.

"But wouldn't you like to have children?" Patty said out of the blue, as if they had been in mid-conversation.

"Pardon me?"

"The internet dating. The falling in love."

"You don't make babies online."

Patty washed her hands and squeezed a dry towel. Then, pressing her lips together, she planted her hands on her hips. "You work in the NICU, for crying out loud. Is there any part of you that wants a baby? Are you really happy living like this? I don't get it. It's not like you couldn't knock on a random door and get a man to marry you on the spot. Why are you not married? Why don't you have any kids?"

They looked at each other, wide-eyed, neither saying a word. Colette broke the silence. "Can I show you something?"

"Of course."

She led Patty down the hall and paused at the closed door. "I don't want you to get the wrong idea, like I had a miscarriage or something. Just to clarify, I've never been pregnant." Then, slowly, she opened the door to the second bedroom.

The color scheme was sage-green and white, all the way down to the stuffed animals. To the left was a crib, to the right a wooden rocking chair she bought at the Scandinavian Festival.

Toys filled the three shelves she had put up herself, and the curtains matched the bedding, the wall hangings, and the rug.

"What is all this? You did this?"

Shutting the door, she led Patty to the living room. "You remember how we met up on a Saturday?"

"I remember."

"The following Monday I was supposed to pick up a foster baby. Bryce and I had a huge fight about it when I got the call. I didn't care. No matter what, I was going to take home that baby and I wasn't going to let him stop me."

"Does he not want children?"

"That's not the point. It's a long story. That's not what upset him."

"It was me."

"No, Mom. It wasn't you either. Anyway, that Monday, I told the caseworker I changed my mind and asked her to remove me from the list. I knew she'd never call me again after begging her for a baby and then not taking the one she offered."

"Coco, I had no idea."

Picking up a couch cushion, Colette smirked. "You're the reason I haven't been knocked up yet. It's all your fault."

"How do you figure?"

"Do you remember how you ended each letter when I was a teen?"

"I do. I told you to guard your heart and protect your body."

"And you told me not to give dogs what is sacred."

She nodded. "Don't throw your pearls before swine. You're a beautiful girl who had been through so much, and I couldn't bear the thought of someone using you in that way."

"Those words have always stayed with me."

Patty blinked back tears. "I shouldn't be, but I'm surprised to hear that. That means a lot."

"I'm glad I didn't go all the way with Bryce. He's a good guy, but look at us now. We're not even friends. The next guy is going to have to wait until we're married."

Tears were in Patty's eyes as she cupped Colette's knee. For the longest time they both sat there, each caught up in their own thoughts. Then, without warning, Patty got up and returned to the kitchen. She began humming as she washed the dishes.

"Mom, the dishes can wait. We need to get going if we're getting popcorn."

"Go on and get yourself packed. I'll finish up in the kitchen."

"Wow, mom. So cryptic. And why should I be packing?"

"You're going to California."

Colette swallowed hard. Bryce was in California. Was it possible that her mom was in contact with him, that the two of them had been scheming? "Why California?"

"Didn't you say that Bryce is there? You're going to pack your bags, get in your car, and you're not going to return until you get him back."

CHAPTER 36

Southern California was busy and exciting, the sun shimmering down on exotic palm trees, with gorgeous mountains just a short drive from the ocean's mist. So this was where the sun went during the Willamette Valley's nine months of gloom.

After weeks of pestering, Colette's lovely bosses finally agreed to give her a two week sabbatical, plenty of time to chase down her man and patch things up. The ticking clock did a fabulous job cheering her on, so much so that she actually believed she was going to pull it off.

Signaling for the next exit, she squeezed between the bumpers of two SUVs like a native Californian, and pulled into a gas station at the base of the off-ramp. There she topped off her tank in exchange for restroom privileges. Now that she was in paparazzi country, gorgeous hair and makeup were crucial. Not that they cared anymore. Ever since she gave in and offered a comment on camera, they fled town as quickly as they had come, transforming her reputation into yesterday's stale news.

For the next hour, Colette explored the streets of Hollywood. It wasn't the glamorous city she had pictured, much of it was filthy, but the mansion-lined streets were a dream.

When the light turned green, she accelerated. Turning down the radio, she picked up her phone on the second ring. Her greeting was met with silence, but she could tell the line wasn't dead. Her heart quickened as she pined for excitement. "Hello?" she sang again, this time with a British accent.

"Look in your rearview mirror."

"Who is this?" It almost sounded like Stuart, but if it was, he was doing a great job disguising his voice.

"Did you look in your mirror?"

"I'm not sure what I'm looking for, buddy. Would you like to give me a hint?"

"No."

Something in his tone was chilling. She turned onto a side road without signaling and pulled up to the curb. The car behind her continued on, but the following vehicle, some sort of sports car, turned off, parking right behind her. When she tried to speak, her voice cracked. "Who are you?"

"Do you not see me?"

It wasn't funny anymore. She made a hard left into the driveway across the street and began backing out. "I'm going to ask you one more time who this is, and then I'm calling the cops."

"Wouldn't you like to know how I found you?"

"This is Stuart, isn't it?"

"Correct," he said in a voice she recognized.

Furious, she threw it into park, marched up to his red sports car, and jerked the door-handle. It was locked. "What do you think you're doing?"

Leaving the engine running, he cracked the window an inch. "So you think you're going to get Bryce Rocco back, do you? I figured you would have learned your lesson by now."

"How did you find me?"

"Let's just say that you never should have let me use your bathroom."

"What did you do? You were in there for two seconds."

"Correction," he said, holding up his index finger. "I had access to your apartment on two separate occasions."

"No you didn't."

"Do you recall locking your door before Bryce entertained you at his apartment?"

"You broke in?"

"The door was practically left ajar."

She started to hyperventilate as she wondered how many nude videos stamped with her first and last name were circulating the internet. "What did you do?"

"I borrowed your phone. Then I simply returned it."

"You did something to it, didn't you? You have a tracking device on me."

Stuart's eyes lit up. "Ding, ding, ding. And that's just the beginning. My recommendation is this: destroy it. Kill your phone and go back home. Forget Bryce. You don't belong with him."

"What you did is illegal."

"No proof."

"Trust me, I'll prove it."

"I have an excellent lawyer. Do you?" He got out of his car.

Grinding her teeth, she grunted. "I don't have time for this." There was only one thing to do. She marched back to her car, put the phone under the front tire, and smashed the heck out of it. Stepping out of her car, she yelled, "Are there any other tracking devices I should know about?"

"No."

"You sure?"

"Yes."

She was still yelling. "If any questionable material ever surfaces about me or my family, you'll be sorry you ever met me. Got it?"

"Are you still going to try to find Bryce?"

"That's none of your business."

"But it's going to be difficult without a phone."

Impossible was more like it. As she gathered up the pieces of her phone, she felt defeated.

CHAPTER 37

The restaurant was pricier than she expected, so she chose the least expensive entrée on the menu, a sixteen dollar Greek salad. Her food hadn't yet arrived, but she knew she was getting her money's worth. It was the cutest little restaurant she had ever seen, and ambiance wasn't free.

People-watching in Beverly Hills was quite entertaining. Fashion trends that hadn't yet hit Eugene were modeled on confident women with perfect hair. Colette was surprised at the number of young, successful-looking men she spotted from her booth. What did they do for a living and how did they get there so fast? A touch of jealousy assaulted her. The mesmerizing surroundings made it impossible to appreciate life back home.

Money was never a factor in her attraction to Bryce, but she had to admit, it would be nice to have all that taken care of someday. She imagined a credit card offered by a laid-back husband who expected nothing more from his wife than for her to take care of his babies, keep a tidy mansion, and plan frequent family vacations to exotic destinations. Life as a Rocco would be a slice of strawberry pie.

Every head turned as a loud-mouthed blonde walked into the restaurant on the arm of a confident forty-some-year-old man. She listened as the woman went off about a good-for-nothing nanny with sharp fingernails. It was obvious the woman loved the sound of her own voice, but in her defense, she had some valid points.

The woman stopped mid-sentence to smile at the hostess, and then ran her mouth all the way to the table. When the waitress came by, they ordered their entrées without glancing at the menu. As the server walked away, the blonde quickly excused herself to the lady's room. Colette watched her curvy body all the way up until the door closed behind her.

Then she glanced back at the man. To her surprise he was already looking at her, his eyes squinting almost shut as he smiled. He winked once and then mouthed hello. Colette smiled back shyly before redirecting her gaze out the window.

Thirty seconds later, his date reappeared. "Forgive me, babe," he said. "I need to say hello to an old friend."

The woman looked around the restaurant as if she were being threatened by a fluttering bat. "Fine, but if you're not back by the time the food gets here…"

"If I'm not back, you can start without me." He spoke softly, but in a way that left no doubt who was *really* in charge.

Before Colette knew what was happening, the man slipped into her booth and extended his hand. "Devin," he stated like a salesman.

Instinctively, she shook his hand. "Hello."

"And how is this gorgeous afternoon treating you, Miss Halbrook?"

She tilted her head in confusion. His date looked ticked. "Good," Colette said slowly. "And how are you?"

"Fine, just fine." His head whipped around when the server came out with two drinks. "Excuse me, Miss. Right here." He tapped the table once. "I'm over here now. That's right. Thank you." Nodding, he slipped the paper off the tip of the straw and took a sip. "So what brings you to California?"

She felt herself blush. "May I kindly ask how we know each other?"

"Let's see, how can I put this?" He curled his lips. "It's like this. Months ago I had the pleasure of seeing your unforgettably gorgeous face in some magazines, and poof, just like that, you appear out of thin air in one of my favorite restaurants. I couldn't pass up an opportunity to say hello."

So she *was* famous. *Incredible.* "Thank you for the compliment, but maybe you should go back to your date. She doesn't look too happy."

"You think I'm making a pass at you? Now if you were single that might be another story, but it sounds like you and Bryce might be..." His eyes lit up. "How's my buddy doing these days, anyhow?"

Her mouth curved into a smile, though she doubted he knew Bryce personally. "I wouldn't know."

He narrowed his eyes. "No?"

"Sorry."

"You can't be more than, what, three miles from his home? Just a coincidence? Nah. Impossible." He winked as if he knew better.

Over his shoulder Colette could see his date making her way toward the door. "Aren't you going to say goodbye to your friend? It looks like she has other plans."

"Nah, I'll catch up with her later."

There was something about him she was drawn to. "How do you know where Bryce lives?"

264

"I know a lot more than his address."

"Such as?"

He fished out the lime floating in his water and bit down on it. Then he set it off to the side, licking his lips. "I know what movie your boy's working on right now. I also know who he's in negotiations with as we speak."

"What's he negotiating?"

"The contract for his next film. But this isn't news to you." Without warning, he got up and left. So she thought. He returned with the roll of silverware from his former table. "The reason I asked why you're in town is because I know that Bryce isn't. This strikes me as a bit peculiar."

Her heart stopped as her eyebrows rose. One wrong move and she could burn the only bridge between her and Bryce. "I'm ashamed to admit it, but Bryce and I kind of broke up."

"Kind of?"

"No, not kind of."

"I'm sorry to hear that." He unrolled his silverware and looked over his shoulder toward the kitchen. Then his eyes were back on hers. "Breakups can be rough. How are you holding up?"

She shrugged. "Actually, this is going to sound crazy, but..." Should she tell him? Originally, she set out on this adventure reminding herself she had nothing to lose. Her reputation couldn't get any worse at this point. And she wasn't about to spend an additional ten years hiding out in her apartment feeling sorry for herself.

"I don't know about you," he cut in, "but I still think about my exes from time to time. You want to forget and move on to the next one, but you can't quite shake the memories."

"I want him back," she said plainly. "That's why I'm here."

He laughed a long drawn out chuckle, followed by a sigh. "The sole purpose of this vacation is to get Bryce back?"

"I'm a fool. No need to remind me."

He laughed again, this time louder. "I think that's outstanding." He began applauding for all to hear. "Go get him, girl. I personally guarantee that as a man, he's not going to be able to walk away from a creature like you."

Her face was redder than paprika as she looked around at the not-so-subtle glances. "You make it sound so easy."

As he cleared his throat, his face grew serious. "I can help you."

"Help me what? Find Bryce?"

"Precisely."

"How?"

He pulled out a pencil and a miniature notebook from his jeans pocket. "Don't let this frighten you, but I'm in the movie business. I stand behind a camera for a living."

Her eyes lit up. "Have you worked with him? That's perfect. I bet you've got all kinds of connections. How lucky am I that I bumped into you?"

"I take pictures of movie stars. I sell them. I'm very good at it. And occasionally, I go back to my roots as a journalist."

"You're a paparazzi?"

"A paparazz-*o*, yes." He opened the notebook. "I'm going to help you, free of charge, all expenses paid. I'm not only going to get you to Wyoming, but I'm going to slay the dragons until you're face to face with your man. The dragons being bodyguards and security, of course."

"I don't know about this."

He put his hands up, wiggling his fingers. "Ah-ah-ah. Stay on track, babe. We're not doing anything illegal here. First things first. The airport. That's the easy part."

She closed her eyes momentarily, considering his offer. "I'm not thrilled with the idea of flying."

His eyes were the size of smoke detectors. "Imagine getting interrupted in the middle of your workday to find that Bryce Rocco has somehow bypassed security because he loves you so much. How do you feel?"

Her lips curved into a smile.

Devin pointed his finger in her face. "That, Colette, is exactly how Bryce is going to feel when he spots you."

Her stomach churned. Was it really going to be that easy? She eyed Devin contemplatively and noticed that he didn't blink once. "Let me get this straight. You're going to fly me to Wyoming?"

"Not personally, but yes."

She narrowed her eyes. "For free."

"You want breakfast in bed? Add it to the tab." He took a sip of water and peered over the edge of his glass. "And a separate room for myself, of course. No funny business."

She laughed under her breath. It all sounded exciting, but there was obviously a catch. "You don't expect me to believe you're just a nice guy who believes in love."

He put his hand over his heart. "I'm a nice guy who believes in love and wants to write a story about it. You and Bryce are going to live happily ever after and I'm simply going to document it for your coffee table scrapbook. Your future children will love it. These stories will be some of your most valued possessions. Think about it."

"You're going to publish this?"

"While America cheers you on." Standing up, he squeezed into her side of the booth. Then he swung his arm around her. "You may not realize this, but people love you. You're a nurse to babies. Do you know how many people have connections to kids who have spent time in the hospital? People *love* that about you. *I* love that about you, and I didn't care much for my own babies."

The more he talked, the warmer the heat of the spotlight felt on her face. This was the first she heard that there were those who actually liked her. "Did you happen to catch the story about my mom?"

"I almost cried when I read that story. It was tragic, the entire thing. I'm ashamed to admit it, but I myself have been behind the wheel after a few too many. More than once. People do it all the time knowing better, and then once in a while it happens. The worst possible outcome. Someone loses their life. And do you think it's ever the driver? Nah."

She couldn't believe what she was hearing. This was a whole new perspective she hadn't considered. "That's the main reason Bryce and I broke up. I couldn't do that to his family. I didn't want them to be reminded of that horrible night every time they looked at me."

"I punched a girl in the second grade. You know what that is? History. To this day I've never touched a woman out of anger. Do you think I'm going to let that define me for the rest of my life?"

"But that girl you hit, she's fine now."

Exhaling, he returned to his side of the booth. "Life is full of mistakes that we can tie around our necks like a twenty pound chain for the rest of our lives. But why? Who wants to live like that? We all make mistakes along the way. Maybe they're judging your mom, but certainly not you. It's just one of those unusual stories that people like to ooh and ah over. Trust me. Nobody is looking down on you."

"And if Bryce says no? If he says he doesn't want me back? Are you going to write about that too?"

"I wouldn't be doing my job if I didn't finish the story."

His bluntness sucked the wind right out of her. He was a charmer, a negotiator. Colette's happiness was the furthest thing from his mind. "It's Devin, right?"

He nodded just as the server set down their meals. "I'll flag you down if we need anything. That will be all for now, thank you." He scowled at Colette's salad. "You don't really want that, do you? Here, try this." He slid his plate next to hers, stabbed the salmon, and waited for her to accept the bite. "Good, right?"

"Very."

"It's yours. I'm going to leave you to your lunch while I do some research. I'll be back in an hour."

"I won't be here that long."

His jaw tensed as he studied his watch. "I never, in a million years, would have pegged you as feisty. Fine. Have it your way. Thirty minutes, but that's pushing it."

Stuffing a bite of salmon into her mouth, she felt no shame in declining his offer. "This is all about the money, isn't it?"

"It has to be."

She slouched back in her seat, setting down her fork. "You didn't actually believe that I'd go for any of this, did you? I enjoyed our chat, but I'm not going anywhere with you."

Staring straight into her eyes, he smirked. "You know that's a lie. Thirty minutes." He walked away without looking back.

CHAPTER 38

Devin tossed a cigarette butt onto the pavement and squashed it with the toe of his shoe. "What do you think of Yellowstone now that the sun's up? Pretty cool?"

Colette yanked the price tag off a wool scarf using her teeth. "I hope I see a grizzly. This place is unreal."

The Old Faithful Inn towered above the surrounding pine trees, boasting of the number of guests she had welcomed for more than a century. The rustic architecture quickened Colette's spirit, transporting her to an era she had never experienced, yet it felt like home. The crisp Wyoming breeze tantalized her senses, making her feel as though she was one with nature. The glow on the faces of tourists couldn't be missed, and love was drifting in the air like mint.

As she looked across the miles of trees fortified by wavy mountains, she pictured the wildlife she had seen in the brochures; bobcats, coyotes, mountain lions, and bison going about their morning, waiting to be discovered. If she was lucky, Colette would be granted time to visit the steamy pastel pools colored by the hand of God. And if she was really lucky, she'd experience the magic later that night in the protective arms of the man she loved.

Devin pointed across the parking lot with his eyes. "See those semis parked way over there? One of them is Bryce's trailer. That means he's here." He snapped a picture of Colette's startled expression.

Flinching, she turned toward the flash. "Do you see him?"

"The crew's on the other side of the lodge. I'm surprised you didn't hear the buzz and see it for yourself."

Covering the lens of his camera, she brought Devin's arm down. "It's too early for pictures. I didn't fall asleep until five this morning and I'm not convinced this isn't a dream."

"Believe it. You ready for this?"

She exhaled, fog dissipating as it left her mouth. "I don't deserve him."

"Everyone deserves a second chance."

"You don't know what I did to him."

With raised eyebrows, he lifted his sunglasses. "It can't be that bad. What'd you do?"

Laughing loudly, she gave him a knowing look. "I'd sit on that geyser with a pan of hot oil before I'd hand over that kind of ammo. You've got a magnetic personality, but I haven't forgotten what you're about." She linked her arm with his and sighed. "C'mon, Devin. Let's go get my heart crushed."

"You got it."

"Just so you know, I'm going to hate you by the time this is over."

"That's your prerogative."

The walk toward the other side of the lodge felt like sidestepping a log near the top of a waterfall. One mistake and it was all over. After hours of tossing and turning, she had yet to devise a plan. Should she get Bryce's attention with a cheerful smile and voluptuous cleavage? Her pushup bra was already in position, waiting for a subtle tug to the base of her shirt. Or should she allow her tears to do the talking? Crying was risky. Maybe she could declare her love with a flamboyant shout, or pull him aside for a heart to heart talk.

She couldn't shake the feeling that she was somewhere she didn't belong. What if he had already moved on?

As they approached the point of no return, she urged her muscles to propel her skeleton just a little bit further. At the last possible second, she released the grip she had on Devin's forearm. "I can't be seen with another man. I'll take it from here. Thanks for everything."

Touching her elbows, he turned Colette's body toward his. "If it doesn't work out with Bryce, I'll be your rebound this weekend. No joke."

Pushing him away, she grinned. "If it doesn't work out with Bryce, I'm going to hate you, remember?"

"Impossible."

"You'd be surprised." Exhaling sharply, she fluffed her curls and adjusted her scarf. "Wish me luck, Devin. I can't believe I'm doing this." Taking a step forward, she willed herself to be brave. Forcing herself around the corner, she stopped in her tracks. The scene off in the distance was not what she had pictured.

There were people and equipment everywhere. As she got closer, she was able to make out more detail. She saw three crane-type vehicles, each one different in structure and function, and two motorized vehicles resembling golf carts. Tents and umbrellas were strewn about, and a shortened railroad track housed a man perched alongside a camera. Stretched sheets of canvas were set up among ladders, cameramen, and lights. Off to the side were three boxy trucks.

As Colette approached the taped off area where a crowd was

gathered, she watched in awe as one of the cranes began spewing rain. The director yelled action, but there was no sign of Bryce. Where was he?

She looked over her shoulder in search of Devin, but she couldn't spot him either. She was on her own. Maybe Devin had gotten misinformation, and Bryce was still in Los Angeles. What if Devin left her there alone? It would cost a fortune to get back to the airport without a car. Her greatest fear was no longer rejection. It was abandonment. She pushed her way to the front of the crowd.

Seated at a table next to the largest tent was a girl who looked to be thirteen. To the left of the girl was a woman with commendable posture and frizzy hair, tracing a piece of paper with her finger. Colette's heart leapt at what she saw next—Gage emerging from the tent!

She didn't know whether to be frightened or relieved. One thing was for sure. Gage's job was to know where Bryce was at all times. Without thinking it through, she reached across several people and tapped a security guard in the center of his back. "Excuse me, sir?"

A short-haired *woman* whirled around, her expression angry. "What did you call me?"

"Hi. Sorry. Will you please get Gage Rocco's attention? I need to speak with him."

The woman curled her lips inward and grunted. "Sorry. Not my job."

"But I know him personally and it's really important."

"If you two are such good friends, why do you need my help? Can't you just call him yourself?"

"I would, but I don't have my phone."

"Of course you don't." Rolling her eyes, she walked away.

Colette stomped her foot. Why were people so uptight? Did she think her job was so significant that she couldn't trust the other security guards to handle things for two seconds? She waited for Gage to look up from his spot next to the young girl, but after several minutes, he still hadn't spotted her.

Enough was enough.

Colette cleared her throat and yelled Gage's name loud enough to be heard on the first attempt. Gage didn't flinch, but the security guard sure did. Colette yelled his name again as the woman marched over. Moments after Gage looked up, he spotted her. He leaned into the young girl as if they were a couple, and she looked up too.

"What do you think you're doing?" An artery in the security guard's neck bulged as if it couldn't handle the pressure.

When Colette looked back at Gage, her jaw dropped. The thirteen-year-old was sprinting toward Colette, Gage trailing behind her. Colette looked at those around her, thinking the teen must be mistaking her for someone else. After catching her breath, the girl giggled. "You're Bryce's girlfriend, aren't you?"

A confident "yes" was the easy response, but Gage was standing right in front of her.

"What are you doing here?" Gage looked confused rather than angry.

"I'm trying to find Bryce."

By now the spectators had shifted in such a way that Colette was the main attraction. Whispers combed the crowd until everyone was up to date. As cameras flashed in her face, her heart wept for the senseless death she represented. The security guard called for backup as the thirteen-year-old ducked under the caution tape. "You're here to get Bryce back, aren't you?"

"We love you, Charisma!" shouted a voice in the crowd. Several others agreed as the teen thanked them in a way that made her seem older than she really was. Gage followed Charisma to the other side of the tape and urged her to get back to her schoolwork.

"I know where Bryce is," Charisma said with an eager smile. "Do you want me to show you?"

The concern in Gage's eyes was throwing her off. "I don't know. You should probably listen to Gage. I don't want to get you in trouble."

Gage put one arm around Charisma and the other around Colette. "Come with me. Let's talk."

Nodding, she followed his lead as he brought her closer to the action. Her knees shook as she waited for someone to call her out. "I shouldn't be here. You're trying to get me locked up, aren't you?"

When he finally stopped, he folded his arms. "Bryce is really mad at you."

The director yelled cut, causing Colette to jump. "I know he is," she said, looking around frantically. Security was eyeing her with distrust, but they kept their distance.

"Regardless of what happens with Bryce, you need to know that our family forgave your mom a long time ago."

She studied his face expecting his expression to harden into contempt. The fake rain stopped pouring, making her aware of the silence. Charisma looked back and forth between Colette and Gage as if she were about to burst at the seams. Colette shoved her hands into her pockets. "Why are you telling me this?"

Running his fingers through his hair, he looked around

275

nervously. "I don't dislike you, Colette. I did at first, but then you sort of evolved into a pesky little sister."

She shook her head. "A part of me is glad to hear that, but the last time I saw you, there was definitely some hatred in your eyes."

His cheeks reddened as he looked around. Then he surprised her by taking a step closer. "I can't explain why I turned on you like that. I really can't, except that we were all in a state of shock. And then you suddenly showed up. It was terrible timing. Totally not your fault though. But it didn't take long for the guilt to set in. I can tell you that much."

For the first time she could see the goodness that everyone else saw in him. He was genuine. She felt as though her protective big brother was towering over her, making sure she was okay. "You have no idea how much this means to me, Gage."

"Don't get me wrong. I'll never stop harassing you. It's too easy to get a rise out of you."

"I'd smack you, but I'm guessing the outcome wouldn't be in my favor." More and more eyes were on her, but where was Bryce? She turned to Charisma. "You know where he is?"

Her eyes grew. "Sure do! Come with me and I'll show you. He's in his trailer."

Colette could picture the condemnation on Bryce's face as they took her away in handcuffs for kidnapping a child actress. "I better not. I have a friend here that will help me find him, but thanks."

"Whatever," she sang. "Follow me." Charisma took off in another sprint, leaving Colette no choice but to powerwalk after her. Gage caught up to his client in seconds, but he didn't seem intent on stopping her. When Colette got to the corner of the lodge, she upped her pace to a jog. Charisma was stopped in the middle of the parking lot, urging Colette on with flamboyant arm gestures. She finally caught up to them about twenty feet from the trailers.

Out of breath, Charisma hung on Colette's arm. "Bryce's trailer is the big one on the right. I have to get back before my mom finds out I'm gone, but promise me you'll let me know how it turns out. I *love* love."

Colette rested her palm on Charisma's back. "I will, but I can't promise you a happy ending. Thanks, girl. And good luck with the film."

"In three days they're killing me off," she giggled. "Oops. I wasn't supposed to tell anyone. I know you won't get me in trouble. It was lovely meeting you, Colette." She ran off, Gage's tall frame jogging behind her.

Colette studied the trailer for a good minute, hoping Bryce would fling open the door wearing a smile that said he was touched she had traveled so far to find him. Her mind flashed back to the way she had ended their lovemaking abruptly, turning on him as if Bryce were the enemy. An untimely shift in focus had destroyed her two biggest dreams all at once. Trust was compromised that day, and forgiveness would be the only path to redemption.

Making her way to the door, she climbed the steps as quietly as she could, her senses picking up the nuances of nature. Heart pounding, she knocked softly, hoping her heart would know what to say when the time presented itself. Glancing over her shoulder, she knocked again. Minutes later, it finally sunk in. Nobody was home.

CHAPTER 39

Colette cracked open the door to his trailer and froze, listening for any sign of life. With all the security on set, it was mindboggling they had neglected Bryce Rocco's trailer. At a minimum, the door should have been locked. She glanced over her shoulder feeling like a police officer attempting a jewelry heist. A man who was unloading a stroller from the trunk of his car nodded at her. His wife pulled two toddlers out of the car simultaneously and shouted at her husband. When he turned in the woman's direction, Colette plunged into the trailer and slammed the door.

Panting as if she had exerted herself, she took in Bryce's extravagant man-cave. She was more terrified than ever, but that didn't keep her from laughing under her breath in amazement. She was not only blown away by the magnitude of the space, but by the smart interior design and flashy lighting. A song she didn't recognize played in the background, its peaceful guitar having little effect on her nerves.

"Bryce?" Removing her coat and scarf, she readjusted her shirt. "Don't mind me. I'm just breaking and entering." She hid her boots beneath a chair in case she needed to make an inconspicuous escape and had a look around.

She tiptoed through the living area and touched the climbing gear spread out on the largest couch. On one of the cushions was a bowl of blackberries, raspberries, and sliced kiwi. She stole a raspberry. Eventually Bryce would have to return to his trailer.

She sampled a kiwi and messed with his climbing gear. If she waited long enough, he'd find her dozed off on the couch, breathing peacefully. She was so exhausted, the sound of the door might not even wake her. Then he would have plenty of time to watch her, remembering why they first fell in love. She yanked at the base of her shirt, revealing a nice amount of cleavage. On second thought, it looked too obvious. She tugged at her shirt until it was just right.

"I'm eating your delicacies," she said at a bold volume. "And I'm looking at your bed thinking dirty thoughts." As soon as she said it, she wondered if there were hidden surveillance cameras mounted in the room. After scanning the ceiling, she laughed at herself.

She sat there a good ten minutes before boredom set in. There was a curled staircase in the back corner of the trailer, and she was dying to know where it led. After a quick look out the windows, she passed through the kitchen to the office. That was the first she had seen of Bryce's desk. There was no telling what treasures were filed away in there.

When she tried to open the top drawer, it wouldn't budge. Her luck wasn't any better with the other three. It was just as well. She never should have tried it in the first place. After stealing one more peak out the tinted windows, she made her way up the staircase. When she went around the corner, she was confused. It led to nowhere. After pushing on the ceiling with the palm of her hand, she went back down the stairs.

When she looked up, she saw Bryce standing in the kitchen. Blood rushed to her face. "Bryce! What are you doing here?" He was holding the bowl of fruit she had eaten from. He set it down on the counter and looked at her like she was nuts. His dark hair was now surfer blonde and she could tell he had gained a few pounds. "I didn't hear you come in." Not that her ignorance justified the snooping, but it was odd how quickly he showed up without making a sound. "I thought you were filming in L.A."

"You're right, mostly."

She could tell he was awaiting an explanation, but she didn't know where to begin. "I'm confused that I didn't hear you come in. I feel like you appeared out of thin air."

He took a seat on the loveseat and patted the spot next to his. "Before I respond to that, let's not forget who belongs here and who doesn't."

Her whole body was perspiring as she took cautious steps toward him. "Gage knows I'm here. I didn't know where to find you, and I needed to see you. I know we're on bad terms, but I didn't think you'd mind if I waited around for you."

"While you downed my snack?"

Her heart sighed with relief when she saw a flicker of a smile. "In my defense, I warned you I was here. It's not my fault you didn't hear me."

His smile grew. "Maybe I did."

"No you didn't. Did you?" Had he been spying on her? "Where were you?"

He leaned forward, balancing his elbows on his thighs. "In the one place you forgot to check while you were casing the joint."

"The bathroom?"

"You're lucky you're so cute, because I didn't have anything nice to say when I saw you and Gage in the parking lot without a care in the world."

She didn't know whether to be flattered or upset. "What if I hadn't barged in? Were you going to let me walk away?"

He grabbed her hand and pulled her onto the loveseat. "I need to know why you're here." Intertwining his fingers with hers, he caressed her skin, gazing at her as if he were an artist studying for his next sketch.

"To see you, of course."

"More specifically?"

She let go of his hand. "It's hard to explain." The background music filled the silence that hung between them. How could she ask for forgiveness when she knew she wasn't worthy?

Bryce rubbed his forehead and sighed. "I'm tired of the chase, Coco. I can't chase you anymore."

Her heart dissolved into fragments as she nodded. Guilt was so heavy upon her, she could barely breathe. Isn't this what she had expected to happen when she started out on this venture? Devin and her mom had made it sound so easy.

Sitting up, she nodded at Bryce, the solemnness of his face stinging her to the core. She slipped into her boots and gathered her coat and scarf. Tears welled in her eyes as she opened the door. Flashes of light struck her repeatedly. When she looked again, she saw Devin.

"Bryce doesn't want you?" he said with pouty lips.

She saw concern in Devin's eyes, but wasn't fooled. As if to solidify her suspicion, he snapped a second series of pictures. Covering her face with her forearm, she took a step backward and slammed the door. "No," she said firmly, her eyes aimed at Bryce's.

Throwing her things onto the floor, she dropped to her knees. Then she crawled forward until her hands were seared to Bryce's thighs. "I don't expect you to chase me anymore. That's why *I'm* chasing *you*." She dabbed the tears welling in her eyes and felt a rush of calm as Bryce's warm palm covered her hand like a glove. "I'm sorry for being emotional over not having a baby of my own. That was selfish of me. Nobody *needs* a baby."

"Colette, that's not true. You—"

"But it *is* true. I ruined our intimate moment. Not a day goes by that I don't feel terrible about what I did to us. I cringe at the way I turned on you when you've been nothing but constant. You've never let me down, Bryce, and I realize that now more than ever. I don't deserve you, but I love you. I can't stop loving you. And I know that you used to love me with the same intensity."

Touching her arms, he guided her onto the loveseat. His hands were shaking. "I appreciate that you've come so far. I really do. That says a lot. But I've pictured an apology similar to this one a thousand times since we broke up. I also challenged myself to stay true to my decision."

His words couldn't be clearer, but something within her demanded that she not let him go so easily. Crossing her legs Indian style, she squeezed his hands. "Gage confirmed what you said about everyone forgiving my mom. I'll always be sorry for what she did, but going forward, I'm going to trust in your family's forgiveness and do my best to follow their example. I'm not going to be ashamed of my mom anymore. I'm not going to live in fear that someone will find out what she did. And how could I anyway? Everyone knows."

He scooted away from her as if he were merely getting more comfortable. "Did you end up taking that baby?"

Her eyes grew larger. "No, Bryce. No. You were right. I was

doing things in the wrong order."

"I shouldn't have said that. The order wasn't the problem. It was the way you sprung it on me."

He moved to the chair across from her. Pressing his lips together, he held eye contact for a long time before speaking. "After weeks and weeks of hoping for a second chance for *us*, there is only one solution that I could come up with. This is so politically incorrect, I'm afraid to say it." He laughed under his breath, but there was no indication he was amused. "Here it goes. I need to know that you're more committed to our relationship than you are to yourself. What do you think about that?" He studied her as if he was afraid.

She wiped her tears and nodded in a way that let him know she was willing to do anything. "One-hundred percent, I am."

"This is going to be so much to ask of you. And trust me. This isn't meant to be an ultimatum." He hesitated. "You've hinted from the beginning that you're afraid of commitment."

"Not anymore. Not to *you*."

"I'm not going to keep chasing the woman I love if she doesn't want me just as badly."

"I'll do anything to prove I'm committed. You name it."

He stood up and walked to the office. He returned with a folded sheet of paper. She had never seen his face so red. "I wrote this letter last month. This will give you plenty of time to think it over before you make a decision. Sleep on it if you have to. In fact, I hope you do."

He made a phone call alerting someone that he was about to leave his trailer. Then he zipped up his coat and paused with his hand on the door. "But if I've asked too much of you, please don't tarnish my reputation by telling anyone. Get rid of the letter and we'll go our separate ways with good memories. Agreed?"

"Yes, but that's not going to happen."

He extended his arm. "Here you go, babe. Whatever happens, just know that I love you more deeply than you'll ever understand."

When she stood up to take the letter, he hugged her as if he'd never have the pleasure of touching her again. He smelled like a good make-out session. She would have to be out of her mind to walk away from the man she wanted to do life with until they were old and grey.

"Call me when you've made a decision," he said, kissing her cheek. "And don't you dare leave Yellowstone without saying goodbye."

"I don't have my phone."

"Where is it?"

"In a dumpster in southern California."

He laughed. "I'd ask for more details, but my stomach is in knots knowing what you're about to read. I'll see you soon."

The flash of Devin's camera struck him like lightning bolts, but Bryce seemed unfazed. When the door slammed, Colette peered out the window. So much for sleeping on it. He and two body guards appeared to be sticking around for her decision. She sat down, dying to know what was written in that letter. He could ask anything of her, and she would never judge him for it. Bottom line, he still cared about her, and that's all she needed to know. Inhaling one good breath, she began reading.

Colette,

If you're reading this letter, that means I'm the luckiest man in the world. My best friend is still in love with me. I would trust you with my life, but I also need to trust that you're committed to us. I need you to consider making a life-altering decision, but my biggest fear is that you might interpret this as a way for me to control you. I would never ask you to do something you didn't freely decide on your own.

You continue to amaze me with how emotionally connected you are to your patients. Saving lives is the definition of a hero, and you take it a step further by investing in the lives of the dads and moms of those babies. I know you love what you do, but I also know that you want a family of your own.

Here's my question. I'm shooting a film in Australia this coming February. I would love nothing more than for you to be there with me. Will you consider it? When I signed my contract, I went out on a limb for you. I asked them not to fill one of the set medic positions until I gave them the go ahead. Treating a sprained ankle might be the most rewarding work day when it's all said and done, a sharp contrast from saving newborns and hugging distraught parents, but I'm hoping that you'll accept this job so we won't have to be separated during those months.

This is probably selfish of me, but I don't think I'm ready to give up acting quite yet. But if at some point my "wife" feels it's too much time away from her and our "baby on the way", I will gladly give it up for my family. That's a promise.

Run away with me, Colette. Let's see the world together. Teach me how to live my life with the goal of helping others. You're the most amazing woman I've ever met, and I can't fathom living without you. I love you, Coco. I do.

Your biggest fan,
Bryce Rocco

CHAPTER 40

Colette tied her bikini top and put on a freshly ironed baby blue sundress. Then she opened the curtains for another amazing view of Sydney, Australia. After two-and-half weeks of waking up in paradise, the dazzling skyscrapers never ceased to amaze her. The beauty of the city was unparalleled, and the Pacific Ocean glistened as if its sole purpose was to touch the lives of those who paused to behold it.

Three months ago, with tears of joy rolling down her face, Colette jumped on the opportunity to follow her true love to the next chapter in his life. Resigning from the NICU was bitter-sweet, but she clung to the feeling that a family of her own was on the horizon, just a ways off in the distance. The Roccos welcomed Colette back into their lives with hugs and laughter, and the NICU threw her a rockin' going away party. Patty was proud that her daughter had followed her heart and been blessed with a second chance at love.

Looking back, Colette never could have guessed how exciting her life was about to become. The passion between her and Bryce was so strong she could hardly stand it, and each day she arrived at "work" she felt as though she had been swept up and dropped off in an amazing make-believe world all over again.

The first day or two on set had been more intimidating than she had feared, but it wasn't long before she embraced the fact that she was one of them. The organization and creativity of the crew was extraordinary. There were so many details to orchestrate, yet they were pulling it off without a glitch. To sit back and watch it unfold was mesmerizing. And thanks to several members of the cast and crew, she had never laughed so hard in her life.

As much as she loved her new job, Colette was ecstatic for the day off. When she heard the knock on her hotel room door, she took one last look at herself in the mirror and jogged over to open it. Her tall, dark, and handsome man was grinning at her. "Are you ready to play?"

"Eighty degrees and sunshine? Might as well." She reached up and grabbed the bill of his cap. "You look cute. Give me two minutes and I'll be ready."

He pushed her further into the room, pulled back the bedspread, and forced her down slowly. "I missed you last night, baby." He kissed the base of her neck, his lips moving upward until he was near her ear at the spot that always made her giggle. "You look extra pretty this morning. You smell good too."

She melted beneath the weight of his body as she moved her hands along his biceps. "I missed you too. Where are you taking me today?"

His lips went to hers as his hand moved down her side. "Somewhere you're going to remember forever."

"You're making it harder and harder to keep that promise I made myself."

"How do you think *I* feel?" he laughed. "Let's go. We're burning daylight." After one last kiss, he helped her off the bed. "Did you pack your tennies? I thought it would be fun to do some hiking later on."

"It's all here." Love-struck, she handed him her backpack. He looked so happy she expected confetti to burst from his ears. She headed to the bathroom. "Give me two seconds. I'm just about ready." She put on earrings, a bracelet, and a final spritz of body spray.

"Oh man, Coco. Today's going to be fun." He whirled her around as he hugged her. "I could get used to living here with you. Our kids would have Australian accents. Who knows? Maybe we would too."

When he set her down, Colette looked at him with a sarcastic smile, as if the mention of children didn't quicken her spirit. "Don't get any crazy ideas. I would like our kids to grow up on the same half of the world as their grandparents and aunts and uncles and cousins." She kissed his cheek and retied the strings to her bikini. She liked the way he was watching her. "Bryce, you should marry me. I'd be a good wife."

He took a step closer and touched her hips. "I can see that happening. I bet you'll be just as vivacious when you're seventy-five."

"I think you're right."

Out in the hall, they passed a co-worker, an orange-haired *key grip*. He let out a flamboyant laugh. "Well, well, well. Looks like Mr. and Mrs. Prude had a good night last night."

Bryce grinned as if he were guilty as charged. "Watch it, Tony. You and your blowup doll should mind your own business."

Tony put his hands up defensively. "Hey, I'm not judging. Ain't no shame in loving your woman."

Colette could feel herself blush, but she didn't fire back the way she normally did when Tony teased her. After what the press had done with news of her virginity, she didn't feel like discussing her romantic life with anybody. "See you around, Tony. And don't get yourself eaten by a shark."

He pointed at himself with his thumbs. "You won't catch this guy swimming with those things. I hate sharks." Tony cocked his head. "No bodyguard today?"

Bryce grinned. "No need. I don't anticipate too many crowds where we're going."

"Well, have fun Down Under. Don't do anything I wouldn't do."

Just outside the lobby, an off-road vehicle awaited them. Giggling, she looked at Bryce. "Great. Something tells me I shouldn't have worn a dress today."

"No way. That dress is smokin' hot." Bryce opened the door to the backseat. With a gentle touch to her shoulder, he stopped her from getting in. There was something odd about the look on his face. "I have a question for you, Colette."

She grabbed his hand and laughed. "I've never seen you with that expression before."

"Really? What do I look like?"

"I don't know. You look... happy."

"I *am* happy."

"And you look nervous." She curled her lips inward. "Like you're about to propose or something." It was a bold statement, but there was no other way to describe it.

He raised his eyebrows. "What would you say if I did?"

She gave him a look that said she knew better. "I won't give an answer to that question until it's asked."

He grinned like he was enjoying the game. "You don't know if you're ready to be Coco Rocco? It has a nice ring to it."

Laughing, she kicked the side of his shoe. "You said you have a question for me. You better ask it before you forget."

"How do you feel about helicopters?"

Her eyes grew as she laughed. Helicopters were a terrible idea to begin with. It was no wonder so many of them crashed. "Why do you ask?"

"You're not a fan of flying, that's why."

"Can I hate them and love them at the same time?"

Three teenagers and their parents approached Bryce with pens and paper. After turning his back on Colette, Bryce made conversation with the family as he signed his autograph. The youngest teen handed her paper to Colette and spoke with a delightful Australian accent. "Will you sign your name next to his?"

Colette glanced at Bryce who was smiling back at her. This wasn't the first time Colette had been asked for an autograph, but it was just as surreal as the first. Her mom would be impressed if she could see her now, strutting around Australia like she was someone special. "What's your name, sweetheart?"

"Charlotte."

"That's pretty." Colette wrote a short message and signed her name.

When the family continued on to the parking lot, Bryce looked at Colette with pleading eyes. "Will you let me take you up in one today?"

"A helicopter?" How could she say no to that face? Her heart started to pound. Bryce possessed a brand-spanking-new piece of paper that told him he had the skills and the right to fly. He obviously had big plans and was hoping she wouldn't squash them. "It depends. How seasoned is the pilot? I trust you, babe, but I'm not about to be your test run guinea pig. I'm in my prime."

He took her hand and helped her into the back seat. "Coco, you know I can't fly helicopters." His patronizing grin turned into laughter.

Covering her face, she laughed at her own stupidity. "Okay, okay. In that case, I'm in."

*

The Blue Mountains National Park was the most beautiful place she'd ever seen, and from a birds-eye view! The door on her side of the helicopter had been removed for a more vivid experience, but she somehow felt completely secure in one of the most unsecure modes of transportation. If the thing malfunctioned, she'd probably go down with a smile. Despite the seatbelt and safety harness, she felt like an eagle flying freely beneath the sun.

They hovered in front of the Three Sisters, a trio of massive rock formations overlooking a bumpy canyon forested with Eucalyptus trees. She wanted to ask the pilot to land so they could explore Jamison Valley and maybe spot a koala, but she refrained. Time was limited and there was no telling what Bryce had penciled in on the itinerary. She snapped a few pictures with her cell phone so she could text one to her mom later. The way the sun was hitting the sandstone, the Three Sisters looked like they were coated in gold.

The third passenger, an Australian photographer named Gus, motioned for Colette and Bryce to look his way. Colette placed her hand on Bryce's leg and smiled. When Gus brought his camera back down, Colette extended her arm into the open air. In that moment she knew God had to be real. Everywhere she looked, nature was proclaiming it as if she should have known all along. And if God created the mountains, he must have created her too.

Bryce wrapped his arm around Colette's midline and did his best to kiss her cheek, despite the nuisance of the headsets they were wearing. "What do you think?"

"I've never seen anything like it," she said louder than she needed to. "The view is spectacular."

He laughed, kissing her once more. "Are you up for some hiking? There's somewhere I've been wanting to take you."

"As long as hiking isn't code for rock-climbing."

"Not this time," he said loudly, his deep voice pulsing through her veins. "There's a waterfall I want you to see over in Blackheath, and then we'll check out Wentworth Falls. That's where I want to spend most of the day."

"I can't wait."

When the chopper picked up speed, Colette squeezed Bryce's hand. It wasn't long before they were moving at a steady pace. Bryce didn't have much to say, but his smile let her know he was very much present. Before she knew it, they were approaching a cliff made of layered chunks of flat rock, with natural vegetation growing out as if a landscaper had arranged it that way. A thin waterfall cascaded unevenly down the front, bringing movement to the tranquil scene. Gus positioned his camera once more.

"Smile, you two."

Bryce flashed his perfect teeth while Colette grinned from ear to ear at her man. She never would have thought to invite a photographer. What a great idea. Joy was radiating from their faces, and she had full confidence Gus was capturing it all.

Bryce leaned in closer. "Can you guess the name of the waterfall?"

Colette pressed her lips together and laughed. "I have no idea."

"One guess. You can do it."

"You know I'm not creative like that. Blue Mountain Falls? That's the best I can do. I give up."

Bryce reached for her hand as he looked into her eyes. Her heart started to pound. He had that funny expression on his face like he had earlier. She wasn't sure, but it almost felt like his hand was shaking. She broke eye contact and set her gaze back on the waterfall, but her mind was stuck on Bryce—and his motive.

He cleared his throat. "Colette. Look at me."

She obeyed. He looked like he was about to be sick. "Are you okay?" Her jaw dropped in objection when she saw him take off his seatbelt. Luckily he left his harness in place.

Bryce shifted his body until he was seated sideways. "It's not called Blue Mountain Falls, but that was a good guess." He squeezed her hand like he meant it. His palm was definitely shaking and his forehead was sweaty. "The name of the waterfall is Bridal Veil Falls."

She felt herself blush, then swallow. "Oh. Woops. I was wrong." She had a strong hunch he was about to pop the question, and it was terrifying. They hadn't even discussed getting engaged. Not seriously anyway. It wasn't like him to ask such a controversial question on a whim. And risk rejection? No way. She looked away and tried to steady her breathing.

Bryce stood up, partially hunched over, and reached up front to where the pilot was. Curiosity struck Colette full force. She couldn't look away. When he turned back around, he went straight to one knee. A small blue box, already opened, was in his hand. A sparkling diamond ring was in the center. "Colette?"

As she tried to catch her breath, tears welled in her eyes. She watched Bryce's lower lip quiver, the most vulnerable she had ever seen him. He looked above his head momentarily and then his eyes were back on hers. "One lucky man is going to get *you* for a wife. I'm just hoping that man is me. I love you, Coco." His knee wobbled as he steadied himself. "Will you marry me?"

Tears were streaming down her face, but she didn't care. She never could have prepared herself for how loved she felt in that moment. The most amazing man she had ever met, the prince studying her with honest eyes, wanted to spend the rest of his life with *her*. "Yes," she whispered, unsure if the headset had picked up her voice. Bryce exhaled in a way that told her he got the answer he was hoping for. She watched in awe as he carefully slipped the exquisite rock on her finger. "It's gorgeous, Bryce! I love you."

"I love you too." He kissed her hand, and then he was by her side again, seatbelt fastened. He looked at her and sighed. "You said yes. Now I can relax."

"When I imagined you proposing to me, you weren't strapped to a helicopter."

"You wanted adventure. Be careful what you wish for."

"Don't worry. I'm not complaining."

"I know you're not." He cleared his throat and gave her a cryptic smile. "So, my soon-to-be wife," he grinned, his hand moving slowly up her thigh, "when would you like to get started on that baby you've been wanting?"

Her eyes tripled in size as she shoved his arm away. To her humiliation, Gus and the pilot were both chuckling. "Not until the wedding bells have chimed. And I'm not hearing anything."

Bryce looked over his shoulder. "Hey, Gus? Do you know anyone around here who sells wedding bells?"

Colette shoved him playfully. "If you don't mind, I'd like an actual wedding."

"You sure?"

"I'm sure."

"Bummer." He scooped up a handful of her curls and let them fall down her back. "I'm kidding. I want you to have your wedding."

She rested her head on his shoulder as he played with her hand the way she loved. She didn't flinch as Gus continued snapping picture after picture. Bryce twisted her ring as his fingertips drifted across her tan skin. The intimacy was eating her alive. "Now I know why you brought our friend, Gus, along," she grinned.

"We'll pack our own camera for the honeymoon."

She pressed her lips together trying to hold back her giddiness. "Good call."

Bryce took off his headset before removing hers. Then he put both arms around her and squeezed. He continued to hold her as he spoke into her ear. "I want you to know that I'm serious about giving you a baby. I've given it a lot of thought, as you can imagine, and I'm one-hundred percent ready when you are. I'm ready to be dad."

Beaming with delight, she kissed his cheek. "I'm sorry to burst your bubble, but I wouldn't mind a year or two of just you and me. Babies will come soon enough."

He gave her a curious look. "Really?"

"We could do more movies together like we are now. And maybe you could get a producer to give me a speaking role, like a line or two, in one of your films. You're not the only one in this relationship who wants to be famous."

"I'll see what I can do."

Bryce put their headsets back on and told the pilot they were ready to head over to Wentworth Falls. When the helicopter was moving at a steady speed, Colette squeezed Bryce's hand. "I always thought I needed a baby to be happy. I think it just boils down to needing a family."

He pulled her closer and laughed. "Knowing you, I think we better try for a baby on our honeymoon, just in case you change your mind."

"That works too." She reached for her fiancé's hand, taking it all in.

"If a family is what you were after, it looks like you hit the jackpot this year. You've got your mom back, plus a mom-in-law, and a whole clan of crazies."

"And don't forget the best part. A soon-to-be husband. Or, as I like to call him, my adventurous half."

Bryce grinned. "And I won't ever let you forget it."

THE END

Afterword

Thank you for reading *Chased by Fame*. If you enjoyed it, please take a moment to write a review or share on social media.

As you know, this is a work of fiction. The actions and words of the characters were merely to enhance the entertainment value. I have the utmost respect and admiration for nurses, doctors, and social workers.

Both of my children would not be here today had they not been cared for by nurses and doctors at birth. Their skills, knowledge, and compassion were remarkable, and I will always hold a special place in my heart for all that they've done for us.

Another group of people I greatly admire are CPS workers. Their caseloads are full, yet they go above and beyond to do everything in their power to protect children and restore families when possible. Oftentimes they are blinded to what goes on behind closed doors, and they do their very best to sift through allegations to discover the truth.

While I have your attention, I would also like to add that there is a shortage of foster homes in our nation, as well as a lack of families willing to adopt. Do you know what happens to children when there is no foster home available to them? They are separated from their friends at school, and sometimes even their siblings, and sent to foster homes in other cities. Some aren't so lucky and end up in group homes. Please ask yourself how you can prove to these children and teens that they are valued and loved when our society tells them otherwise.

Thanks again for reading *Chased by Fame*. I hope the story took you on adventure far different from everyday life.

Best wishes,

Melissa

Acknowledgements

A special thank you to Bethany Page, Brandye Hughes, and Sandy Fackler for polishing the final draft.

About the Author

A hopeless romantic, Melissa began her quest for a husband and her happily ever after before she had even gone on a first date. A few days shy of her twentieth birthday, her dream of getting married came true. Together they have two children, a boy and a girl.

Though a piece of her heart will always be in Oregon, Melissa has planted roots in Texas. She and her family enjoy road trips, theme parks, and spending time outdoors.

www.ingramcontent.com/pod-product-compliance
Lightning Source LLC
Chambersburg PA
CBHW020235180626
46810CB00006B/2209